the **O**pposite of love

ALSO BY HELEN BENEDICT

Bad Angel

The Sailor's Wife

A World Like This

Many of the characters in *The Opposite of Love* also appear in *A World Like This*.

the **O**pposite of love

a novel by helen benedict

Viking

VIKING
Published by Penguin Group
Penguin Group (USA) Inc., 345 Hudson Street, New York, New York 10014, U.S.A.
Penguin Group (Canada), 90 Eglinton Avenue East, Suite 700, Toronto, Ontario, Canada M4P 2Y3
(a division of Pearson Penguin Canada Inc.)
Penguin Books Ltd, 80 Strand, London WC2R 0RL, England
Penguin Ireland, 25 St Stephen's Green, Dublin 2, Ireland (a division of Penguin Books Ltd)
Penguin Group (Australia), 250 Camberwell Road, Camberwell, Victoria 3124, Australia
(a division of Pearson Australia Group Pty Ltd)
Penguin Books India Pvt Ltd, 11 Community Centre, Panchsheel Park, New Delhi – 110 017, India
Penguin Group (NZ), 67 Apollo Drive, Rosedale, North Shore 0745, Auckland, New Zealand
(a division of Pearson New Zealand Ltd.)
Penguin Books (South Africa) (Pty) Ltd, 24 Sturdee Avenue, Rosebank, Johannesburg 2196,
South Africa

Penguin Books Ltd, Registered Offices: 80 Strand, London WC2R 0RL, England

First published in 2007 by Viking, a member of Penguin Group (USA) Inc.

10 9 8 7 6 5 4 3 2 1

LIBRARY OF CONGRESS CATALOGING-IN-PUBLICATION DATA
Benedict, Helen.
The opposite of love / by Helen Benedict.
p. cm.
Summary: When seventeen-year-old Madge, a bi-racial girl living in a small Pennsylvania town
populated by bigots, decides to change the world for the better, she starts by "adopting" a four-year-
old boy she finds abandoned in New York City.
ISBN 978-0-670-06135-8 (hardcover)
[1. Racially mixed people—Fiction. 2. Prejudices—Fiction. 3. Abandoned children—Fiction.
4. Family problems—Fiction. 5. High schools—Fiction. 6. Foster home care—Fiction. 7.
Pennsylvania—Fiction. 8. New York (N.Y.)—Fiction.] I. Title.
PZ7.B43175Opp 2007
[Fic]—dc22
2006037898

Printed in U.S.A.
Set in Perpetua

for Emma

*The opposite of love is not hate,
it's indifference.*

—Elie Wiesel

one

I'M THE OLIVE in the peanut bowl, the black button in the white button box. It hasn't been easy, but it's taught me how to fight. And it's given me a story that's made me half proud, half ashamed.

The story began about a year ago, if it's possible to trace when anything begins, on one of those dank days in March when the wind scrapes your skin like a knife. I'd just come home from a long day and a thirty-minute walk, cold and hungry. I climbed the stairs to the top of our three-story apartment house and kicked open the door.

"Mom?"

No answer. I turned on the lights, threw my backpack on top of the boots and newspapers choking up our hallway, and went into the kitchen. Piles of dishes in the sink, junk mail all over the table. Bags full of bottles and cans on the floor. Normal, for us.

I opened the fridge: beer and jam—nothing else. No bread in the breadbox, either. Mom never had been much for domestic organization.

"Why the hell don't you ever have any food for me when I come home?" I yelled at her once.

She looked me up and down, her square face rumpling into a grin. "Food? What do you want that for? You eat up every penny I make as it is," she said in her gravelly cigarette voice. "Only joking!"

No matter what meanness she laid on me, Mom always said she was only joking.

If you stood Mom and me side by side, you'd never know we were related. For one thing, she's white. For another, she's English, which probably explains her bizarre sense of humor. By the time this story of mine began, she'd been living in our little corner of Pennsylvania for eighteen years, but she still sounded like she'd hopped off the boat an hour ago.

As for my dad, he was a Jamaican construction worker who knocked up my mom back in England when she was twenty-four and just out of prison. Nobody's seen him since.

That's why I'm the olive in the peanut bowl: half black, half white; half foreign, half American; half belonging and half a complete stranger.

I searched every one of our kitchen cupboards till I found an old can of chicken noodle soup. I heated it on the stovetop, still wearing my purple bubble coat and warming my hands over the saucepan—Mom must have stopped paying the heating bill again. Then I sat down at the table to eat. Mousy, my basketball-sized orange cat, ran up to me and rubbed his head against my ankles, moaning. (I named him Mousy because he'd never caught a mouse in his life.) That's when I saw her note.

"*Got to split. Call Liz. Love ya, Mum.*"

I jumped up and ran into her bedroom. The mess in there was even worse than usual—underwear and socks all over the floor, drawers hanging open like panting tongues. Right away I could see her suitcase was gone. I sat on the bed and stared at the few ugly men's shirts she'd left dangling in her closet. All Mom ever wore was men's shirts over jeans. The house felt empty and suffocating at the same time; it felt like it wanted to swallow me up. I pressed my fingertips against my chest, the way you touch a bruise to see if it hurts.

When I called my aunt Liz, she answered right away. She lived in a nearby town called Riverbend, where she ran a beauty shop and managed to keep her life together without resorting to stupid insults or unexplained disappearances. She was the opposite of my mom in every other way, too. Mom was squat and square like a mailbox, Liz tall and slim. My mother wore her hair in a bristly graying crop, Liz kept hers long and dyed lemon blonde. Mom's face was heavy and scarred from acne, Liz's was long and narrow. And Mom had spent her teens in and out of prison, while Liz, as far as I knew, had never broken a law in her life. The only likenesses between them were their little flat noses and the sly expressions on their tight, skinny mouths.

"Aunty?" I said down the phone. "She's gone again."

"Oh, for God's sake." Her accent was exactly the same as Mom's, singsong and gutsy and pitched low like a growl. "Brandy's got no more sense than a tree stump. Listen, I'll come straight over to fetch you. And don't you worry, you can stay with me as long as you want."

Brandy. What kind of name was that for a mother?

While I was waiting for Liz to arrive, I threw away the chicken soup—no more appetite—and packed. Mom had disappeared so many times before I knew there was no way of telling how long I'd have to stay away. So I stuffed the yowling Mousy into his traveling box, where he glared at me indignantly through the bars, like he thought he was a tiger I'd shrunk in the wash. I folded my favorite clothes into a green duffel bag, along with my journal. And I shoved all my books and schoolwork into my backpack because when you're the only black person in your family, your school, and your whole damn town, you don't let yourself fall behind, no matter what chaos chooses to rain down on your shoulders.

After that, I pressed my forehead against the grimy living-room window and gazed out over Hollowdale: rickety clapboard houses spilling down the hill; the main drag below nothing but an empty strip of asphalt lined with boarded-up stores; and a cluster of abandoned brick factories across the other side of the valley, windows broken and roofs dangling, looking lonesome and useless as a cardboard box in the rain.

I may have been only seventeen, but I knew there had to be more to life than this.

The minute I saw my aunt's muddy Ford chugging up our hill, I grabbed Mousy and my bags and ran downstairs. She hadn't even yanked up the parking brake before I was climbing in.

"You all right then?" she said, her narrow blue eyes crinkled up and worried. Her nose was red with the cold and her lemony hair was pulled into a shiny, tight bun.

I shrugged. "You think they've got her this time?" Mom couldn't get American citizenship, like Liz had, because of her prison record back home, so she was living here illegally, which is why I was always expecting her to be caught and kicked out.

"I'm sure she's fine." My aunt patted me on the knee. "She's wily as a fox, she is."

"But where's she go when she disappears like this?"

"I don't know, Madge. Perhaps she's got a little love interest tucked away somewhere. But look, I'm happy to have you stay with me. It's been lonely on me own."

That made me sad. Liz's husband, my uncle Ron, had died only the year before, when some moron on his building site had run him over with a backhoe, squashing him like a bug. None of us were over the shock of it yet, least of all her.

I stayed with my aunt for the next three weeks, and Mom never called once. That was typical but we worried anyway, even though we never said so. Liz kept glancing at the phone like she expected it to stand up and tell her something, but I knew better. All the times Mom had disappeared before, she'd never called either.

I loved my aunt, but I couldn't stand living in her town. Riverbend was a cute little village on the Delaware River, with rows of wooden houses in pastel colors and a fancy pink hotel overlooking Main Street like a fussy grandma, but it was even smaller than Hollowdale and about as lively as a cinderblock. The only stores were one pharmacy, two sleazy saloons, and my aunt's beauty shop, and most of the town residents were cranky old white people over sixty. The only exceptions were some Latino men who'd moved there to work in a chicken factory (they were from El Salvador, I think), but nobody mixed with them.

To make matters worse, Riverbend was a forty-minute drive from Hollowdale, so I had to rely on the yellow bus our school sent for students who lived far away. I dreaded that bus. I'd dreaded it ever since the day in junior high when I'd clambered aboard and some smartass had said, "Hey, who burned you in the oven, Madge?" After that, kids were always trying to be funny. ("How come you got that ugly name, huh? Is it from Aa-frica?") That's why I always walked to and from school when I was home in Hollowdale, even though it took half an hour each way.

I couldn't walk from Riverbend, though—it was way too far. So I dragged myself on to that bus every day, spent hours on the phone with my best friends Krishna and Serena, read about fifty books, watched way too much TV, and turned so crabby and mean that when spring vacation arrived, Liz said, "I'm sending you to stay with Bob for a week, no questions asked. You need to get out of here."

The morning of Easter Monday, she drove me to Hollowdale and put me on a Shortline bus to New York City. The bus smelled of bad breath and rug cleaner, but I was too excited to care. I hadn't been to New York since I was twelve, when Bob, Liz's son and my one and only cousin, moved there to become a newspaper reporter and we'd gone to visit him. Even in the middle of my excitement, though, I felt a pang at how alone my aunt looked waving me good-bye, and at how her lipstick was way too bright for her pale face.

The bus arrived at Port Authority a couple hours later, but Bob wasn't there yet. I had to wait under the glary white lights, hugging my green duffel bag and trying not to stare at the raggedy-ass man snoring beside me on a bench. The place was big and unfriendly, grimy as a parking garage, and stuffed with people scurrying about, looking sad and mad and yelling into their cell phones. Cops were checking me out. A couple of creepy guys said something obscene to me. I wished my cousin would hurry up and get me out of there.

Then I saw him walking toward me with that little bounce he'd always had, and it made me smile. Bob may have turned into a big-city reporter by then, but in that bus station he looked like the country boy I'd always known: wide shoulders over short legs, a broad pinkish face, nose round as an elevator button, and the shiny head-knob that comes from going bald way too young.

"Hey, where's your hair gone?" I said. "You look like a Ping-Pong ball." We always teased each other like that.

"Welcome to the Rotten Apple," he replied, laughing, and wrapped his arms around me. (I'm the same height as him, five-foot-ten, so when he hugged me we almost bumped noses.) He smelled of stale beer and too much deodorant, and he didn't sound like either of our moms. He sounded American, like me.

He stepped back to look me over. "You look different." We'd been real close when he was still at home, but now that we hadn't seen each other since his dad's funeral, we had to get used to one another all over again. "Wow, all that yellow. You're getting prettier every time I see you."

"Thanks." I tossed him my bag, trying not to show my smile. Earlier that morning, I'd put on black jeans, a bright yellow shirt, and matching yellow beads in my dreads. I'd figured long ago that if people were going to stare at me, I might as well give them something to stare at.

"It's great to see you again," Bob said. "Now let's get out of this hellhole."

Outside, it was as cold and windy as it'd been in March, though by then it was the beginning of April. Even the cardboard Easter bunnies hanging in store windows looked shivery. I hunched up in my bubble coat, my hands in my pockets, and hurried alongside Bob on our way to the subway. Litter scooted around us; newspapers grabbed our shins. A row of tall buildings frowned down at us, and a woman in skimpy clothes and matted hair shouted curses into the air. I stared down at the sidewalk. I was a small-town girl. I wasn't used to this.

On the train I took a seat across from my cousin so I wouldn't look as clingy as I felt, and watched the passengers come and go. Next to Bob sat an elderly African American woman in a navy blue suit and matching hat, her head bent over a Bible and her feet pressed together in shiny black shoes. Beside her sprawled a Latino man, brown and muscular, with his legs spread and his eyes closed, his Adam's apple poking out like a knuckle over a golden chain. A couple stood nearby, the man tall and brown as me, the woman slender as a leaf and Chinese. Nobody looked at me, nobody noticed me. And I loved it. In Hollowdale and Riverbend, I was never ignored like this. I never blended in, with nobody staring or pretending not to stare, with nobody wondering how a person like me got to call that place home. I never had the chance to be just ordinary.

I turned back to Bob and sent him a grin. I was glad to be there with him—after all, we'd lived together so much he was more like a big brother than a cousin. The first time Mom took off, when I was four, she dumped me at Liz's house for two months. Then it happened again when I was six, and then seven (Mom was gone the whole winter that time), and twice more over the last five years. I'm tougher now, but when I was little I used to crawl into my aunt and uncle's bed at night and huddle there, just so as I could have a body beside me instead of a nothing. And when I missed Mom too much not to cry, Bob, who's ten years older than me, used to hold me on his lap and tell me funny stories till I was laughing instead.

My cousin's building turned out to be near the corner of West 113th Street and Amsterdam in Manhattan, which he told me is a neighborhood just below Harlem full of frat boys and panhandlers. All I knew was that I'd never heard such a racket. Fire engines screaming, trucks blasting their horns, sirens and car alarms busting your ear drums. If Mousy had been there, he would've crawled under the bed covers to hide. At home all we ever heard at night were crickets and peepers, dogs barking, and sometimes the snorty squeal of a raccoon. We couldn't even hear the drunks because they always made their ruckus down on Market Street, not up on the hill where we lived. The whole thing made me feel shocked and shaky, like Mousy does on the Fourth of July.

Bob led me through the entryway and up a marble staircase to the second floor. "Ta-da!" he said, flinging open his door. "Here it is—my new pad."

I walked down a skinny hallway and out into a big living room. He had just moved there, so I'd never seen it before. It smelled of fresh paint and was still almost empty, its wooden floor bare and its few bits of furniture looking naked and embarrassed in the glare from the windows. He didn't even have curtains yet or anything on the white walls. But compared to the garbage heap Mom and I called home, it was a palace.

"I like this cool kitchen thing here," I said, my voice echoing. The kitchen was separated from the living room by an open counter. I'd never seen that, except on sitcoms. "You live in all this space alone? Not even with Julie?" Bob had been dating Julie for two years now, but my aunt said all they ever did was break up and make up every other week, like those fools in soap operas.

"Julie has her own apartment. Much nicer than this. You can sleep in my study here." He opened a door to a small room with nothing in it but a single bed and a desk, and tossed my duffel bag onto the floor. "Listen, you want some lunch? I'm starving."

After I'd washed the bus grime off of me, he took me to a pizza restaurant around the corner, a worn-down, family-type place where we sat in a red plastic booth and ordered a sausage pizza to share and a cup of hot tea each. He watched me load up my tea with three sugar packets. My aunt would've freaked if she'd seen me do that—she was paranoid about people getting fat, being skinny as a knitting needle herself. But I wasn't fat, I was just solid, with broad shoulders like a swimmer's and long, sturdy legs. I was okay with this, but Liz thought to be beautiful a girl had to be as anorexic as the models in her hairstyle magazines.

"So what's going on with you and Julie?" I said, wrapping my hands around my teacup.

"Nothing." Bob stared into his cup. "She dumped me again."

"Again? Why?"

He sipped his tea without answering. "Hey, your hair looks a lot better," is all he said. "Last time I saw you, you looked like a porcupine."

I frowned down at the table. I knew he was trying to be funny, but my hair was something of a sore point for me. It'd taken fifteen years of my life to figure out what to do with it. Mom dealt with my hair by not dealing with it at all: she just cut it short and let it sit there on top of my head, a halo of nappy frizz, for my whole childhood. Brillo-head, the kids called me then. After I'd come home all beat up from fighting

11

about that enough times, Liz tried braiding me some corn-rows, which always came out looking like the corn had been through a drought. That got me called noodle hair. Finally, she bought a copy of *Black Hair* magazine and we figured out how to separate and twist my hair right so it would grow into the long, slender dreadlocks I'd had for the past year. ("How you keep your hair like that, Madge? You never wash it?") I knew from reading books that girls who grow up in black families have this whole ritual with their hair. They get to sit down at their mother's knee and she divides the hair into little squares, then combs and oils, twists or braids it for hours. I read it can hurt like hell having your hair pulled like that, but it still sounded cozy to me, with the smell of oils and perfumes, and that soft, quiet talk you can have with a mom or a grandma while she fusses with your head. The most my mother ever thought to do about my hair was yank at it and say, "Looks like your dad fucked the blonde right out of me."

"I was asking about your girlfriend, asshole, not what you think of my hair," I muttered.

"Cool it, Madge, okay?"

That made me feel bad. I didn't want to fight with Bob. I just wanted to have fun the way we used to and forget about my stupid mom.

"I'm sorry about Julie," I said more calmly. "I know you like her a lot."

He tightened his mouth and shrugged. "Yeah, well it's been over for a while. I'm seeing somebody new now. Ruth. She's a photographer at the paper."

"That was fast. You serious about her?" He didn't answer so I poked him in the arm with my spoon. "Hey, I asked you a question."

"Cut it out, will you? What about you, anyway? You got a boyfriend?"

"Nope."

"Oh, come on. I bet you have ten boys running after you." He winked at me. Bob always talked like this, even though I'd told him for years that the boys in my town wouldn't be caught dead dating me.

The waiter came over then and slammed a platter of pizza down in front of us. He was an old man, tall and stooped, with a potbelly and greasy hair so black I was sure he'd dyed it. He looked like it would kill him to smile. I thanked him anyway and crammed a slice of pizza into my mouth.

"Slow down," Bob said, laughing. "You remind me of your mom. She's always bolted her food like somebody's about to snatch it."

I didn't answer. If anybody wanted to insult me, all they had to do was compare me to my ex-con, disappearing, juvenile delinquent of a so-called mother.

"Madge?" Bob said then, leaning over the table. "You haven't heard anything from her yet, have you?"

"Nope."

He reached out to take my hand. "I'm sorry she's taken off again. I know it's rough."

I yanked my hand away. Nobody likes to be pitied. "How about showing me the town?" I said to change the subject.

He sat back. "I can't, not today. I have to go back to the office, and tomorrow I need to get up at the crack of dawn to do a story."

"What kind of story?"

"Child welfare. It's about a little girl who got bumped from one horrible home to another, and now this foster mother's trying to rescue her and the city won't let her. I'm doing a series."

"I didn't know you covered stuff like that. I thought you only did stories about quintuplets and celebrity divorces."

Bob paid the bill and put on his coat, a brown bomber jacket that made him look surprisingly cool. "It's like that on a tabloid newspaper. I'm trying to reform. Let's go."

When we left the pizza place, it was colder than ever. We walked past a huge stone cathedral by the side of the road, which Bob said was called Saint John the Divine. I'd never seen a building so beautiful. It looked incredibly old, like a fairy-tale castle, with ornate pillars, a whole mess of stained-glass windows, and a row of skinny stone saints on either side of the door wearing the bleakest expressions, like they were staring right into the end of the world.

"Can I go with you on that story tomorrow?" I said.

Bob looked at me, his eyebrows lifted. "Why would you want to do that?"

"I don't know." But I did. I wanted to find out about that poor kid and the foster mom who was trying to save her. I was interested in people like that. "Well, can I?"

He frowned as he unlocked his front door. "I guess so. It's

kind of unusual, but I suppose I could bring you if you stay out of my way."

I wonder what that foster mom is like? I thought. I wonder why some women want to be mothers, and some don't.

When we got inside the apartment, Bob took a subway map out of his desk, along with two twenty-dollar bills, and handed them over to me. "My lunch hour's long over, so I've got to skedaddle. What're you gonna do this afternoon? Go see Times Square?"

"I was thinking of going to Harlem."

"Harlem? Why?" He opened a drawer in his desk and took out a bunch of keys.

The reason was I wanted to stand on a street without a single white person in sight, but I didn't think he'd understand that, so I only shrugged and asked him how to get there.

"Just walk north. We're practically there already. Or you can catch the subway up to 145th and go to the park on top of a sewage plant."

"They built a park on a sewage plant? Doesn't it stink?"

"Of course it stinks. But it's got great views. Here." He tossed me two keys on a ring. "Lock up when you leave, okay? I'll be back at seven or so and we can grab some dinner. Don't do anything I wouldn't do."

Mom used to say that to me all the time. Pretty ironic, given that she'd spent half her life in the clink.

After he left, I took the subway uptown, like Bob said to, and wandered around in the cold for a while, taking in all the brown faces. I never did come across a street with no white people at all, but it still felt good to blend in instead of stick out. It made me feel free and a little crazy, like I could do whatever I wanted and nobody would notice.

It didn't take me long to find the sewage park. I only had to follow the signs, and it was pretty obvious up there on a roof, jutting out over the Hudson River. I was surprised at how big it was, with grass and trees, playgrounds and ball courts, an ice-skating rink, and a cafeteria. Only a few people were around, though, walking or playing ball, maybe because it was so cold. The wind was certainly strong enough to blow away the stink.

I walked over to the far edge to look down at the water. The Hudson was much wider than the Delaware River near my house, with silvery waves like an ocean's and even some seagulls gliding on the wind. It looked wild and open, like it led to the rest of the world. I leaned on the wall and gazed at it a long time, squinting into the icy wind and thinking of all the places it could take me, places I'd never been, as far away from Hollowdale as I could get.

I'd been dying to get out of Hollowdale for years. All my friends were—we knew it was stifling, we knew it was dead. Where else could I have gotten all the way to seventeen without ever having a boyfriend? Mom said it was my own fault. She said I was too outspoken and feisty and I scared boys off, and sometimes I was afraid she was right. But other times I was sure it was prejudice. After all, everybody in Hollowdale was descended from Scots, German, or Irish. They didn't exactly take to those of a darker hue. At school, the kids wanted me on their basketball teams, even if they'd never seen me play ("You're a natural, right?"), and invited me on school committees to make them look "multicultural." (How can one person be multicultural all by herself?) But when it came to dating, I might as well've been a lamppost. I'd explained all this to my family for years, but they couldn't deal with it, couldn't take it in. Their idea of fighting racism was to pretend they were so color-blind they didn't even recognize it when it bit them on the nose.

Uncle Ron was different, though. He used to tell me that ever since the town's pipe-making factories had failed in the seventies, the good citizens of Hollowdale had turned small-minded and bigoted. "The fewer jobs there are, the more they hate outsiders," he said to me once. "It's not your fault, love, whatever your mum says." I missed my uncle. He was a boozer and a Commie, but he had a way of opening my eyes to things I might never have seen otherwise.

A scream jolted me out of my thoughts, and I turned around to see where it came from. A tiny black boy was collapsed by a playground fence like a pile of sticks, cradling his ankle and rocking. I scanned the playground for a nearby adult but didn't see a soul, so I walked on over.

"Hi there." I crouched beside him. "What's the matter?"

The boy looked up at me, his little face twisted in pain. His hair was a dusty mop of curls, and he was dressed in shabby sweatpants and a jacket way too big for him. His skin was a dark reddish brown, like nutmeg.

He was gasping too hard to talk. He wasn't crying, though.

"Let's see." I peered at his leg but his hands were clutched over his ankle, hiding it. He shrank away from me.

"Don't be scared, I won't hurt you. But I can't help unless you let me see what's wrong."

He shook his head, shivering.

"I won't touch it, promise. Look, I'll put my hands behind my back, see?"

He eyed me a moment, then slowly pulled up his pants leg. His ankle was already turning purple and it was puffy with swelling.

"Wow, looks like you twisted it pretty bad. Can you move it?" He shook his head again. I paused, wondering what to do. "Listen, you want me to carry you over to that bench? It's in the sun—you'll be warmer. It's pretty cold in this wind."

"No."

"But you're shivering! I'll be real careful, honest. If it hurts, just tell me to stop."

He didn't say anything this time, but since he didn't protest either, I picked him up. He was surprisingly light, even for a child that small, and so skinny he felt hard as bone, much harder than the two little girls I babysat for at home. He didn't smell too good—his clothes clearly hadn't been washed for quite a while—but when he wrapped his arms around my neck so trustingly like that, it made me feel tender and protective. I put him gently on the bench and sat next to him.

"What's your name?"

"Timmy." He huddled up beside me, like a sparrow in its nest. "You live near here?"

He nodded. He had a sweet face, a little brown oval with sharp cheekbones, a narrow jaw, and a round, full mouth. But it was the look in his eyes that got to me. They were huge and black and lonely, like the middle of the night.

"How old are you?" I asked him quietly. He held up four fingers. "Four?" He nodded, then added a fifth. I smiled. "Okay. Now who are you with? We've got to get you home." He didn't answer. "Who did you come here with, Timmy?"

"Nobody."

"I tell you what. I'll carry you and we'll go find someone to help." I moved to stand up, but he grabbed me and dug his fingers into my wrist. His hands were scrawny as bird feet.

"No!"

I patted his little back. "We can't stay here, sweetie. What'll your mom say if you sit out here in the cold with your ankle hurt so bad, huh?" He wouldn't answer, so I began lifting him off the bench, but he yelped and shuddered. "I'm sorry," I said quickly, and picked him up more carefully, settling him on my hip. "This okay now?" He nodded.

I carried him over to some older boys playing basketball nearby, on a court surrounded by a hurricane fence. "Excuse me!" I called. "Any of you know this kid?"

The boys looked at me, and one of them, about my age, tall and muscular and pretty damn cute, dribbled his basketball over to where I stood. He took a peek at Timmy through the fence and laughed. "Oh, that kid, yeah." He turned around.

"Hey, Joey!" he yelled so loud I jumped. "Your homeboy's found a hot mama!"

"It isn't funny," I told him. "He's broken his ankle or something."

A pudgy boy ran up, about nine years old, who said he was Joey. "Whazzup?" he said. Timmy stuck out his leg to show him his ankle, proud of himself now. Joey whistled. "Whoa, that's nasty." He looked up at me. "You want me to take him home? I know where he lives."

Joey was only a few inches taller than Timmy; I didn't see him getting very far if he had to carry the boy. "Why don't you show me the way and I'll carry him?" I said. "He's too hurt to walk." Joey agreed and led me out of the park.

"You kids came here all by yourselves?" I asked him, panting to keep up. Timmy didn't feel so light anymore, and his smelly clothes were getting to me.

"Yeah," Joey said. "We come here every day." That surprised me. Even my on-again, off-again mom hadn't let me out on my own when I was as little as Timmy.

Joey led me down some piss-stinky steps out of the park and across the road to a block of old apartment houses and almost no trees. He stopped in front of number 548, a shabby brick building with a gray, graffiti-covered door, ran up the stoop and pushed the door open—the lock must have been busted. Then he trotted up three flights of stairs while I followed more slowly, Timmy getting heavier by the minute. When we reached a door with a brass fish nailed to the middle of it, Joey stopped. In the center of the fish was a spy hole. Timmy hid his face in my neck.

"Yo, open up. Timmy got hurt!" Joey yelled, banging on the door with his fist.

I heard footsteps inside, then the cover of the spy hole lifted and a magnified eye stared out at us through the fish's belly. The door opened a few inches. A man with an unshaven white face and a gray mustache poked his nose through the crack.

Joey turned around and ran down the stairs.

"Who you?" the man said.

"Uh, hi," I answered quickly, wondering why Joey had scooted away so fast. "I found your son here with a hurt ankle, sprained or broken or something. He can't walk."

"He not my son."

"Oh," I said, confused. "Is this the wrong apartment?"

"No, no. Come." The man opened the door. He was middle height with a belly so big it looked like he'd swallowed a pillow. He was wearing a white undershirt stained yellow under the arms, and loose brown pants with no belt.

"Come," he said again, and shuffled ahead of me, muttering to himself in such fast Spanish I couldn't understand a word. (So much for my seven years of Spanish class.) I followed him down a long, dark passageway into a living room with ratty furniture, no rug, and a bare lightbulb in the ceiling. Timmy was still clinging to me with his face hidden. The man pointed to an orange couch. "There."

Carefully, I lowered Timmy to the couch, but he wrapped a hand around my wrist like a claw. I had to pry his fingers loose before I could stand up again.

The man turned to me. "Now go."

I was shocked. No thank-you, no questions, no welcome—

what kind of a person was this? "But shouldn't he go to a doctor?" I stammered.

"This not your business. Go."

Soon as he said that, Timmy started to cry. I bent over and stroked his springy hair. "Hey, I'll come back soon and see how you're doing. Don't cry, okay?"

He looked up at me, tears running down his little face. But he didn't say a word.

When I got back to my cousin's place late that afternoon, I was pretty upset. I didn't like that man I'd left Timmy with, I didn't like how scared Timmy had seemed, and I didn't like the look of that apartment, either. I made myself some hot, sugary tea and turned on the television while I waited for Bob to come back from work. I wanted to zone out and forget all the troubles in the world.

Bob didn't have cable, so the only program I could find on his stupid TV was a whites-only sitcom, the kind where the characters don't even have any black friends. I turned it off in disgust, took a book out of my backpack, and was just settling down to read when the phone rang. I picked it up.

"Hello?" drawled a snooty woman's voice. "May I speak to Robert Dunbar?"

"Who's this?" Of course I knew.

"Julie Winters." She sounded impatient. "Is he there?"

I'd met Julie once. She was tall, stunning as a model, and arrogant as hell. Bob had brought her down to Riverbend to have dinner with the family, and she'd spent the whole time tossing around her long red hair and criticizing Liz's taste in that same snooty voice I recognized on the phone. She'd made Bob real unhappy, too, dangling him on a string for two whole years while she went out with other guys, telling him she loved him one week and not the next. She was the kind of woman who takes pleasure in screwing men over and making every female around her feel ugly as a walnut.

"No," I answered. "He's out."

"Who am I speaking to?"

"I'm Madge. You met me once."

"Ah."

Wow, the buckets of contempt a person can put into one little syllable.

"Well, please ask him to call me when he gets home."

"Maybe I will, maybe I won't."

I hung up and started reading my book.

Half an hour later, Bob banged into the apartment and collapsed into an armchair. "What a shit hole of a day. I need a drink."

I looked him over—rumpled gray suit, tie askew, wisps of hair flying about. I went behind the kitchen counter and picked up the mop. "Here," I said, "your hair needs combing."

He laughed. "You're such a pain in the ass, Madge. Why don't you get me a beer from the fridge?"

"Okay. Can I have one?"

"No way. I'm not about to contribute to the corruption of minors. Where the hell did you get that T-shirt? It's hurting my eyes."

I'd changed into a neon-green T-shirt with the words I'M RIGHT YOU'RE WRONG scrawled across it. I shrugged, handing him the beer.

"Did I get any phone calls?" he said.

I paused. I really didn't want Julie messing Bob up again. "Madge?"

"Uh, yeah, I just remembered. Julie Iceberg called. So, what was wrong with your day?"

"Julie! When?" Bob jumped up and grabbed for the phone, but just then it rang again. "Yeah?" he said eagerly. He listened awhile, his face all confused, and then he laughed. "Sure, no problem." He talked a moment more, then turned to me. "It's your mom. She's back."

When I heard that, my heart jumped with relief. She was safe! But then it thumped right back down. It was a horrible, sickening feeling, like my guts had dropped out of me. Mom always made my insides bounce around like that.

I waited a few beats and took the phone. "Hi."

"So, big-city girl, how d'you like New York, then? Been having a good time with Bobby?" Mom was the only person in the family who still called my cousin by his baby name.

"It's been okay."

"Is that all you've got to say? Well, it's time to drag your arse home. Bobby said he can drive you back Saturday, all right?"

No, it's not all right! I wanted to yell. *You can't just disappear, then act like nothing's happened!* But I'd learned long ago it was

24

no use complaining, let alone asking Mom where she'd been. She would never answer.

"I don't want to come home Saturday, it's too soon."

"Don't be daft. When I say come home, you come home."

"Then *be* there for a fucking change!" I shouted, and slammed down the phone.

two

MY COUSIN WOKE me the next morning by banging into the room and barking at me. "Ruth's arriving any minute. Shake it!" He snapped up the window shades. "Want some breakfast?"

I blinked in the sudden sunlight. For a second there, I had no idea where I was. "Course not. I can't eat while I'm asleep."

"Well then, move."

I pulled myself out of bed and stumbled to the bathroom, clutching my clothes. The bathroom was just as white as the rest of Bob's place—the walls, the shower curtain, even the towels. It couldn't have been more different from his home in Riverbend. My aunt had decorated it in so many bright colors you practically needed to wear sunglasses inside the house.

I gave my face a scrub and took a peek in the mirror, then quickly turned away to take a shower. Mirrors bothered me. When you've grown up different from everyone around you, even your own mother, it can be disconcerting to look in a mirror. It makes you see yourself the way most people only see strangers.

I went through a phase of staring in the mirror every day when I was nine. Mom used to tease me about it. "You falling in love with yourself, Madgy? You getting vain on me?" But it wasn't that. It was that I wanted to work out whether she was really my mom at all. Kids were always telling me I was adopted. Why else would I be there, they said, the only "wool-head" in town? I hit anybody who said that, but it didn't get me any answers. So I stared in that mirror for hours, trying to find Mom in my face. She was there in my green eyes, but where else? Mom had a square face, eyes high and narrow, lips a thin line, blonde and gray hair straight as brush bristles. I had the same high cheekbones, but where was the rest? Dense black curls, full mouth, tea-brown skin, and a long oval face—all that had to have come from my dad, but I'd never even seen a picture of him. That was why I didn't like mirrors. They reminded me of everything I didn't know.

"Am I adopted?" I used to ask Mom all the time.

"Of course not," she'd say. "You take after your dad, that's all."

"Then why am I brown when you're pink?"

"Because people come in all colors, like dogs. All that counts is what's on the inside." And when I asked what my dad had looked like, she always answered, "He was tall and gorgeous, like you." Last year, though, that changed. "Look," she finally told me, "I don't remember, all right? I was too sodding pissed. All I know is he was Jamaican 'cause of the way he talked. Now leave me alone."

Up until I was ten, I would tell any kid who'd listen that

my dad was going to show up any minute to get me. Sometimes he'd arrive in a big green car with a teddy bear in his arms, and he'd be tall and shiny, like he was polished. Other times he'd come out of the clouds in a helicopter and land on the roof. (I think I'd seen that on TV.) But he was always smiling and he was always a beautiful dark brown. "Hey, little girl, sorry I been gone so long," he'd say, his voice booming, and he'd lift me up for a hug. "You're coming with me now." And we'd go off to the city, where I'd have a huge bedroom covered in a pink shag rug, a school full of kids who looked like me, and a dad who loved me so much I never had to wonder who I was again.

Oh, well. Those were kid dreams. I gave up on them a long time ago.

"Madge, I need to shave!" Bob banged on the bathroom door just as I stepped out of the shower. "Hurry up!"

I yanked on my clothes and pulled open the door so fast he fell in. When I walked back out into the living room, a white woman was standing there, gazing out the window.

"Hi," I said.

She turned around. "Oh, hi," she said casually, but I wasn't fooled. She was wearing the same startled expression I always saw when my family's friends met me for the first time. I dropped onto the couch and stared at her. I could outstare anyone if I wanted to. I'd had plenty of practice.

She walked over, smiling. "You're Madge, aren't you? Bob's told me about you. I'm Ruth." She shook my hand. Her fingers felt bony and cool. She was one of those fragile types who never looks warm enough, with a delicate face, a heap of bushy brown hair, and legs long as a spider's. I thought she was pretty, but a touch too gawky to be beautiful.

"Are you Bob's girlfriend?"

"Well . . ." She blushed.

"Leave her alone, Madge," Bob said, emerging from the bathroom freshly scraped and pink. "We ready?"

Ruth picked up her heavy camera bag and gave him the sweetest smile. I didn't know whether to trust her yet, but I could tell right away she was nuts about my cousin.

She drove the three of us up Broadway in her battered white Honda while I stared out the back window, amazed. I could not believe how crowded the street was. Thousands of people were rushing around, cars were double-parked, every single building was an open store. In Hollowdale, our main street was empty as a bigot's head, except for weekend nights, and even then you only saw one or two whale-sized women lumbering in and out of their cars, or winos falling out of bar doorways. (Mom wouldn't let me go downtown on weekend nights because she said that was when all the nutcase Nazi types came in from the boondocks to get drunk.) Hollowdale had been built in a swamp at the bottom of a valley and Uncle Ron used to say it never would've existed at all if it hadn't been for greedy capitalists needing to stick their factory workers in cheap housing. But it was like a ghost town now. Almost all the stores had failed or moved out to the mall, and nobody had any money to spend anyhow, so all we had was one overcrowded school, a failing racetrack, and a lot of alcoholics. It was like any American town, I guess, once you take the hope out of it.

When Ruth finally pulled over to park, she said we were in a neighborhood called Washington Heights. "It's poor but respectable," she told me, slinging her camera bag over her shoulder and locking the car. She was dressed all in black, pants and a fitted leather jacket, which made her look narrow and graceful, like a winter branch. "This woman we're interviewing this morning, for example, Mrs. Henderson, used to be a nurse. Let's go."

She led us up the block and into a huge, gray apartment building. "Madge?" Bob said on the way. "Keep quiet while we do this, all right? No butting in or sassy remarks. Deal? It's weird enough bringing you along."

"Screw you! What in the hell do you think I am?"

"No, I think it's good she came," Ruth said quickly. "And I don't see why she shouldn't ask questions. This woman's a foster mother, she loves kids—she'll probably relate to Madge much better than to us."

Bob shrugged, looking a little ashamed. "Guess so."

Ruth caught my eye and winked.

Mrs. Henderson turned out to be small and dark, and dressed up like a churchgoer. She looked incredibly old, but Bob told me later she was only forty-five. She had big brown eyes that bulged out a little, and a round droopy face. My own eyes soaked her up. Back then I didn't really know any other black people, just the daddy of my imagination and that girl who stared out at me from the mirror.

Bob told the woman I was his cousin and she seemed surprised, the same way white people always were. But then she ushered us in, sat us down, and offered me a box of doughnuts right away. Normally I would've eaten about four, having skipped breakfast, but I didn't want to act like some fool kid, so I let the box sit unopened on my lap. I wanted to pay attention so I could ask some smart questions and prove to Bob I wasn't the idiot he thought.

After we'd all made our introductions, Mrs. Henderson began to speak, her voice quiet and a little shaky. "I'm glad you folks are gonna tell my story 'cause it needs to be told," she said. "Here, take a look at this picture. It's Marissa. Just look at the poor child."

She passed around a photo of a girl about ten years old: round face, serious eyes. Her hair in a topknot, gold hoops in each ear.

"I been a foster mother for a whole bunch of years and I loved every one of my babies, but Marissa, she captured my heart."

"She looks real sweet," I said, gazing at the picture before I handed it back to her.

Bob frowned at me to shut me up, but Mrs. Henderson only smiled and turned her sad, droopy eyes to mine. "Yes, honey, she is. I'm glad you can see it. But her mama never wanted her, you know, all she wanted was her dope." And then she told us that when Marissa's mother was arrested and put in jail, Marissa was given to her for the next six years.

"I loved her like my own and she was so happy here! But

when that devil woman got outta jail, those Children's Services people wanted to give Marissa right back to her. I fought against it, but those people, they wouldn't listen. 'Biological mother,' those are magic words to those folks. So they took away Marissa—didn't matter she was happy with me. And they put her back with that crazy junkie. Oh, she cried and cried, poor little baby. And me, I cried, too. How could they be so cruel?"

Mrs. Henderson stopped talking, her lips twisting. Ruth fiddled with the camera and Bob wrote in his notebook. I stared down at the box of doughnuts on my lap, trying to think of a question, but I couldn't. It felt wrong sitting in this woman's home, poking into her sadness like this. It felt nosy and rude.

She spoke up again. "After only eight days, Marissa had a smashed nose and burns on her arms. The neighbors and teachers reported her mama to the authorities a whole bunch of times, but they didn't do nothing for months. She only got rescued 'cause a housing inspector happened to visit, and he found her locked in a closet with her belly bloated from hunger and welts all over her poor little arms and legs, Lord help us."

I'd heard stories like this in Hollowdale about parents abusing their kids, backwoods types who beat the boys and messed with the girls. I even knew one boy in third grade who came to school every week with long red streaks on his back where his daddy whipped him with a belt. I knew something about how evil the world could be. But still, every time

I thought about people being this cruel to kids, I wanted to punch out the wall.

"Is that when you got Marissa back?" Bob said. Mrs. Henderson didn't answer—she was gazing at the photo in her hand, too upset to speak anymore. "Mrs. Henderson?"

I shot Bob a look. Did he have to be so pushy?

She raised her head and sighed. "No. I tried, but I couldn't get her back. They put the poor baby with another foster family instead, this one with five older kids and not one of them with a heart. One boy, he raped Marissa, and the foster mother, she just turned a blind eye. That boy abused Marissa for two years before somebody at her school noticed a problem. And then, you know what they did?"

I swallowed because her words were making me want to cry.

"They put her in another home with strangers."

"How could they?" I burst out. "Why didn't they give her back to you? That's terrible!"

Bob glared at me again, but Mrs. Henderson nodded. "I know, baby. You're right. But this time, I found out early enough to fight till I got her back." She pulled at her scrawny hands. "I'm nursing that child now like she's my own. But she's turned so scared. She used to be a smiley thing, bouncy like a bubble, full of sass. All that's gone. She's just big-eyed silent, waiting for the next bad thing to get her."

Mrs. Henderson paused again, shaking her head from side to side. "Now I'm trying to adopt her so they won't never take her away again. But the city won't let me. They want to give her to some other foster family, all over again, like they learned nothing at all."

"That's crazy! How can they do that?" I said.

"I don't know, honey pie. It's just the system. Anyhow, that's when I got hold of the Children's Rights folks and now we're in a lawsuit. You know what it's called? Marissa versus the mayor. That says it all, don't it? One poor child against the boss of the whole city."

"You think you'll win?" Bob asked, still scribbling in his notebook.

She looked over at him, her mouth tight. "We got to win. If we don't, Marissa's gonna die." There was a flash and a click and we all jumped.

"I'm sorry," Ruth said quickly. "I had to take a picture."

"Where's Marissa now, Mrs. Henderson?" I asked after we'd all blinked enough to see again. "Is the poor kid okay?"

"She's right here, sweetie. She's back there in the bedroom watching TV. You want to meet her?"

When I said yes, Mrs. Henderson did something I never would've expected. She stood up, took the doughnuts off my lap, and said to Ruth and Bob, "You wait here, if you don't mind. Marissa ain't gonna want to deal with you reporter folk." And she led me down the hall to the back of the apartment. "You like kids?" she asked.

"I love kids. I babysit for my downstairs neighbor all the time at home."

"And where's home for you?"

"Hollowdale, Pennsylvania. You've probably never heard of it."

"Well, no, but that don't mean it ain't some place that matters. Now here's my baby. Don't be shocked. She isn't all better yet, but she's getting there."

She opened the bedroom door and I found my heart knocking hard. I was scared I'd see something terrible, like a skeleton instead of a kid, or some poor rag of a thing covered with scars and bruises. But there on the bed, curled up around a pillow and watching TV, was this cute little girl in blue jeans and a white shirt, those same golden hoops in her ears. She seemed so normal.

Mrs. Henderson didn't say anything, she just let me stand there and look. And the more I looked, the more I saw. Marissa was way too small for ten. Her legs and arms were frail, her face was a narrow patch of brown. And on one arm I saw a row of ragged round scars.

"Marissa, honey?" Mrs. Henderson said.

Marissa blinked and glanced over at us.

"Say hi to . . . what's your name again, sweetie pie?" I told her. "Say hi to Madge."

Marissa put her thumb in her mouth and stared glassy-eyed at me for a moment. Then she turned back to the TV.

On the way home in the car, I told Ruth and Bob what I'd seen. "Could you write that down for me when we get back?" Bob said. "It might help my story."

"Okay, I'll try."

"It's nice the way Mrs. Henderson trusted you, Madge," Ruth added, looking at me in the rearview mirror as she drove.

"You were so respectful of her. I think she appreciated that."

"Thanks," I said, pleased. "But is it normal for a kid to end up in so many bad foster homes?" I was thinking of Timmy and wondering if that's what had happened to him. The man who'd answered the door had said he wasn't the father, after all. Suppose I'd left Timmy in a cruel foster home like the one where Marissa had been raped?

"It is pretty common, yeah," Bob answered. "That's why I'm doing this series. The system has to change."

I stared out of the car window, seeing Marissa in my mind, sucking her thumb like a baby, her growth stunted by cruelty. I couldn't get over how long and hard Mrs. Henderson had been fighting to rescue that girl. If you were a person like that, I thought, you could hold your head up in the world. You wouldn't mind not having a boyfriend. You wouldn't mind that your mom bounces in and out of your life like a tennis ball. You wouldn't even mind being the only black button in the white button box. You'd just be proud.

three

AFTER WE GOT home from visiting Mrs. Henderson, I wrote down my description of Marissa for Bob before he went back to the office, and Ruth invited me to stick with her for the rest of the day. She shot a five-alarm fire in Brooklyn and a collapsed building on the West Side, and the whole time she took the trouble to explain what she was doing. She even let me help a little, holding her cameras, taking down people's names, and making notes on what was happening. By the end of that afternoon, I'd decided Ruth was a hundred times better than Julie, and that Bob would be a fool not to hold on to her as long as he could.

That night, the three of us met up in Chinatown and ate some kind of stringy mush I didn't recognize at all. Then Ruth came back with us to stay over. I had to turn up the TV real loud when she and Bob went into his bedroom so I wouldn't hear what was going on. Still, I was glad. The only drawback was that I was pretty sure Bob wasn't over Julie yet. I hoped he wouldn't hurt Ruth. And I hoped Julie wouldn't hurt him.

When Saturday rolled around, Bob and I climbed into his old blue Toyota so he could drive me back to Hollowdale. I didn't want to go, and the weather didn't help—it was one of those cold, gray days when the sky looks like a saucepan lid clamped over the world. I pulled my coat tight around me and stared through the windshield, while he talked excitedly about how his story might help Mrs. Henderson's case. He sounded pretty pleased with himself.

"I found a kid with a sprained ankle the other day," I said when he'd finally shut up. I wanted Bob to know he wasn't the only person in the family who could do good in the world. "He'd hurt it real bad. He was only about four."

"Oh, yeah? Were you able to help him?"

"Yeah. I got this older boy who knew him to take him home." I decided not to tell Bob I'd done it myself. He would only yell at me for going into a stranger's house.

"Good for you."

Bob didn't say anything after that, so I went back to staring out the window. I wondered how Timmy was doing. Was he outside playing in this horrible weather? Was his ankle any better? Did he have anyone to look after him besides that scary man I'd met in his apartment? I should've gone back to see if he had a home as bad as Marissa's. I'd been in New York for four whole days since I'd met him, but I'd gotten so busy seeing the sights and helping out Ruth that I'd forgotten all about my promise to visit.

"Madge?" Bob said after a while. "How do you feel about seeing your mom again?"

"Not great."

He pulled a face. "What about school, though? Is that going okay?"

I paused. I didn't like it when he gave me the third degree like this. Did he think he was my dad or something?

"I mean, do they still bother you about being mixed and stuff?" he went on.

"I'm not 'mixed and stuff,' I'm black!" I yelled. Then I went silent. Bob had asked me this a few times before, and he always did it in this same hushed voice, like he was asking how I felt about missing a leg, or something. When I was little, I trusted him, and I would tell him about the kids calling me names and the ugly things I heard them say about black people. But I stopped doing that years ago because either he got all preachy about how color didn't matter, like Mom did (if color didn't matter, then how come I was treated like that?), or he questioned me so closely about what exact words the kids used and what their parents believed that I felt turned into a specimen for some kind of sociology class. When he questioned me like that, I felt like a pinned-down bug under a microscope. It made me feel like I wasn't me.

"Well, do they?" he prompted.

"Yeah, they still bother me," I muttered. "It's no different than it's always been."

Bob shook his head. "You'd do much better in a big city. It isn't right making you go to an all-white school. I've told Brandy a million times she should move the two of you to Philly."

I didn't answer that. I was pretty sure if I moved to Philadelphia and went to an integrated school, like Bob was suggesting, I wouldn't fit in there any better than I fit in at Hollowdale High. The white kids would reject me because I looked black, just like happened to me so often already. And the black kids would call me an Oreo because they'd be able to tell that all I really knew about being black was from what I'd read or seen on TV.

Truth is, if you ask me, there's no such thing as being mixed race in this country. Nobody will allow it. They make you choose sides—either you're black or you're white. You can't be in the middle, and you can't be both.

By the time we reached the northeast corner of Pennsylvania, we'd been in deep country for a while, and the gray sky was bringing out all the colors. Electric green fields, sugar-white farmhouses, rust-red cows. The Delaware River was a silver ribbon in the valley below, and the trees were apple green with early spring. We drove over the top of a hill, where the road ran straight through farmland and past an old house. Bob slowed down so as not to run over anything. Four goofy-looking geese peered at us, their heads small and suspicious on top of their long necks. Bob waved hello to a fat farmwife taking down her washing.

"I love it here," he said. "I never appreciated how beautiful it is till I moved to the city."

I looked out the window. What I saw was a farmhouse falling apart, an obese white woman doing mindless chores, and acres of boring emptiness.

When we drove into Hollowdale, I pointed to a weed-cluttered space behind Mom's rusty Chevy and told Bob to park there. Mom and I lived halfway up a hill overlooking the valley, in a skinny clapboard house that was listing like a capsized fishing boat. Its gray paint was chipped and blistered, its front porch sloped so steeply that whenever you stepped on it you almost got pitched right off again, and the roof was always raining asbestos shingles. The house looked like it was about to somersault right down the hill.

Bob parked and we walked up the sloping front steps. I squeezed my duffel bag to my chest, my guts tight and aching. Then I wrenched open the crooked door and walked in.

Even though it was still afternoon, the foyer was dark as a broom closet. I could barely make out the wooden staircase disappearing into blackness. But I could hear the muffled sounds of television voices coming from upstairs.

"Mom?" I called. "She's got the TV on too loud to hear us. Come on." I led Bob up the creaking stairs past the other two apartments in the house: one on the ground floor, where Maggie Donahue lived, this blowsy single mother who Mom liked to smoke and drink beer with; and one on the second floor, which belonged a crotchety old guy called Mr. Henig, who banged on his ceiling with a mop handle whenever I played music. We lived on the third floor, in a pokey, low-ceilinged apartment right under the roof.

I unlocked our door. "Mom? You here?"

"Madge, is that you?" she called in her croaky smoker's voice, and stepped out of the kitchen, drying her hands on a dishcloth.

She looked no different from the last time I'd seen her,

though for some reason I'd thought she would. She was wearing the same black jeans she'd had on then and her usual blue work shirt. Her hair, which had turned gray a few years ago, was as short and bristly as ever, her face heavy and pale.

"Well, well, look at this, my favorite nephew." She loved that joke, Bob being the only nephew she had. She made it every time she saw him.

"Hi, Brandy." He gave her a hug.

"It's been quite a while, hasn't it?" She stepped out of his arms to look at him. "I've not seen you since your poor dad's funeral. What a fuckin' mess that was, eh?" She shook her head.

"How are you doing?" is all Bob replied. I knew he didn't like talking about Uncle Ron's accident. It upset him too much.

She shrugged. "Same as always. Bit of this, bit of that. You coming in for a beer, then?"

"No beer, thanks, I have to drive back to the city. Here's Madge, safe and sound."

Mom glanced at me and turned back to Bob. "Sure you don't want one for the road?" She pulled him down the hallway and into the living room by his wrist.

"Well, maybe a little one." He looked over at me. I was standing near the door with my green duffel bag in my arms, frowning. Mousy waddled over and rubbed against my ankles—Mom must've picked him up at Liz's. At least somebody had noticed I was back.

"Make yourself at home, then." She went into the kitchen

and returned with a bottle of beer in each hand. "Sit," she said, waving at the worn-out red couch facing our TV set. The volume was up so loud I realized we'd all been shouting. The rest of our tiny living room was littered with furniture Mom had found in the street or at the dump: a battered coffee table, three mismatched armchairs, and a rickety black side table covered with her souvenir knickknacks and ashtrays, which I hated and she loved. Under it all lay a scattering of rag rugs in dull oranges and browns. After Bob's bare apartment, the room looked like an overstuffed closet. It didn't help that we hadn't washed the windows in five years.

"Want a fag?" Mom held out a cigarette packet.

Bob shook his head. "I've quit."

"You and the rest of the world. Go on, take one for emergencies."

He shrugged and took one, slipping it into his shirt pocket. Mom lit one for herself. Switching off the television, she plopped down on the couch, her legs spread apart like a man's, and grinned up at him through a stream of smoke. "Now then, sit yourself down and tell me what life's like in the Big Apple."

I was still standing by the hallway, clinging to my bag.

"Madge, come sit with us," Bob said.

Mom twisted around to look at me. "You were all right with Aunty Liz, then?"

"What the fuck do you care?"

Mom sighed. "Look, love, don't start. It's nothing to make a fuss about. I was only gone a month."

"You could have called!" I dropped my bag on the floor

and kicked it. "Why won't you ever tell me where you go? You might've been dead for all I knew!"

"Do all teenagers exaggerate like this?" Mom said to Bob. She patted the seat beside her. "Come on, lovey, sit here with me and don't sulk. You know I can't stand sulking."

Scowling, I trailed over and flopped down beside her. She put an arm around me and pulled my head on to her shoulder. She felt thick and solid, like a rubber tree trunk, and she reeked of cigarettes.

"So, what did you two do in New York, eh?" She patted me on the head, fiddling absently with my dreads. "Had a good time, did you?"

"Madge came with me on a story," Bob said. "We ate in Chinatown, went to some movies, saw the sights."

"I met his girlfriend. Or one of them. I went on a photo shoot with her."

Mom turned to look me in the face. "Then what're you so grumpy about? Sounds like you had the time of your life."

"If you can call seeing a beat-up kid the time of my life."

"Beat-up kid?" My mother raised her eyebrows.

"I took her with me on this story about foster care," Bob said, leaning forward and rolling his beer bottle back and forth between his hands. "It could be an important case. Some people think it might change a lot of things about child welfare in the city."

"Huh, listen to you! I didn't know you were turning political, Bobby. You're getting more like your dad every day, you are."

"Well, you can't watch the way the world's going and not do something."

"But what can we do? It's all up to the government and they don't give a rat's arse what we think."

"Bullshit!" I said, pulling away from Mom. "That's the kind of attitude that got the world in this mess. If you sit there like a bathmat and let them walk all over you, nothing will ever get better and there will never be any revolutions."

Mom shook her head and took a swig from her beer bottle. "Yeah, well, revolution's all right for some place like Russia or Africa. I mean, those places have had real oppression and starvation and all that. If that was going on here, I'd be with you all the way. Out in the streets, waving me fist and shouting rhymes about love and peace." She chortled. "But the U.S. isn't like that, is it? A lot of prejudice, I admit, just like at home, but most people here are comfortable, know what I mean? Look at me! An ex-con, been in and out of the nick more times than I care to remember, but here I am anyway with a nice home, free education for my daughter, a car—we live very decently. I feel lucky. We couldn't have a revolution here. There's nothing to revolt against."

"God, you should hear how selfish you sound!" I said. "'I'm all right, so screw everybody else.' What about all the poverty in this country, and the innocent people we keep killing in wars? What about the racism and those abused kids Bob's writing about?"

"Calm down, love, you'll give yourself a brain tumor." Mom chuckled. "I said the prejudice is bad, didn't I? And I know those poor kids need help. But that's nothing revolution is going to cure."

"What will, then? Letters to the editor?"

Bob raised his eyebrows at me. "So you're planning to start a revolution, huh?"

I crossed my arms. "Whose side are you on, hypocrite?"

"Well, this is fun. I'm going for a piss." He went into the bathroom.

While he was gone, I gave Mom a piece of my mind about her political apathy, she told me to shut the fuck up, I told her the same thing, and by the time Bob got back I was fuming and she was biting her fingernails and getting cigarette ash all over the couch.

"You talk some sense into her," I said to him, and marched off to the kitchen to see if Mom had bought anything to eat for a change. I'd been home for all of fifteen minutes and I was fed up with her already.

"Look, Brandy." Bob lowered his voice, but our apartment was so small I could still hear him. "Madge was real upset when you took off like that. You have to stop. It's too hard on her."

I heard my mother thump her legs on top of the coffee table. "I know, I know. That was the last time, I swear."

"I hope so. It upsets us all. My mother, too."

"Look, I didn't have any choice, all right?"

"Why don't you make it so you do have a choice, then? Whatever you mean by that."

"You don't know what you're talking about, Bobby, and

I'm not going to tell you, so you can stop your preaching. You sound like a fuckin' priest."

"I can hear every word you're saying, you know," I said, coming back into the room, munching an apple—amazingly, Mom had actually gone shopping.

"We're only discussing you, darlin', and your wonderful qualities."

"Oh, shut up."

"Don't give me that cheek, young lady." But then she laughed.

Bob stood up then and said he had to leave. Mom looked disappointed. "I never get to see you anymore," she said, her square face suddenly anxious. "You have to go already?"

"Yeah, my mother needs me to help with the insurance papers." He walked toward the door. "They owe her for Dad's accident and I want to make sure she gets it. Thanks for the beer."

Mom bounded up off the couch. "Hold your horses." She lumbered toward him. "Give your aunty a hug, then, before you take off." She held out her arms and he stepped into them. "Bye, you old sod," she said gruffly. "Give us a ring now and then, all right? That's what telephones are for."

"I will. I'm glad you're back." He opened the door and looked at me. "See you, Madge."

"Bye, Bob. Thanks. I had a great time. Tell Ruth thanks for me, too." I tried to smile but it didn't come out right. I felt panicked. I didn't want to him to go. I didn't want him to leave me alone with Mom.

❖　❖　❖

After Bob closed our door behind him, Mom and I stood in the hallway without saying a word, listening to his footsteps clump down the staircase and out the front door. I stared at my feet and the frayed bottoms of my jeans. My sneakers, blue and orange, had gotten so dirty in New York the laces had turned gray.

"All right," Mom said, rubbing the palms of her hands together with a sandpapery sound. "It's back to real life now, eh Madgy? You better go unpack that body bag of yours." She poked my duffel bag with her muddy boot.

I wasn't in the mood for her jailhouse humor right then, so I picked up the bag without answering and lugged it into my bedroom.

My room was by far the coolest place in the house. It used to be the attic, so it was shaped like a slice of cake lying on its side, with the ceiling sloping all the way to the floor in the back and my bed against a wall opposite the window. Two years earlier, when I was fifteen, I'd painted it red all over. Not cherry red, but a bluish blood-red so intense it seemed to pulse when you looked at it. I'd covered one wall with posters of my favorite hip-hop and movie stars, and another wall with antiwar slogans, photos of my friends, and a snapshot of Snake Eyes, our school rock band, playing at a dance. On the slanting ceiling over my bed was a big American flag with a peace sign painted on it, dripping tears, which I'd tacked up when we started bombing innocent kids and civilians in Iraq. I thought my room looked like the inside of a heart. Mom said it was more like a stomach.

"Every time I walk in here, I feel like I'm being digested," she liked to say.

I was slinging my bag on to the bed when I noticed a package sitting there, wrapped up in newspaper and tied with a pink Easter ribbon. "Hey, what's this?" I called.

Mom came to my door and propped herself against the doorjamb, her thick arms folded across her chest. "Aren't you going to open it, then?"

I picked up the package and shook it. It was lumpy and square. "Is it a present?"

"No, it's a bomb. Go on, open it."

I undid the ribbon and tore off the paper, and what I saw was pretty amazing. Inside was a big hamburger bun, only made of cloth, with sleeves to hold CDs where you'd normally put the lettuce and onions. And in every sleeve was a new CD. There was hip-hop, rap, reggae, a whole bunch of my favorite girl bands, and the kind of hard rock Snake Eyes played. . . . I'd never realized Mom paid attention to the kind of music I liked.

"Jesus, these must have cost a fortune!" I said. Mom was grinning at me from the doorway. "Where'd you get them— off the back of a truck?"

She stood up straight at that, dropping her hands to her hips. "Is that all you've got to say? Give them back, then, if you feel that way about it. Go on, hand them over." She strode up to me, holding out a nail-bitten hand. Back when she'd been a teenager in prison, she'd tattooed the letters L-O-V-E on the knuckles of her right hand and H-A-T-E on the knuckles of the left. The words looked like faded pen scratches by now, but you could still read them.

I didn't move. I wanted that present real bad, but I wasn't going to keep it if it was stolen goods. Mom was always giving me stuff she had acquired under dubious circumstances. Once, when I was six, she'd made me take home a doll stroller just because it was lying on somebody's lawn. And another time she'd picked up a kid's bike from an empty playground and stuffed it in the trunk of our car. "But what if the kid comes back to get it?" I'd said, and I remember she'd laughed.

"Madgy, listen." She'd crouched down to chuck me under the chin. "You ever heard the phrase 'finders keepers'? Anyone who can afford a shiny new toy like this and then leave it lying about can afford another one. The poor shall inherit the earth, eh? I'm just redistributing the wealth of the land, that's all."

I had no idea what she was talking about. I only knew, bad as I wanted a bike of my own—I'd never had one and never would—that it didn't feel right. "Put it back," I said. "It's gonna make somebody cry."

She looked at me a moment, shrugged, and pulled the bike back out of the car. "I've got a goddamn nun for a daughter," she muttered. "Mother sodding Theresa." I was eight at the time.

So in my bedroom, I wasn't about to let her bluff her way out of this. "Tell me where you got all these," I said again.

"I fuckin' well bought them with my own hard-earned moola, thank you very much," she replied indignantly. "Ask your mate Krishna if you don't believe me. Jesus bleedin' Christ." And she stormed out of the room.

four

THE NEXT DAY was Sunday, when Mom always went to help Liz at the beauty shop while I stayed home to do chores. My best friend Krishna had come over, and he was sitting on my puke-green bedroom carpet, helping me fold some laundry, and sharing a bottle of cola I'd spiked with what I called Brandy's brandy, while I told him about Marissa and Timmy.

"I feel so bad about not going to see Timmy again," I said, downing a swallow. "He was crying when I left."

Krishna stretched out on my floor, his head propped on a pile of Mom's humungous underpants. He was the same height as me, with broad shoulders and a bony body, and he had such a narrow face that he reminded me of those statues I'd seen on Saint John's Cathedral in New York. His eyes were like those statues' eyes, too, wide and sad, even when he wasn't.

"Don't feel bad," he said, reaching for the bottle. "You helped all you could. Maybe he was only crying because his ankle hurt."

"Anybody home?" our friend Serena yelled just then from down in the foyer, so I went to let her in. I watched the top of her long, inky hair while she panted up our three flights of stairs. Serena's hippie parents had moved her here from Philadelphia in eighth grade to get her away from bad influences, and she'd had her revenge by turning goth. Now she put so much energy into dying that hair and shopping for her dozens of spooky black outfits that she had none left for stair climbing. Plus, she smoked.

"Hey there," she said, giving me a breathless kiss. She dropped like a black cloud next to Krishna, who was still lying on the floor, cradling the bottle and yawning. "You asleep already?" She poked his stomach. Krishna wasn't supposed to drink on account of being Hindu, so he only did it at other people's houses, but he was so unused to booze it always put him to sleep after about three sips.

"I'm not asleep," he said sleepily.

Serena flung back her hair, which she wore parted in the middle and draped over her little white face like a curtain. "Hey, you wanna crash Sophie O'Brian's party next Saturday?" she said in her sultry voice. None of us were invited too often to the parties in town, but we tended to crash them anyway. All the kids in Hollowdale did.

"Good idea," Krishna mumbled. "You want to, Madge?"

"Maybe." I felt wary of parties because I usually had such a bad time at them, but there was always the hope that the next one would be different. A chance to meet someone new, someone who might buck the trend and want to be my boyfriend.

Jamie walked in then, the fourth corner of our little

crowd, his head a flare of orange. "Hey guys, don't hog all the booze," he said, settling cross-legged on the floor. He grabbed Brandy's brandy from Krishna and took a long swig. Jamie was a freckle-faced Irish-American who liked to infuriate his farmer parents by ranting about vegetarianism and animal rights. Serena had a thing for him, but it seemed pretty hopeless. Jamie treated her like another boy, though I figured if she could ever bring herself to wash off that horrible purple lipstick and the eyeliner that made her look like a raccoon, he might actually realize she was alive. As it was, she mooned after him, Krishna mooned after her (I could tell by the way he stared at her all the time), and Jamie mooned after me. Well, it made life interesting.

For a couple of hours we lay on my floor, working our way through Mom's brandy and a joint, courtesy of Serena's hippie parents. Jamie fastened one of Mom's enormous white bras around his head, the cups like giant mouse ears, and we put on a CD of Stylofone, my favorite new rock band, the volume up so high we could barely hear Mr. Henig thumping on his ceiling again with his mop handle. I loved times like that with my friends.

I never would have found Serena and Jamie if it hadn't been for Krishna. When I think of how I was at school before he was around, I always think of those wooden nesting dolls they make in Russia. I started off okay, like the doll on the outside, because at least I had friends up through third grade, even though they were always wanting to touch my hair like I was a freak in a zoo and asking me why I was so brown. In fourth and fifth grades, though, they began snickering about Mom and how I must be adopted, which was when I started getting into fights. That shrunk me down a doll or two. Then along came junior high, and that's when the girls got so mean on the bus and the boys discovered teasing, big-time. ("Are your tits as black as your face?") I felt like I'd shrunk down to the littlest doll by then—the one with no face left and only a couple of dots for eyes.

Krishna arrived in ninth grade. He was fifteen, I was at the end of fourteen, and we were the only brown-skinned people in that school. But that's not what made me like him. What made me like him was that he was the most together person I'd ever met. When some of the kids took to calling him a rag-head terrorist because they didn't know the difference between terrorists, Muslims, and Hindus, he never got bitter, like I would've. He only shrugged and said, "That's their problem, not mine." Within one week he'd found Serena and Jamie, who I'd always ignored, and pulled us all together. He'd lived in Queens, New York, for years after his family had come from India when he was little, so I guess a small town like Hollowdale was sugar cake to him.

"Well, well, look who's having a party."

Startled, I looked up from Krishna's lap, where I seemed to be resting my head. Mom was standing there, her hands on her hips. Serena was lying flat out on the floor like Krishna, and Jamie still had Mom's bra perched on his head like a bonnet.

Mom sniffed. "Smells like a pot factory in here." She marched across my room to throw open the window and spotted the brandy bottle in Jamie's hand. "You little thieves!" Grabbing it from him, she chugged down every last drop.

I closed my eyes. "Go away, Mom. This is our scene. You're not invited. You're too old."

Krishna pulled himself upright. "No, no," he said, his voice a little slurry. "Please stay, Mrs. Botley. We don't mind at all."

Mom barked out a laugh. "You are a polite little bugger, aren't you?" She bent over and plucked Jamie's cigarette packet from his shirt pocket, extracted a cigarette, and tossed it back at him.

"You look very good like that, Jamie. I always knew boys had nothing but tits on their brains."

Jamie snatched her bra off his head, blushing neon orange.

"Five more minutes and the lot of you are out of here," Mom said then. And she banged out of the room.

"Madge, I can't believe the way you talk to your mom," Krishna mumbled, sounding like his mouth was full of peanuts. "Mothers should be respected, even if they are a little . . ."

"Fucked up?"

"Well, yeah."

"If I had a mom like yours, I'd respect the hell out of her. I mean yours is the real thing, you know? She cooks for you, she dresses nice, she talks nice. And she's beautiful. I'd love a mom like that." Krishna's mother was beautiful, I meant it, and kind, too. She and his dad worked incredibly hard running their motel just outside of town, but on the few occasions when she'd found time to allow Krishna to bring us over, she'd fed us about twenty dishes of delicious Indian food, and pots of tea.

"Madge," Krishna said, "I don't feel so good."

I led him to the bathroom and handed him some Tums and aspirin. He liked to drink, maybe a little too much, but it always made him sick. Krishna wasn't really made to be corrupted.

When next Saturday finally rolled around, I spent half the day trying to figure out what to wear. Dresses and skirts made me feel way too girlish and silly, so I chose tight black jeans and an orange spaghetti-strap with the words WHAT'S YOUR PROBLEM? scrawled on it. I threaded a few orange beads in my hair to match, and put on my gold hoop earrings. My hair was looking the best it ever had, the slim dreads all shiny and even, exactly the right length to curl under my jaw. I smeared a little gloss on my mouth and tried some eyeliner, then washed it off again. It only made me look surprised and scared. Then I stepped back to see what I'd done.

There I was again, the question mark. Tall, kind of athletic around the middle, wide shoulders, big boobs, and a face I didn't understand. The orange shirt made my green eyes look as angry as Mousy's. I slumped down on the bed, the hope slumping with me. What made me think I'd meet anyone new at this party? I never had before. Why the hell had I expected this one to be any different?

The doorbell rang, so I went downstairs. Serena was there in one of her long black dresses. Jamie looked scrubbed and orange, like a newly washed carrot. Krishna was wearing a pearly white Indian shirt, which made him glow in the dark like a moonbeam.

"I'm not coming," I said. "I hate parties."

Krishna took me by one arm, Serena by the other, and without a word they marched me down the hill. "Hey!" I said. "I don't want to go!"

"Course you do," Krishna said. "If you don't go, none of us will want to, and then what? We need you with us."

I was so touched I didn't say another word.

Sophie O'Brian lived on the rich side of town, or I should say what passed for the rich side in Hollowdale. Instead of a railroad track dividing the rich from the poor or the white from the black, what we had was Market Street dividing the Have Littles from the Have Nothings. Sophie's dad owned the only kitchen-appliances store in town—one of the few stores that hadn't closed or moved to the mall—and because all our families bought our refrigerators and ovens from him on layaway, the whole town owed him money. He had another advantage, too. Having installed all those appliances, he knew what the inside of every house looked like, which gave him a kind of power over us, like he knew all our secrets. This gave Sophie a similar power at school.

When we arrived at her house, we found the front door open, so in we traipsed, invited or not. We said a quick hello to Mr. O'Brian, a fat blob glued to his TV chair, and followed the noise downstairs to the rumpus room in the basement. It was pretty packed already, with the music so loud you had to yell to be heard. A lit-up disco ball was sending dots of light all over the room, but otherwise it was too dark to see anything except the dim shapes of clumped-together bodies. Serena disappeared into the crowd pretty fast, because even though she dressed so creepily, she did have this purring voice and slinky way of moving that pulled boys to her like ants to a picnic—except for Jamie, that is. Soon as my eyes had adjusted to the dark, I saw her dancing opposite Dave Kruger, this muscly little guy built like a bulldog I recognized from school.

"Let's find some alcohol," Krishna said in my ear. Taking my hand, he threaded through the crowd, Jamie following us. We all liked a drink and a joint, but one of the many things that held us together was our refusal to take the harder stuff. That year everyone was doing Ecstasy, crystal, or ground-up Ritalin, which kids would get on prescription and then sell to their friends. Krishna said he couldn't reconcile brain-altering drugs with keeping his A's at school straight, Jamie believed in staying as pure as his veggie juice, and Serena said she wanted to keep her brain intact so she could think about the dark side of life. I just wanted their respect.

"Watch it, klutzball," I snapped at Jamie, who kept stepping on my heels. I wasn't in the most generous of moods. I'd just noticed Gavin Winslow, the guitarist from Snake Eyes, grinding with some girl whose clothes were so tight she looked like she'd been grabbed by the ankles and dipped naked into a vat of dye. I didn't know much about Gavin except he was a phenomenal musician, tended to go his own way at school, and was so hot that every time I looked at him I felt like melting all over the floor. Guys like him, of course, never danced with me.

"Hey, don't bite my head off," Jamie said behind me. "Listen, grumpy, you wanna, you know . . ." He was still talking when we got to the booze table, which was covered with nothing but soda and fruit juice to please the parents. Only we knew it had all been spiked with vodka, gin, whiskey—whatever Sophie and her friends had been able to steal. That was how it always worked at the parties in my town.

Jamie was still trying to ask me to dance and Krishna was pouring me something brown and fizzy when Sophie O'Brian wiggled up to me. She had on so much eye shadow I was surprised she could keep her lids open, but otherwise she looked pretty good. Her brown hair was pinned up in the back, with strands straggling over her sticky eyes. I'd seen that look in my aunt's hair magazines.

"Hey, Madge, I didn't expect to see you here," she said, swinging her hips to the music. "I like your shirt." She squinted at it a little too long, in case I hadn't caught the sarcasm. "Did you bring any CDs?"

Ever since seventh grade, the kids in my school had conceived the notion that I knew more about music and dancing than anybody else. I guess they thought music came wired in my genes, along with all the other things that made me "multicultural."

"No, I didn't."

"Too bad. Next time you crash one of my parties, at least you can bring some of your music." And she turned and left.

"Hey, Sophie, your inner bitch is showing," Jamie shouted after her, but it didn't help. There are some things a body can never get used to and one of them is the rudeness of others. I turned away to hide my face.

"We all crashed this party, why's she have to pick on you?" Krishna said, handing me the drink he'd made. "Come on, let's dance."

I turned to see if this was okay with Jamie, but he'd taken off somewhere, so I squeezed onto the floor with Krishna. It was okay dancing with him, but I wasn't really into it. It wasn't exciting, it wasn't romantic. It was like dancing with a brother.

I looked around for Serena but she'd been swallowed by the crowd, along with Jamie. Gavin Winslow was still there, though, pressed up close to the girl dipped in dye. I couldn't quite see but I thought he might be kissing her. I never had luck like that. Nobody but Jamie and Krishna and a few guys I'd known since I was little had ever danced with me at parties, let alone kissed me. The only exception was once in eighth grade, when Ricky Campbell, football star, took me into a corner at a party just like this one. I was so excited—I was going to get my first kiss, and from the hottest boy in the grade, no less! He kissed me quickly on the lips, then spat and wiped his mouth on his sleeve. "I did that for a bet," he said, screwing up his face like he'd tasted something bad. "I get a quarter for kissing a jungle bunny."

"You're not having any fun, are you?" Krishna said in my ear.

I shrugged, my mouth tight.

"We don't have to stay here. You wanna go?"

I didn't know where we could go at this time of night in dead old Hollowdale, except to one of the bars full of redneck drunks, and we were too young for that. But Krishna was right. With every beat of the song I was feeling worse. It wasn't only the memory of Ricky Campbell, it was the way I was being looked at. Some people were eyeing me warily, others were flashing me these nervous little smiles. The older I got, the more I could read the faces of the people in my town. I was making these kids uncomfortable, I was upsetting the balance of their little white world. I should've paid attention to my instincts and stayed at home.

"Yeah, let's get out of here," I said.

Krishna pushed his way through the crowd, while I followed. Somebody knocked into me from behind and cursed me for spilling his drink. "Asshole," I hissed, and kept going. I was mad at everyone at that party by then, with their small-town prejudices and their wanting everybody to be exactly like them. Then someone grabbed my arm, so I turned, ready to explode. And my kneecaps almost clattered to the ground. Because at the end of my arm was Gavin Winslow.

I stared at his fingers on my wrist, my body turning weak as a noodle.

"Hey, Madge," he yelled over the music. "How you doin'?"

I couldn't look up. "Uh," I said.

"That was my drink you spilled, you know."

It was? Oh, shit.

"It was me you called an asshole, too."

Double shit.

"It doesn't matter. Listen, I been lookin' for you. You wanna dance?"

That surprised me so much I did look at him then, right in the eyes. They were the color of an early summer morning, just at that moment when the sky's remembered its blue. He looked back at me a moment without saying anything more. Then he tossed his long brown hair off his forehead and I felt a pang shoot right down from my chest to the bottom of my stomach.

"Well, will you? You owe me now, since you spilled."

I still couldn't find any words, so I nodded. I didn't know what he'd done with that other girl, but he was with me now and excitement started bubbling up inside of me like a pan of boiling milk. I tried to push it down. There were only three people I trusted in that room, and Gavin Winslow wasn't one of them.

He found an open spot in the crowd and we danced without touching. He was a good dancer. Maybe it was being up on a stage when he played guitar, but he knew how to move his feet and his hips so he looked graceful and easy, not like a chicken with a bee sting, the way most boys dance.

"What do you mean, you were looking for me?" I said finally, my voice having decided to come back for a visit. "You don't even know me."

He smiled, his long hair swinging. "Sure I know you. Everybody does."

Oh, yeah, of course. "Still, we've never talked before."

"True, but I been wanting to for a while."

I was too surprised to respond to that, so I concentrated on dancing, hoping I wouldn't make a fool of myself. I could dance, kind of, but I didn't feel too comfortable doing it.

"I like how you dance," Gavin said then, as if he was eavesdropping on my brain.

I glanced at him suspiciously. He smiled into my eyes, did a twirl, and dipped down near the ground, fast and smooth. His body was strong and sinewy. I smiled back. I felt like a sucker but I couldn't help it. I wasn't in charge of myself anymore.

I tried to think of something to say. *You play that guitar pretty good.* Dumb. *Hey, you and Snake Eyes can play a mean rock and roll.* Considerably dumber. *I've been noticing how well you play that instrument.* I opened my mouth, then shut it again. Help!

Gavin moved up close to me again. "That's a crazy shirt you're wearing, by the way. Color's real pretty on you."

A hot flush shot up my neck when he said that, and I felt that pang in my guts again. I could see the words CAUTION, CAUTION flashing across my eyes like a traffic warning, but the pang was erasing them fast.

"Thanks," I just managed to croak, then I clammed up. I wasn't doing too well at making conversation here. I was too scared to speak.

The music slowed down then, so Gavin slipped his arms around my waist and moved his body an inch away from mine.

We danced like that awhile and he kept looking me in the eye, but I couldn't make myself look back. I stared over his head, behind one ear, at the wall and the ceiling and the floor. I think I stopped breathing, too. But he didn't seem bothered. Every time my eyes slid back to his—and I couldn't seem to stop them—he gave me the sweetest smile and pulled me even closer. Finally, he pushed one leg between mine, so we could sway together to the rhythm of the music. He did it so naturally it felt natural to me, too, even though I hardly knew him. His hair brushed my face and it smelled of shampoo and something spicy. The whole of him smelled so good I couldn't even think.

"You feel nice," he said, pulling me up even tighter against him. His body was narrow and hard but supple, like nothing I'd ever felt before, and even though I was still wary, it made the pangs inside of me turn into hot waves. He stroked my hair while we swayed together, his hand big and warm on my head. The sweetness of his shampoo, that tangy scent only boys have—they filtered into my head like smoke till I forgot about everybody else in the room. I forgot to even remember.

As soon as the song ended, though, and we stopped dancing, I panicked. I turned to leave before he could sneer like Ricky Campbell or say something cruel. I was afraid to even see the expression on his face. But he grabbed my hand again and stopped me.

"Where you goin'?" And something in his eyes seemed to soften. "Hey, don't go yet."

I stared at my feet, feeling mixed up and foolish. But then the music started up again and he pulled me close for another dance. "It's okay," he said, and his voice was so gentle that, somehow, I knew it was.

After that we kept on dancing together whether the music had stopped or not, our bodies pressed close. We danced a long time, so long that most everyone else was off in a corner by then, cuddling or making out, including Serena, who seemed to be wrapped around Dave Kruger like an octopus. Finally, Gavin and I ended up on a pile of pillows ourselves.

The only boy I'd ever seriously kissed before was Jamie, which we'd tried once at a school dance for the practice. Jamie had opened his mouth so wide I'd felt like he was trying to swallow me whole and I hadn't liked it at all. But Gavin's kisses weren't like that. He started off gently, with little soft pecks on my cheeks and around my mouth. And when he got to my lips, he kissed only the outside of them first, nibbling at me softly, the way ponies nibble at the grass in your hand. I didn't have to worry about whether he liked kissing me, either, because he kept making these little moaning sounds and telling me I was great. It made those hot waves inside of me come on so strong I hardly knew what was happening. And his kisses weren't slobbery like Jamie's. His kisses were like words, as if he was talking to me, as if our lips were telling each other all our best secrets, secrets so good that when he began exploring me with his hands, I didn't even mind. In fact I wanted him to.

Serena was the one who made me go home. She came up to us on the couch and kicked me on the ankle. "Ow!" I yelled, pulling back from Gavin. "What the hell are you doing?"

She was standing over me, her eyeliner smudged and her mouth pale—that Dave must have kissed off all the purple lipstick. "Hey," she said, "I called your name three times and you didn't hear me. Mom's waiting outside." Mrs. Jenkins was always ferrying us around from one house or another when it was too late to walk. My own mom never took a turn, of course. Too busy with her nightlife, I guess, whatever that was. Or else too damn lazy.

I tried to focus. I felt completely drunk, like I do after a few shots of Brandy's brandy, even though I'd never had one sip of alcohol that entire night. My eyes were blurry and my lips felt swollen, but in the nicest way. Gavin's arms were still around me, and so was his smell, and I didn't want either of them to go away, ever. I looked around the dark room. It was much emptier now. "Where's Krish?" I managed to say.

"Don't know. I think he went home. Come on!"

"Okay, okay." I looked at Gavin, who was lying back on the pillows, his eyes closed and a goofy smile on his face. I took a moment to examine him close up, while I could. I couldn't really believe he wasn't a dream. "I gotta go," I said quietly.

He opened his eyes. "No you don't," he mumbled, pulling me to him.

I giggled. "Yeah, I'm afraid I do."

He gave me a last kiss, then I dragged myself reluctantly out of his arms and stood up. "Okay, I'm leaving now." I hesitated. "Bye."

He didn't say anything more, just raised a hand in a little wave and sent me the sexiest wink. It was so hard to walk away from him. I wanted to step out of my body and leave myself behind.

On the way home in the back of Mrs. Jenkins's car, Serena and I couldn't tell each other anything on account of the listening ears behind the steering wheel. I liked Serena's mom. She talked politics and actually wanted to know my opinions. But party autopsies were Off-Limits around adults, even adults who wore long hippie dresses and dangling earrings, and who grew marijuana in their backyards. Still, I knew Serena was pleased with the evening, for herself and for me—she kept giving me these secret little grins. It was so odd she held on to that spooky goth act of hers, because her heart was tender as a petal.

I looked out the car window at the sliver of moon, the clouds wrapping it up, then unwrapping it again. I felt so happy. It was the first time in my life I'd had a good time at a party, the first time I'd ever felt sexy and beautiful. I wanted to hold on to that moment forever and ever, because even in the middle of it, I knew life didn't get that sweet that often.

five

"COME ON, MOVE your bum!" Mom barked at me the next morning, poking her head through my bedroom door. "I'm taking you to work at Liz's instead of me today. I've got some business to take care of. Hurry up!"

I was sitting at my glass-topped dressing table, which doubled as my desk, all steamed up over an essay for English class about how Zora Neale Hurston had died forgotten and poor. I wrote everything by hand because we couldn't afford a computer. Couldn't afford an answering machine or a cell phone either. According to Mom, we couldn't even afford the rent.

"What business?" I said.

"None of your beeswax. Get going, come on."

"But I've got too much homework. I can't leave."

Normally I would have jumped at the chance to work with Liz instead of doing stupid chores, but that particular Sunday I wanted to be home in case it occurred to Gavin to look up my number and call. I also wanted a chance to talk over the party with Serena.

"Tough titties. Get in the car. We're late." Mom was just

shutting my door, when she opened it back up again and took a long, hard look at me. "You had a good time last night at that shindig of yours, then, did you?"

I looked down so she wouldn't see my smile.

She walked over and stared at me. "Some boy's been sucking on your mug, by the look of it. I knew I'd be fighting off the lads sooner or later. Hah!" And snorting with laughter, she left the room.

I jumped up and looked in the mirror. My lips were kind of puffy, it was true, and I had a serious hickey on my neck. I touched it and shivered.

On the way to Riverbend, I was in the greatest mood. I didn't fight with Mom over the radio for a change—she always picked these old-fogy stations that played nothing but the Bee Gees, who all sounded castrated to me. And I didn't even tell her to shut up when she started singing one of the hymns she was always croaking in her loud, off-tune voice, "Bring me my bow of burning gold! Bring me my arrows of desire!" She gave me a lewd wink at the last line.

"Where'd you learn all those hymns anyway?" I asked after she'd screeched her way through about fifty verses.

"Oh, we used to sing them all the time in Borstal. Best day there was Sunday, 'cause you got to go to chapel instead of working. Anything was better than standing all day in that fuckin' factory, shoving thermos flasks together."

I squeezed my eyes shut. I knew Mom had served three different sentences in Borstal—that's what they called the prisons they had those days in England for hopeless teenagers.

I knew she'd been a runaway and a juvenile delinquent, getting into trouble for stupid stuff like shoplifting and thieving. But still, every time she talked about it, a pounding started up behind my forehead.

"You know what we used to do in chapel?" she said with a chuckle. "We used to stick filthy words into the hymns instead of the real ones. Made the words rhyme, an' all. The priest got so angry he almost popped his buttons." She looked over to see if she'd made me laugh, but I turned my head away so as not to encourage her. I hated Mom's prison stories.

My aunt ran her beauty shop out of the front of her house on Main Street, right opposite the fussy pink hotel. Years earlier, she'd hung a sign over the sidewalk—HAIRLINE—a name she'd taken from her salon back in England, and recently she'd repainted it with wiggly black letters on a bright gold background. Her front window was gleaming, too, not like the other few dusty storefronts on the street. Liz had always known how to run a good business. Lucky somebody in the family had.

The beauty shop wasn't open yet, so we walked around to the private entrance down a side alley. Mom rang the bell. "Move it!" she shouted up at the window. "I need a piss!"

When Liz opened the door, I squinted at the blast of color that greeted us. She was wearing a cherry-red sweater over a matching tight skirt. Her hair was coiled so neatly behind her head it looked varnished, red plastic spheres were clipped on to each ear, and her long, thin face was blotchy with way too much makeup. She'd always overdressed like this, but ever since Uncle Ron had died it had gotten worse. It was like she was trying to cover up her sadness with paint.

"Oh, hello, Madge," she said, looking surprised. "Nice to see you. Come on in, then. I've just put the kettle on." She led us down her narrow hallway to the kitchen, which smelled of coziness and toast. Her kitchen was bright and overdone, just like her: blazing yellow walls, white ruffled curtains, and little moralistic samplers hanging over the sink. The worst was, "Women who keep clean kitchens keep clean minds." Knowing Uncle Ron, he must have given that to her as a joke.

"I can't stay long," Mom said after she'd dashed to the toilet. "Madge'll fill in for me today, all right?" She gulped down a mug of hot tea, holding it in her fist like she'd never heard of handles. "I'll be back around five." And she banged out of the house.

Liz sighed and put down her cup. "You got much homework, then?"

"Some."

"Well, it'll be a quiet day, so you can do it till we get busy, all right?"

"But, Aunty, at least I should clean the equipment for you." Liz paid Mom to do that every Sunday, something that filled me with shame. I knew we needed the money because Mom never held on to a job for long. She'd pumped gas, cleaned out people's basements and garages, sorted the recycling at the town dump, and now she had a new job in the stockroom of a supermarket. But since she had the habit of fighting with her bosses and skipping town for weeks on end, none of her jobs tended to last too long. Still, after all Liz had done for her, the least Mom could do was help her out for free.

"It's all right, lovey. Schoolwork is more important than learning how to sterilize a sodding hairbrush. Off you go."

I took my tea and climbed up the narrow staircase to the room my aunt had kept for me ever since Mom had started disappearing, a small bedroom in the back of the house. She'd papered it in pale yellow with chiffon curtains and a bedspread to match, which made it look like a buttercup. What with her kelly-green living room, candy-pink dining room, and the blazing kitchen, it was the only room in the place that didn't shout at you.

Bob's old bedroom was across the hall from mine (Liz had done that one up in electric blue) and the shelves were still packed with his boyhood trophies and toy cars. The family had lived in this house ever since he was eight, when they'd moved here from England so my uncle could work for a cousin's construction company and make more money than he ever could back home. Mom hadn't joined them till later, when she was pregnant with me, because she'd been stuck in that Borstal again for her longest sentence yet. I didn't know what she'd done that time—I only knew it was more serious than anything before. I'd asked her over and over to tell me about it, but she wouldn't, just like she wouldn't tell me where she went when she disappeared.

I put my school bag on the bed and wandered to the window, too restless over Gavin to work. The woods out back were purple that day, sprinkled with buds of pale green, and the river was a pewter gray under the cloudy sky. Was the party a one-night-stand thing or was I going to be Gavin's girl-friend now? Was he going to call me or wait till we saw each other at school? I wished Mom had let me stay home so I could find out. I brushed my fingers over my lips, remembering the velvet pressure of his kisses. Even with being away from the phone and my stomach fluttering like a moth, I felt good.

After I'd forced myself through my homework, I went down to help Liz. I could get my work done pretty fast if I had to—all the classes in my school were easy. Most of my class-mates were more into guns, God, and cars than into studying, so the standards weren't too high, but I made myself try hard anyway. Some of the teachers were fine, my English teacher Mrs. Gough in particular. She was always reading my stories and essays out loud and posting them up on walls. But a lot of them assumed I was stupid soon as they saw the color of my skin, which is why I always had to prove them wrong. As a result, I was one of the academic stars of the grade, along with Serena and Krishna. Jamie would've been, too, if the teachers had given out A's for goofiness.

I found my aunt trimming the hair of Mary McAlister, an old lady who clutched her purse each time she saw me, like she was sure I was going to mug her. Whenever my aunt left the room, I stared the old crab right in the eye till she squirmed.

"Aunty," I said once Liz had stuck her under a dryer where she couldn't hear anything, "I was thinking upstairs. Why was Mom in Borstal when you moved over here? What had she done that last time? She won't tell me, but I have a right to know."

"I've told you before, Madge, that's not for me to say." She handed me a bottle of blue Barbicide for sterilizing brushes and combs, then swept Crabby McAlister's wispy white hair off the linoleum floor. Everything in the beauty shop was one shade of gory pink or another: the walls, the chairs, the ceiling, even the gowns for the customers. It looked like the inside of somebody's mouth.

I concentrated on drying a bunch of combs, then lining them up inside a drawer in perfect little rows. "You have to tell me sometime. I'm not a baby anymore."

My aunt shook her head. "I'm not the one to tell you, ducks. It has to be your mum who does that. Go get the old bag out of the hair dryer, would you? Before we have a shrunken head on our hands."

We both smelled a whiff of singeing hair just then, so I whipped the dryer off Crabby McAlister's head and pulled her to her feet. She looked terrified and tried to yank her arm out of my hand. I leaned down and whispered, "Watch out, I bite."

By the time Liz had closed up the beauty shop at six, Mom was an hour late, which was typical. We waited for her in the kitchen, eating one of my aunt's anorexic dinners of fish and salad while the house sat empty and hollow around us. It felt so lonely without my uncle there. He'd always filled it up with his blustery voice and big stomach and his friends who came over every night to yell about sports and politics while they got drunk on his beer. Liz had gone so quickly from having a house full of men to being there on her lonesome, I didn't know how she stood it.

"Aunty, do you think Mom might be stealing again? Or getting up to something at the racetrack?" I said after she'd finished boasting about Bob all the way through dinner.

Liz took a swig of the second beer she'd poured herself since work. "I hope not. Why do you ask?"

I shoved my knife around the yellow plastic tablecloth. "Because she gave me these presents when I got back from New York, stuff she can't afford. And the phone hasn't been cut off for two whole months."

Mom had once let it slip that the reason we lived in Hollowdale and not Riverbend with Liz was because of the horse racetrack. "I like racetracks," she once told me. "I learned the ropes at the one in Brighton when I lived there with Liz. It's how I made my income back then, no questions asked." And when I did ask, she just said, "Babes in the woods, ducky, babes in the woods." I had no idea what she meant.

My aunt frowned and smoothed back her shellacked hair, her polished fingernails gleaming red as her clothes. "No, she gave up that nonsense years ago. I wouldn't worry about it. And she does have that supermarket job now, so she's not entirely broke."

"But why's she have to be so screwy? Why can't she be normal, like you?"

My aunt didn't answer right away. "Get me another

beer, would you, love?" is all she said. "I'm knackered."

I fetched her another from the fridge—it was her third by my count—and sat back down while she took a gulp. She was getting pretty relaxed, her lipstick eaten off and her eye makeup smudged.

"It was your grandma's fault," she said after a pause. "You know she was a serious drunk, don't you?"

I nodded. Mom and Liz talked about that all the time.

"Not like this." Liz held up her beer can. "I mean falling-down, brain-shriveling, never-remembering-where-you-are sort of drunk. And once our dad left, she wouldn't give poor Brandy the time of day. She was too busy going down the pub and passing out."

Liz fell silent then, gazing at the leftover lettuce leaves on her plate. I'd heard all this before, but something was hurting in my chest anyway, the same hurt as when Mom disappeared. It half made me want to tell my aunt to stop, but the other half needed to hear it, over and over.

"I got out by leaving with Ron when I was sixteen," she went on, "but Brandy was only twelve then, so she had to stay behind. And our mum never did a thing for her but nag and criticize."

"Is that when Mom got into trouble that last time?" I asked quietly.

"Yeah." Liz heaved a sigh. "It happened when she went home just after she'd been released from one of her spells in Borstal. She and Mum had the most dreadful row. And well, Brandy lost control, I'm afraid. She was just out of the nick, after all, and that's not exactly a place that teaches you rational behavior."

"What do you mean, she lost control?"

Liz glanced at me, rubbing her brow. "I don't know, Madgy. I promised your mum I wouldn't tell you."

"Please, Aunty, I'm old enough to know now. I can take it. It's not fair to keep me in the dark like this."

"I suppose that's true. You are seventeen, after all." Liz frowned a moment, gazing into space. "All right," she said at last with a sigh. "What happened is this, Madgy: Brandy got so angry she attacked Mum and, well, she tried to strangle her. Mum called the police, and that's how Brandy got put back inside for so long. So there you have it."

I stared, trying to take in what she'd said.

"Don't tell your mum I told you, all right?" Liz murmured. "It makes her too ashamed."

We both went quiet after that. The kitchen clock ticked, the refrigerator hummed. A light rain tapped at the window. I'd always known Mom was a fuckup, but I'd never known it was that bad.

"Listen to how lonely it is," Liz said after a long silence, her voice thick and sad. "I miss Ron so much. I'm only forty-six and here I am, already a widow. I feel friggin' tricked."

I was still too shocked to say anything.

"It's so confusing, Madgy. I know it's been a year since the accident, but I still keep thinking we've just had one of our spats and he's stormed off for a sulk. I keep expecting him back any minute. And I'm so alone without him! Bob never rings me up anymore, he hardly ever visits. What's he care about his dried-up old mum, eh? Every night when I get into bed, I still turn to give my Ron a squeeze." And she broke into tears.

I was too embarrassed to move. I wasn't used to seeing my aunt like this. She was usually so self-controlled, hard as her lacquered hair. Uncle Ron's death had really changed her. I sat watching the tears pour down her face, mingling with her makeup and snot. Why didn't the adults in my family ever act their age?

Liz put her head down on the table and sobbed into her arms, so I finally got up and went over to stand by her chair. "Hey, don't cry," I said stiffly, handing her a tissue from the counter. "You're not all alone, Aunty. Bob's busy, that's all. He loves you a whole lot, he really does." I looked down at her polished blonde head, that head that had tried so hard to give me a normal life, and I melted. "I love you, too," I added.

"You do, Madgy?" she howled, and threw her arms around me, wetting my stomach with her tears. I stood beside her chair, patting her, and that made me remember patting Timmy. I hadn't thought about him for days. I'd been so wrapped up in the party and Gavin I'd forgotten all about my promise to visit. Everybody in this world needed some love and attention, I thought, no matter how young or old—including that poor boy and my aunt.

Maybe even my fuckup of a mom did, too.

Never in my life had I dressed so carefully for school as I dressed that next morning. I washed my hair and chose my best white button-up shirt and tightest black jeans. I pulled on my favorite black-and-white sneakers, praying it wouldn't rain and ruin them, and I even put on a touch of mascara, which I never did normally. Then I looked at my tall self in the mirror—at my green eyes and milky tea skin, my strong, no-nonsense body. And for the first time in years, I liked it.

All the way to school, though, while I was walking through the dead streets of Hollowdale, past graffiti-covered store-fronts and dark, neglected diners, I couldn't stop thinking about Gavin. I didn't know whether he'd called or not, since Mom hadn't been home and we didn't have an answering machine, but I couldn't help feeling hope, along with a wiggle of dread. What would he do when he saw me at school? Would he ask me out, or ignore me? Would I get hurt, or feel won-derful? I couldn't even begin to wrap my mind around what Liz had told me about Mom. I mean, the bad news buzzed there in my head, the shame and the anger, like a fly trapped in a room, but I kept swatting it away. If I spent all my life worrying about what a mess she was, I wouldn't have any life left for me, that's what I figured. Her past was her past. I had a future to get on with.

I kept an eye out for Gavin that whole morning. Our school was huge, gray, and squat, like an airplane hangar, with about a thousand kids in it, and it was full of long hallways that seemed to stretch on forever. Each time I walked down one of them, past the endless rows of scratched-up doors and metal lockers, every tall, brown-haired boy I saw made my stomach lurch. But none of them was Gavin. By lunchtime I was in such a state I had to sneak into the girls' bathroom to wash the sweat off my face.

Lunch was always in the school cafeteria—there was no place to go outside—and the room was shaped like a giant fan, so it was easy to see the whole place with one sweep of your eyes. I checked it out quickly. The usual cliques were there: Sally Anderson's Cool Crowd, who looked down on everybody who wasn't one of them. Sophie O'Brian and her little band of girlfriends, whose main purpose in life seemed to be collecting boys and then stealing them from one another. The dorks and the geeks, who spent all their time in the computer lab. The jocks talking sports. The kids who flew Confederate flags on their cars and were obsessed with guns and war. And all the other kids who were just kind of in between, like me and my friends, floating around in our own private worlds. But I didn't see Gavin. Serena was there, though, hunched over like a crow at our usual corner table.

I couldn't face any of the cafeteria food that day, not even the reheated defrosted refrozen frozen pizza, so I bought a little carton of orange juice and headed over to join her. She was in one of her usual goth outfits—you'd think she'd get tired of all that black and wake up one day with a serious craving for color. She looked worried.

"What's happened to Krishna?" she said as soon as I sat opposite her. "He wasn't in chemistry. He never misses school." She peered at me, her gray eyes almost colorless inside her black eyeliner, and her little face ghostly between her panels of hair.

"Maybe he's sick," I said. "What happened to him at the party, anyhow?"

Serena looked down at the vanilla yogurt she always ate for lunch and poked it with her plastic spoon. "He left 'cause of you and Gavin. He couldn't take it. I think he was jealous."

I opened my juice and pushed a straw into it. I didn't believe her. "Hey, wasn't that Dave Kruger I saw you slobbering all over?" I said, leaning forward and lowering my voice. I'd been too busy all Sunday with homework and Liz to get a chance to call Serena about the party, so I was dying to talk it over.

Serena blushed so deeply she looked almost healthy. "Yeah. He's dumb as a plank but he kisses good. He asked me to get some pizza with him later this week. I might do it."

"What about Jamie?"

Serena swallowed a spoonful of yogurt. "Jamie can't see beyond the edge of his veggie burgers. I've given up. But listen, about Krishna. He likes you, I can tell. I saw it at the party."

"Crapola. It's you he's been staring at for months, not me."

"No, you're wrong. He stares at me 'cause he thinks I'm a freak. I mean, Hindu and goth, that's a pretty weird combination, right? No, it's you, it always has been. I didn't see it before, but at the party it was clear. He'd do anything for you."

When Serena said that, I felt bad. I knew she was wrong about Krishna liking me romantically, but it was true I'd abandoned him at the party. The two of us had always had this pact that we'd stick by each other at those things, that we'd get through the cruelty and rejection together, but I'd gotten too caught up in Gavin to even think about that.

"Madge," Serena whispered suddenly, leaning over the table between us. "Don't turn around, but Dave and your boyfriend just walked in."

I froze. My heart started pounding so hard I felt cold and dizzy.

"What's he doing?" I whispered back. Gavin was one of those rare people in school who had friends in all the cliques but didn't belong to any one of them. Sometimes he sat with Sally Anderson's Cool Crowd, sometimes with Sophie O'Brian, sometimes with his band or the jocks, and sometimes alone with another guy. It was one of the things that intrigued me about him.

I watched Serena watching him over my shoulder, trying to read the expression in her eyes, but I didn't dare look for myself. Finally, she dropped her eyes to the table and grimaced. "Boys are such assholes," she said.

I did glance around then. Gavin was sitting on Sophie's table, his legs slung over a chair, talking and laughing. And Dave Kruger was clearly flirting with Sophie, who was tossing her bangs and snapping gum in his face. None of them looked at us. But just seeing Gavin again, his long hair and casual slouch, brought back his kisses so vividly my cheeks burned.

I turned back to Serena. "It's just the usual. Who cares?" But my hands were shaking.

"You wait here. I'm gonna get some water. Don't even think about watching me."

But I did. She took a detour around the room, moving in that slinky way of hers, like Mousy when he was stalking a dustball. She was wearing a long black skirt and a bodice-style top, laced up over her bust, which was tight enough to show off all her curves. Her hair was almost down to her waist and swayed above her hips as she walked—she did make an impressive figure, I had to admit. She filled her water glass and managed to find a way back past Gavin's table, lingering just enough to be noticed. A lot of guys in the room were watching her, but nobody from Sophie's table paid any attention to her, not even Dave.

"Shit," she said when she sat back down. "The male gender sucks."

I was just about to agree when the bell rang for classes.

For the rest of the day, I thought about what jerks those guys had been: Dave ignoring Serena and flirting with Sophie right under her nose; Gavin hooking up with me one day and treating me like a speck of dust the next. But then something happened that made me forget all about it. I was getting ready to go home, stuffing my backpack with homework from my locker, feeling all heavy inside with disappointment, when I heard a voice in my ear say, "Hey."

I jumped and turned around. Gavin was about ten inches away from me, leaning on a locker as naturally as if he'd grown there. "How ya doin'?"

I didn't know what to say. My mind jumbled up in all sorts

of directions but not a single word found its way to my lips. It was just like what had happened to me at the party and I was furious at myself for it. I gaped at him like a blowfish.

"You got anythin' to do after school tomorrow?" he said then. His hair was flopped over one blue eye and a smile flickered on his lips. His whole body, leaning against that locker, curved as gracefully as one of his guitars. I had to concentrate incredibly hard just to remember to breathe.

"Um, no," I barely managed to squeak.

"I got the car. Maybe we could go someplace?" He shifted languidly, like he was made of liquid and not solid matter at all. He'd danced like that, too.

I couldn't speak. I was sure people were staring at us, but right then the hallway, the lockers, the whole school, and every damn fool inside it just disappeared. *Poof*, like it was all nothing but a mirage.

I nodded.

A huge smile spread over his face. "Cool! I'll pick you up here after school. See you." And looking real pleased, he sauntered off.

I floated all the way home.

six

MOUSY GREETED ME at the door when I got back to the apartment that afternoon, frantic for food, as usual. Mom was always forgetting to feed him, but he still managed to stay fat as a groundhog anyhow, with a pocket of glob dangling below his belly and his sides swelling out. Before we'd had him "snippity-snipped," as Mom so delicately put it, he'd been sleek and handsome with his tiger-striped fur and white bib and paws, but now he looked more like a giant pom-pom than a respectable feline. Still, I liked him, blob that he was. He was the only live creature I could count on to be there when I came home.

"Okay, greedy guts, hold on a sec," I said, giving him a tickle between his ears, and went into the kitchen to feed him. A letter addressed to me was lying with a pile of bills on the table. It was from Bob, and inside it were a newspaper clipping and a note.

"Hi Madge. Here's the piece I wrote about Marissa. Thanks for your help. I owe you. Keep on truckin'. Love, your cuz."

I tossed the note aside, wishing Bob wouldn't try so hard to sound hip, and sat down to read his article.

CITY IN FIGHT OVER ABUSED CHILD

By Robert Dunbar

Ten-year-old Marissa spent four months locked in a closet without food or light. She ate a cardboard box to survive, and even her own feces. The Administration for Children's Services received several reports of Marissa's abuse by her mother, according to Children's Rights, Inc., a former branch of the ACLU, but did nothing to stop it.

For six years before that, while Marissa's mother was in jail on a drug conviction, Marissa had been living in the foster home of Katherine Henderson of Washington Heights, N.Y.

"She was real happy with me," Henderson said. "She was a smart, bubbly little thing." Even so, once Marissa's mother was released from jail, ACS returned Marissa to her, over Henderson's objections.

As soon as Marissa was back in her mother's care, her mother locked her in the closet and only let her out to beat her. Numerous reports of abuse were made by ACS caseworkers, but according to Children's Rights, all were ignored. Marissa was only saved by the chance visit of a housing inspector, who found the child with a stomach extended from malnutrition, clumps of hair missing, broken bones, and burns and bruises all over her body.

But instead of giving the girl back to Henderson, ACS placed her with another foster family, where she was sexually abused for two years.

Now Henderson and Children's Rights, Inc., are suing the city to make sure this never happens again.

Bob went on to describe Marissa's case, which was still being argued in court, what it might mean for other abused kids, and what we saw when we visited her. And almost every word of that last part was mine.

It made me proud to see my own words in print, even if they were under Bob's name, but somehow I wasn't satisfied. I'd felt much better carrying Timmy home than writing that description of Marissa. I knew the article was important, but it was Mrs. Henderson and the Children's Rights lawyers who were doing the real fighting. Those were the people I admired.

I folded up the article and put it in the shoe box where Mom kept all of Bob's writings, gave moaning Mousy his rat-pellet food, and headed into my room to start my homework. I wanted to get it done before Mom came home and caused some type of chaos.

Taking out my books, I sat down at my dressing table to work, but I was too excited about Gavin to concentrate. Instead, I gazed at the clutter reflected in the mirror above me: my bed under the rumpled brown blanket Mom had bought at a rummage sale, which had never smelled right; the curtains a dull yellow and badly in need of a wash; that puke-green carpet; and my wonderful blood-red walls. And over on one side of my mirror, the note I'd taped up for inspiration, a quote from Elie Wiesel, this Holocaust survivor who won a Nobel Peace Prize:

> The opposite of love is not hate, it's indifference.
> The opposite of art is not ugliness, it's indifference.
> The opposite of faith is not heresy, it's indifference.
> And the opposite of life is not death, it's indifference.

At least Bob's article wasn't indifferent; at least it showed he cared. I wondered whether Gavin would be impressed if I ever let him read it. Would he think it was as cool as I did to have a newspaper reporter in the family? And what would he make of my family, anyhow? My cousin was respectable enough, and so was my aunt, but I'd always dreaded introducing anybody new to Mom. She wasn't exactly discreet about her time as a jailbird, she dressed like a man, and she was constantly cracking jokes that shocked or offended people. Years earlier, I'd stopped going shopping with her because I couldn't stand the way everybody either stared at or avoided us. What would they say if they found out what she'd done to her very own mother?

I opened my books and picked up a pen, wondering who else besides Liz knew the truth about Mom. It covered me in shame to think that Bob and my uncle had probably been walking around with this secret against me my whole life. And what did it mean that Mom had done such a thing, anyhow? Did it mean she was truly dangerous, a serious maniac? Or did it only mean she'd been an angry, screwed-up kid with a mother as bad as Marissa's? I stared down at my homework binder, trying to figure it out. Mom had never hurt me, at least not physically; she'd never made me afraid of her. But she was so hard and unpredictable. How could I know what kind of a person she was underneath?

No, I decided. There was no way I was ever going to let her meet Gavin.

Sitting in a car with somebody as gorgeous as Gavin Winslow in broad daylight, I discovered the next afternoon, was not at all the same as smooching with him at a party in the dark. I felt like I'd split into two people, the person who'd been in his arms only three days earlier, who now seemed impossibly confident and glamorous; and the person who was sitting like a lump of butter in his car right then, dissolving into goop. The worst was that I still couldn't think of a thing to say. Not one thing.

Gavin wasn't too talkative either. He turned on the radio and drove away fast as he could from the school and all the people staring after us, collecting their gossip. And each minute that passed without either of us thinking of anything to say he turned the volume up a little higher. It was a heavy-metal station, not my favorite, but that was okay with me. I figured he needed to listen to that stuff for his guitar playing.

I shut my eyes for a second to breathe in his smell. That spicy, peppery smell he had, plus the mustiness of his leather jacket. It made me want to swoon.

"So," he finally yelled over the music, "you live up on Willow?"

"Yeah." I'd just told him that.

"That's pretty far. How d'you get to school?" He reached over to turn down the volume with his long, guitar-playing fingers. I thought about how they'd run all over my body, and my face went hot.

"I walk."

"You walk all that way? Why don't you take the bus?"

I paused. Should I tell him the truth or lie? "I prefer walking," I lied.

He glanced at me. I could feel it, though I didn't dare look back at him. I'd tried looking at him when he'd picked me up at my locker at the end of the school day but I'd been too high on excitement to really see him. He'd seemed to shimmer, like a road in the sun.

"Yeah, the bus can be pretty cruel."

He was reading my mind again, like he had at the party. How did he do that?

We fell back into silence while Gavin negotiated the only busy intersection in Hollowdale. "You wanna go down by the river?" he finally said.

I nodded, but then I realized his eyes were on the road and he couldn't see. "Sure." I cleared my throat.

"I like the river, don't you?" he said then, and I could hear in his voice he was as nervous as I was. "I used to fish in it all the time with my stepdad when I was a kid. Used to catch trout and perch. Saw a lotta water snakes, too."

"Me, too. I used to go tubing in it with my cousin."

"Uh-huh. I still do that in the summer," he added kind of sheepishly.

We soon drove over the iron bridge to the parking lot, the car rattling and booming over the metal grate, and Gavin parked in a cloud of dust. He drove a little fast for my liking, but then, he was a boy. We got out and walked down to the river. It was a clear day, the water silvery and the sky blue, with a cold wind blowing. Rows of flat rocks ran along the bank and across the river, so smooth they looked like giant gray pillows. We jumped from rock to rock, till we were in the middle of the water.

"Where did you grow up?" I finally thought to ask. I knew he hadn't moved to Hollowdale till fifth grade or so, but I didn't know where he'd moved from.

"Nashville, Tennessee, home of country music," he said in a jokey Southern accent.

"Is that how come you play guitar?" I glanced at him shyly. He had the collar of his black leather jacket turned up, and his hands were shoved in the pockets. The wind was whipping his long hair over his eyes.

"Guess so. Must be in my blood, since I grew up hearin' it all around me. Played my first guitar when I was five. Electric by nine. Been in bands since third grade."

We'd reached a wide gap between the rocks now, the river rushing through, and I didn't see any way to get across without getting wet. I stopped, thinking we'd have to turn back, but Gavin jumped over the space as if it was no more than an inch wide. He moved like he was made of elastic, graceful and easy. He held out his hand to me. "Grab ahold of my hand and jump," he said.

It was the first time he'd touched me since the party and it felt like an electric shock. I'm not sure how, but I sailed over that water like a bird. And when I got to the other side, he didn't let go of my hand.

"Are your mom and dad musicians?" I asked then. Could it be possible? I was thinking. Could it be possible he likes me?

"Nope. My mom's a receptionist at the hospital and my stepdad's a county sheriff. But they listen."

"You got any brothers and sisters?" I knew this was sounding like an interview, but I had to make some kind of conversation.

"Yeah, I got twin half brothers. They're in second grade. They drive me crazy, always messin' with my guitars and stuff." Gavin paused, his fingers closing tight around mine. "My real dad played banjo, but I ain't seen him since I was ten."

I looked at him again. That long swinging hair, those summer eyes. "That's sad. Do you miss him?"

"Nah. He was fucked up. Got drunk all the time. Beat us up. That's why we moved here, so he'd never find us. If I never see the bastard again, it'll be too soon."

We'd returned to the riverbank by then, and were walking down a path in the woods. The wind blew the trees around us, making them whisper and creak, and the river whooshed and burbled as it rushed along. I don't know if I was cold or not, though. Gavin was still holding my fingers in his warm hand and I couldn't feel anything else.

"I don't have a dad either," I said.

"Oh, no?" Gavin glanced at me. "Mind if I ask why not?"

I shrugged. This was getting too close to talking about Mom, and I didn't want to do that. "He just didn't stick around. I don't know anything about him, except he was from Jamaica. I've never even seen a picture."

"Jamaica? Wow, that's cool. I wonder if he was a Rasta." Gavin began singing a Bob Marley song, "Stir It Up," his voice low and sexy. He let go of my hand to play air guitar a minute, leaning back and swaying his head, just like he did onstage. "Is that where you got your name? Is it Jamaican?"

I smiled and shook my head. "No, it's British. It was my mom's idea. Ugly, isn't it?"

"Oh, I don't think so. I kinda like it. It sounds . . ." Gavin thought a moment, which made me nervous. "It sounds like the name of somebody who gets what she wants."

I didn't know what to say to that.

"Too bad you didn't know your dad, though," he went on. "He could've turned you on to some pretty cool music."

"Yeah, I know. I do listen to Bob Marley, though. Other reggae, too."

"Lookin' for your roots, huh?"

I glanced at Gavin, unsure what he meant. It made me uneasy when white people talked about roots. It always sounded a thread away from mockery. On the other hand, Gavin was a musician, so he probably really did care about things like that.

He took my hand again and we walked on a little. "Did you ever have a dream dad?" I said. "You know, to make up for the real one? When you were a kid, I mean?"

"Sure." He kicked a stone along the path. "I used to pretend my dad wasn't my dad at all, and that my real one would turn up and kick him out on his ass. But then I got my stepdad, and he's pretty cool, so it's okay. What about you? Did you have one?"

I nodded, kicking a stone myself. "Yeah. He always came in a helicopter with a big teddy bear in his arms and whisked me off to a life of riches." Gavin laughed, so I did, too. It did seem funny all of a sudden.

He stopped on the path, then turned to face me. "I'm real happy we got to meet, y'know? You're a very cool chick altogether. I couldn't stop thinking about you the whole weekend after that party." And he pulled me right up to him and lifted my chin. Then he gave me a long, gentle kiss and I thought I'd melt right there in the middle of the woods. Two hundred oak trees, one hundred birches, a single gorgeous guy, and a puddle of me.

seven

THE NEXT DAY at school, I felt like a queen. Gavin had arranged a date with me for the following day and it made me feel more proud and beautiful than I'd ever felt in my life. I didn't care about Sophie O'Brian's catty little tongue anymore, or Sally Anderson's snooty Cool Crowd, or even the whispers from the Confederate flag thugs whenever I walked by. I floated through my classes like I was riding in a chariot, head high, shoulders square. The hottest guy I'd ever met liked me. Who needed more than that?

I made Serena listen to the entire story at lunchtime, then I asked her about Dave Kruger. She told me she'd decided not to meet him for pizza after all because of the way he'd behaved at lunch. "He's a jerk, who needs him?" she said. "I hate it when people act one way alone with you, then another with their buddies. So watch out for yourself, okay? Gavin could be just as bad."

"I know," I said. "I'm not stupid." But the truth is I was so high I didn't even question the fact that Gavin was ignoring me in the cafeteria again. I figured what we were building between us was still private and new, not for school gossip and not for just any old person to see. I figured he was protecting us.

Krishna and Jamie joined us then, and I could tell Krish was mad as hell at me. He avoided my eyes and managed not to say anything to me for fifteen whole minutes. I tried to apologize for disappearing on him at the party, but he looked away and frowned. I thought that was dumb. It was true we were best friends, but that didn't mean he owned me. If he wanted to go out with some girl, it'd be fine with me, so he had to allow me the same freedom. Our little crowd needed to expand anyway. For almost three years we'd stuck together like melted caramels—it was time to break out, 'specially when it came to our love lives. I was sure Krishna would agree when he'd simmered down.

When I got home at the end of that day, I called Bob. I wanted to talk to him about his Marissa story and I wanted something else, too. I'd been wondering about Timmy ever since the day Liz had cried her mascara all over my stomach, and I'd decided to go back to the city and see how he was doing. But I needed the bus fare first.

"Madge! What's up?" Bob said when he answered. He was at work and I could hear voices, electronic beeps, and the whole mysterious world of a newspaper going on behind him.

"Nothing much. I liked that story you sent about Marissa."

"Good. Thanks for your help, by the way. You've got quite a knack for description."

"That's why I'm calling."

"Oh, yeah? I'm on deadline, so make it quick."

I fiddled with the telephone cord. It's not easy to ask for money quick. "Well, I want my pay."

"What pay?"

"You know, for my words you stole for your article? You said you owe me."

"Huh? No, no, he said he wouldn't go on record. Nothing I can do about it . . ." Bob kept on talking to whoever it was, while I kicked at the stacks of newspapers lined along our hallway floor. "Madge? Sorry about that. What were you saying?"

"My pay, Bob."

"Oh, yeah." He chuckled. "I guess that's only fair. How much do you want, Miss Bloodsucker?"

"Fifty bucks."

"Fifty?"

"It's not for me. I need to buy something special for Mom." I was good at lying. Mom had taught me that.

"Yeah, yeah I know," Bob said to someone else. "Listen, Madge? This is a bad time. I'll stick it in the mail, okay? Gotta go."

I was surprised—I hadn't really expected him to pay me at all. "Okay. Say hi to Ruth."

"Uh, I can't do that. She dumped me."

"She did? Why?"

"Don't know. Talk later." And he hung up.

That's terrible, I thought, that's really sad. That was something I was going to have to fix.

My second date with Gavin was after school on Thursday, the next time he could get his stepfather's car. We'd agreed to go to my house so he could see what music I had, and that he'd bring some of his own CDs as well. "We can burn each other some of our favorites, okay?" he'd said. I hadn't had the nerve to tell him that neither Mom nor I had a computer to burn them on.

We chatted about school on the way, but it was still pretty awkward. I was so afraid I'd say something dumb.

"Is your mom home?" Gavin asked as we swung up my hill.

"I doubt it. She usually doesn't get home till pretty late."

"Cool." He put his hand on my leg.

Nobody's touch had ever affected me like that. It made me woozy and helpless. I didn't understand it, Gavin's power over me, and I didn't know how to resist it, either. But then, I didn't want to.

Gavin glanced at me, smiling. I still couldn't believe he was actually there, that I was in a car with him, and that he seemed to want to be with me. I looked over at him and smiled back giddily.

Once we reached my house, however, I was too embarrassed to feel giddy anymore. Gavin's family wasn't rich—nobody in our town was—but compared to mine, they might as well've been billionaires. Everybody knew the Winslows had a house all to themselves, a garage where Snake Eyes could practice, and that Gavin owned at least two guitars, not to mention a stereo system the kids at school were always begging to use for their parties. All Mom and I had was a two-bedroom dump and an overweight cat. So when he parked, I didn't even want to get out of the car.

"This it?" he said, looking up at our listing front porch. "Funky."

I hiccupped nervously.

"So, we goin' in?"

"Um, you really want to? It's kind of a mess in there right now. Maybe we should go someplace else instead?"

Gavin leaned over to me, put his lips to my ear and whispered, "It ain't your house I wanna come up and see, Madge." Then he tickled my ear with his tongue, and I turned back into butter goop.

Soon as I opened our apartment door, Mousy waddled over, moaning and rubbing his head all over my black sneakers, wrecking them up with his orange hairs. Gavin almost tripped over him. "Damn, I better give him some food," I said. "I'm sorry."

"That's cool, I don't mind." Gavin crouched down and tickled Mousy between his ears. "Hey, fatso." Mousy rolled over to present his wobbly white stomach, which Gavin tickled till Mousy was writhing in ecstasy. Gavin could do that to everything, it seemed: Mousy. His guitar. Me.

I shook some food into a saucer and put it down with all the other garbage on the kitchen floor, while Gavin lounged against the door, watching me. I felt so bad about the disgusting mess in there I couldn't look at him. The dingy orange

paint on the walls was cracked and flaking. The brown linoleum floor was worn through in patches. But the worst was
the cup of leftover tea on the counter, with three cigarette
butts and a clump of curdled milk floating in it. Mom was
such a slob.

"Sorry it's such a shit hole in here," I said.

"It don't bother me," Gavin replied. "Quit apologizing,
Madge. It just looks lived in. My mom cleans our house so
many hours every day you can't even move. That's why I took
up guitar—to drown out the sound of the vacuum."

I didn't believe him, but I laughed anyway.

Gavin said he liked my red attic room right away, which
made me happy, though I felt a little jittery when he closed
the door behind us. He looked puzzled when he saw my crying American flag, though. "What's that mean?" he said. "The
peace sign and the tears like that?"

"It means America's messing up. It means we're killing
people just to get oil and make ourselves rich."

"Oh." He gave me a funny look. "But you still believe in
the U.S. of A., don't you? I mean, we got the best music in
the world, right?"

He grinned at me and I found myself nodding yes.

The first thing he did after that was wander over to look
at my CD collection. I watched him, hoping he'd approve.
"Huh, interesting," he said, a compliment way too ambiguous
to make me feel any good. "Not what I expected."

"What do you mean?" I said nervously.

"Well, it's not your usual chick music, y'know? You got

some cool stuff here. Reggae, like you said. Nirvana, Prince, OutKast, Chili Peppers . . ." He kept flipping through my hamburger case, naming the bands he liked out loud, while I cringed. I'd thought the hamburger was cute when Mom gave it to me, but in his hands it looked babyish and dumb.

"Stylofone!" he said suddenly. "You are indeed cool, Missy Madge."

"Thanks," I said, blushing. Then I gasped. Right beside Gavin's elbow, stuck up on the wall over my CD player, was my snapshot of Snake Eyes. I'd taken it at a school dance with Serena's camera and tacked it on my wall because I thought the guys in the band were so hot. I'd never expected any of them to come to my house and actually see it. I felt like such an asshole. I mean, how uncool could I be?

He was standing right in front of the photo, flipping through my CDs. Don't see it, I was praying, don't look up. But of course, he did. I saw his eyes fall on it and linger there for a second, but the thing is, he didn't say a word. He didn't even tease me about it, or ask me why it was there. I thought that was so kind.

"Okay, let's hear some of this music," he said finally, and slipped the Bob Marley into my CD player, choosing "No Woman, No Cry." He turned to me and I pretended to smile, but I knew what he was doing. That was the song people always played at parties to signal the time for making out. I didn't know what to do with myself. I was afraid to sit on the bed, in case that seemed slutty. I was afraid to move around, in case I seemed nervous. And I was afraid to talk, in case I sounded brain-dead. So I stood there like a parking meter, waiting to see what Gavin would do next.

What he did was pull the curtains closed so the afternoon sun was filtered into a gentle, soft light, and walk over to me. Then he took my hand and pulled me down on the bed. "This okay?" he whispered. I nodded yes.

But somehow it wasn't. I couldn't get the same feeling I'd had making out with him at the party, those hot waves that had turned me so giddy. I couldn't even feel as good as I had in the woods. I was too nervous there alone in my room with him, too unsure. Maybe I wanted to talk more first, or maybe I was afraid Mom would walk in at any moment. Perhaps I still didn't trust him enough, I don't know. But it all seemed too fast, too smooth, too sudden. I kissed him back anyhow, and I still liked his smell, the feel of his strong back in my arms, and his body pressing on mine. I was flattered as hell he was there and wanting me. But when he pulled off my shirt and bra, I felt weird and exposed, and when he tried to pull off my jeans, I stopped him.

"I'm not ready yet," I said, yanking my ugly brown blanket up to my neck.

Gavin rolled off of me. "That's okay." He let go of me altogether and lay on his back, his hands folded under his head. "Don't worry, we got time."

I liked the sound of that. But I couldn't help wondering how experienced he was. I was sure the only virgin in that room was me.

"You done it before, though, right?" he said then. Reading my mind, as usual.

"Uh, not exactly."

He turned his head to me. "Not exactly?" He raised his eyebrows. "What's that mean?"

I swallowed. "I guess it means no. No, I haven't." I felt myself blush.

He hoisted himself up on an elbow and looked down at me, his long hair dangling. "You haven't? Never?"

I shook my head.

"Wow, I thought you . . ." He stopped himself and flopped back down on his back.

"You thought what?" A chill ran over me. What did he think—all black girls were sluts?

"Nothin'." He paused. "It's okay, don't worry. I'm not trying to make you feel bad or anything, I'm just curious. Is it that you belong to some kind of strict religion or something?"

I laughed, relieved, though I felt a little bitter. What could I tell him, that nobody but him had ever shown the interest before? "No, I'm not any religion in particular. Are you?"

"Only Presbyterian. Nothin' special." And he told me a funny story about his church for a while, which helped me relax. Soon he was kissing me again, and this time I felt a little better about it. But only a little. He didn't try to take off my jeans again, or touch me anywhere but my ribs, and I was grateful. But I was also afraid I'd scared him off for good.

The next time we took a break, he lay back and said, "Hey, Madge, can I ask you a question?"

"Sure." What was it going to be this time? Gavin had a way, I was finding, of digging a little too deep.

"What's it like for you, living here in Hollowdale?"

"What do you mean?"

"I mean, you know, being different?"

I waited a moment before answering. Every kid I knew had asked me that sooner or later, except for Krishna and Serena, who knew better, and Jamie, who lived in a cloud. They'd asked me on the school bus, they'd asked me in gym, they'd asked me on the playground when I was little and at parties when I was big—and it had always made me furious.

"What do you mean, 'different'?"

Gavin chewed on that for a while. "You don't feel different? For real?"

"It's not me who's different. It's the people who want to see me that way." I could hear my voice getting edgy, but I didn't care. "Anyhow, who doesn't feel different one way or another? I mean, how's it for you? Being so cool up there onstage, having kids worship you for playing guitar. That's different, if anything is."

Gavin was quiet a moment, still lying on his back, gazing up at my sloping ceiling. Rain leaks in the roof had stained it, and patches of my red paint had fallen off. "Guess I can see why that seems different to you," he said then. "To me, it's just normal."

"That's my point. That's exactly what I mean."

He sat up and looked at me. "Hey, no need to get so prickly."

Then I felt terrible. I mean, there I was, lying naked from the waist up, the blanket pulled to my neck, while he was sitting beside me with his T-shirt on, looking just as cool and together as he always did. It made me feel angry and vulnerable. So much so, I didn't say anything.

"Listen," Gavin said then, and he moved off the bed to pull his boots back on. "You know what I mean. You *are* different. You gotta have some recognition. I just wanted to know if it's been tough for you, or cool, or what."

"Why?" My throat was choking up. I felt so helpless. He didn't get what I'd been saying at all.

"Why? I just wanna get to know you, that's all." He stood up and reached for his leather jacket, which he'd thrown on a chair. "Anyhow, we all wonder. It's human. We all wonder what it's like to be somebody else."

That made sense, but somehow I knew that wasn't what he really meant. Somehow I knew it was worse than that.

"You know what you're really saying?" I said, my voice coming out between my teeth. "You're saying you think I'm a different species from you. You're saying I'm so different from you that you can't even imagine what it's like to be me. That's what you really mean, isn't it?"

"Oh, fuck it. For cryin' out loud." And Gavin threw open my door and left.

The rest of that day was horrible. I lay in bed for almost an hour after he'd gone, swinging between rage and tears. I didn't even know if I'd been right or wrong, fair or unfair. Had Gavin stormed off because I'd exposed what he was really thinking, or had I misunderstood him? Was he just like all those other kids who, when they said I was different, really meant I wasn't as good as them? ("Who burned you in the oven, Madge?") Or had I been too angry to see straight?

I didn't know. But I did know that, one way or another, I'd blown a dream.

At last I put my shirt back on and heaved myself out of bed, praying the phone was connected so I could call Serena. I needed a friendly voice real bad. I picked up the receiver and listened. A dial tone. Thank God.

I punched in her number and sank to the hallway floor with all the boots and stacks of papers, hoping Mom wouldn't burst through the door and fall over me. Serena answered pretty quick, and I told her what had happened. "You think I should talk it over with him to see if I was wrong, and apologize if I was?" I asked.

"Well, do you like him?"

"Of course I like him."

"Even after what happened? He seems pretty slick, Madge. You sure you trust him?"

"Why, you think he's a player?"

"Duh. On the other hand, he does seem to like you. It's only that if you don't really like him, it's not worth going to the trouble of trying to talk to him about all this, let alone apologize. Apologizing is tough shit. And so is telling a person they're racist."

"I know." I paused, twisting the phone cord around my finger. "Serena? Do people ask you why you're friends with me? Behind my back, I mean?"

She let out a snort. "Nobody ever asks me anything. They think I'm too weird."

"For real? They don't ask you what it's like being friends with a black person or any shit like that?"

"No, they don't. Not everybody's like that here, you know. You're getting paranoid. Listen, do what your heart says. If Gavin's willing to talk and it looks like you misunderstood him, go ahead and apologize. Nobody loses a thing by apologizing, that's what my peacenik mom always says. It means you're the righteous one, and if he doesn't accept it, he's the asshole."

"I guess so." I took a long breath, a whole crowd of doubts clamoring in my brain. "I'm scared."

"I know," she said. "I would be, too."

Throughout the whole next day, I looked for Gavin at school so we could talk. After all, hadn't he said, "We've got time"? And didn't that suggest he'd wanted to keep seeing me? Perhaps he was being honest when he said his questions were only a way of trying to get to know me. Perhaps he didn't see me the way so many other white kids did, and I was being paranoid, like Serena said. It was so hard to know. All my life I'd watched a race going on in white people's faces when they looked at me, a race between hatred, fear, and guilt, and it had left me defensive and suspicious. With the Ricky Campbell types at least it was clear, because they didn't even pretend not to think I was dirt. I knew they hated me. But with people who meant well, like maybe Gavin, it was painful. If they tried to be kind, they seemed condescending. If they tried to be normal, they seemed phony. I knew white people didn't even want to deal with me sometimes because the very sight of me made them so self-conscious and tangled up. Most people didn't understand how confusing all this was, though, not even my own family. They thought racism was clear and simple, like chicken pox—a person either has it or he doesn't. They didn't know all its layers and complications, how you feel it in a tone of voice or a flicker of an eye, how you hear it in the questions you're asked, and see it when people assume you're a certain way because of stereotypes. Krishna understood because he was always being treated like a type instead of an individual. Serena understood because she'd spent most of her life in Philly, in an integrated school, and because she was smart and sensitive enough to think about these things. They knew how racism works, how it makes you unwilling to trust, how it makes you feel like you're never on solid ground—how it makes you so sure people are out to bring you down that you can't tell the difference between reality and fear.

Perhaps I could explain all this to Gavin. Perhaps he'd understand and we could make up and start over.

Every minute of that Friday inched by as slow as Mousy's brain. I kept looking at the clock all the way through my morning classes, and excused myself a trillion times to go to the bathroom in the hope of finding Gavin in the hallway, but no luck. And with every second that did manage to creep by, I lost more and more courage. He wasn't even in the cafeteria at lunchtime, but I couldn't relieve myself by talking to Serena about it because Krishna was at the table, too, and he clearly didn't want to hear me talk about Gavin. By the end of that day, I was knotted up with misery. I was going to have to go home with no relief at all and face a long, cold weekend alone with my murderous mom. And it was my own damn fault.

I was just passing out of the school gate when a boy I'd seen hanging with Gavin called my name. I didn't know this kid at all, except by sight. I stopped, surprised.

"Wait up!" the boy said, and strolled over to me, his friends watching. I did, wary but hopeful. Maybe Gavin was home sick and had given him a message for me.

The boy was skinny and tall, a basketball-player type, with buzz-cut brown hair, a pug nose, and gangly legs. It didn't take him long to lope up to me. "Hi there, Madge Botley," he said, stepping up so close I backed off. "How you doing?"

I narrowed my eyes. "What do you want?" I didn't like the phony smile on his face, and I didn't like that his friends were watching his every move.

"Oh, nothing. I hear Gavin's been getting a taste of hot chocolate. You gonna gimme some, too?"

The air sucked right out of me. All I could do was stand there, stunned, while he turned and swaggered back to his snickering friends.

But then such a huge rage roared up inside of me I didn't even have to think. I ran up behind him and threw myself against his back so hard he fell down. Then I socked him in the ear. I was a practiced fighter—I'd had to do it so much as a kid—and he was too surprised to react at all, except to raise his arms over his head. I was getting ready to punch his stupid-ass nose right up into his eyes, too, but at that moment I saw Gavin for the first time all day. He'd just come slouching out of the gym in his basketball clothes when he caught sight of us, and he was watching the whole thing from across the parking lot, a surprised lift to his eyebrows. And that lift stripped me of every shred of dignity I'd worked so hard all my life to hold on to, not only with him but with every last soul in that school.

I turned around and ran.

So that's how I found out. Gavin didn't care about me at all—all those nice things he said were lies. He was just using me. He'd danced with me to see how a black girl dances. He'd touched my hair to see how black hair feels. He'd kissed my lips to see how a black mouth tastes. He'd talked to me to hear how a black girl talks. He'd held my body to feel how a black body feels. And he'd done it all so he could tell his friends about me and jeer. He was no better than Ricky Campbell.

The worst thing about hope is how it cheats you. You feel so strong and light when you have it, but that only makes you hurt all the more when it drops away. The difference between how I'd felt at school after that first date and how I felt the very next Friday was like the difference between being a queen and a cockroach. And that girl in the mirror who'd looked so fine with her kissed-up lips and her purple hickey now looked like God's bottommost fool. I took the scissors out of Mom's chaos drawer (we didn't have tool drawers and sewing drawers like most people, we had chaos drawers) and I cut up the photo of Snake Eyes that had embarrassed me so, and the orange shirt I'd worn to Sophie's party. I mashed my shiny lip gloss into the mirror, right over where my damn fool of a mouth was. Then I grabbed the scissors and went to the bathroom and locked myself in.

There I was under the lights, narrow green eyes, a head full of dreads, and a mouth too stupid to speak. I picked up one of my dreads, one right in front, and cut it off. I stared at it a moment, nothing now but a half-inch nub above my forehead. Then I lifted up the scissors again and cut off every one of those graceful dreadlocks it'd taken me so many years to grow, till my hair was no longer than the stubble on a doormat. And it served me right.

I was never going to let myself trust anybody, ever again.

eight

"JESUS, YOU'VE SCALPED yourself!" Mom yelled soon as she came in that evening. She dropped on to the edge of my bed, where I was hiding and crying, holding her hand to her heart. I pulled the sheets over my head.

"Madgy, what the hell have you done? Oh Lord, your hair was so pretty, too! It took you years to get it right, stupid girl! You look like a fuckin' cancer case! Why'd you do that? Madge? Madge, answer me!"

I wouldn't talk no matter how much she yelled. So after blabbing some more, she yanked down the sheet. I squeezed my eyes shut.

"Oh, lovey," she said more softly. "You've been crying your heart out, haven't you?" She stroked my cheek with her rough hand. It stank of tobacco and was so callused it scraped. I pushed it away. "Come on, tell me what's wrong. I do know a thing or two, it so happens. Maybe I can help."

"No, you don't! You don't know anything about me! And you're a stupid-ass thief. That's why this happened! Everybody hates us in this town 'cause of you!"

Mom pulled away her hand when I said that, and for a moment she was quiet. "What do you mean?" she said in a low voice.

"I mean everybody knows you're a goddamn criminal. You can take your dumb presents back! I don't want your shitty stolen goods! I don't want to have anything to do with you! You're a violent maniac and you've got no right to be my mother!" I jumped out of bed, grabbed my new CD case, and flung it at the wall, the CDs spraying all over the floor. Then I stamped on them with my heel, one by one.

Mom stared at me, her square face flushing red. "After everything I've done for you, after all the crap I've taken from the people in this town because of you—you talk to me like this!" And she jumped up and stalked back out of the house.

For a long time after she left, I stood in my bedroom not knowing what to do. So many bad feelings were crowding up inside of me that not one of them could decide which should come out on top. Yes, I was mad at Mom for being a loser and a crook, but I was just as mad at her for the racism in this town, for raising me here, for being white—hell, I was so mad about everything I didn't know where to start.

I lifted my hands to my head and felt what was left of my hair: soft, uneven stubble and a few lumps. It felt like a shaved rug. There was no way I was going to school the next day. I would never be able to face Gavin or anybody else with my head looking like this. I'd have to spend the day by myself, with no escape from the mirror and the consequences of what I'd done. I stared at my blood-red walls. "Fuck!" I shouted.

The phone rang just then, so I took a gulp of air to calm my breathing and went into the hallway to answer it. "Hello?" My voice was shaking.

"Madge?" It was Krishna.

My throat swelled up all over again. It was so good to hear his voice. "Hi, Krish."

"Madge, I know what happened. Serena told me."

"She did? How'd she know?"

"Sophie O'Brian told her. She saw the whole thing."

I closed my eyes. Of course. All kinds of people must've seen it. But why did one of them have to be Sophie?

"Listen, I'm coming over," Krishna said then. "Serena wants to call you, too, but I told her I needed to talk to you first."

"How can you come now? Isn't it too late?"

"Doesn't matter. I'll borrow Dad's car."

Then I remembered my hair. "No, don't. I can't see anybody right now."

"Madge, it's only me. You don't have to hide. I'm coming." And he hung up.

I stood looking over my mess of a room while I waited for him. I couldn't let him see it like this, so I made myself pick up. The hamburger case was fine, since it was made of cloth, but all the disks I'd stamped on were either scratched or cracked. I felt real sorry about that—the day I would be able to afford ten more CDs was too far in the future to even imagine. Then I put on the kettle to make tea for Krishna and spent the rest of the time till he arrived going through

Mom's drawers, looking for something to tie around my head. I rummaged through her piles of giant bras and underpants but I couldn't find anything that would work as a head scarf. She just didn't go in for that kind of thing. What I did find, though, was a long piece of paper that looked like a receipt. It was from the department store in the mall: one CD case, ten CDs—$189 total, plus tax. Paid.

By the time Krishna ran up the stairs, I had on my gray sweatshirt with the hood over my head and shame in my eyes. He arrived at the top step and stood for a moment, looking at me. Then, without saying a word, he put his arms around me and held me for a long time, till I broke down and cried into his bony shoulder.

"Don't worry, Madge, those people aren't worth it," he murmured, still holding me. "They're not even worth the Kleenex you need to blow your nose on right now."

I giggled and sniffed. He was right, I did need to blow my nose. I stepped back, laughing and crying at the same time, and pulled an old tissue out of my pocket.

"Thanks," I managed to say, wiping my nose, my breath still shuddering. "Come have some tea." I sat him down in the kitchen so I could pour it for him. I couldn't do it with the style his mom did but I wanted to try my best. "Did you have dinner? I'll make you some toast, if you'd like. Mom forgot to go shopping, so we don't have anything else except raisins."

Krishna looked up at me with his sad brown eyes. "Toast and raisins sounds perfect. Did you do something to your hair?"

I clutched my hood. "Don't ask."

"Okay, I won't. Go on, make us that toast."

I made the toast from an old loaf my mother had left in the fridge, and served a little pile of raisins on a plate for us to share. There wasn't any butter but I did find some raspberry jam—if there was anything at all in our house to eat, it was usually something cheap and sweet. Then I sat opposite Krishna, surrounded by the garbage that always cluttered our kitchen, and we drank our tea with milk and sugar, the way Brits and Indians like it.

"You know," Krishna said after a few moments, "in only one more year we'll be done with this school and we won't have to deal with Gavin Winslow and his type anymore."

I sipped my tea. A year felt like such a long time I couldn't stand to think about it. "What happened to you the night of the party?" I said to change the subject.

Krishna looked so embarrassed I was sorry I'd asked. He cradled his tea mug, shivering a little. It was freezing in my house, as usual, and he was still wearing his coat, a puffy, ugly thing his mom must have found on sale somewhere.

"I walked home early. I wish I hadn't. I wish I'd stayed and stopped what happened, somehow. Today, as well."

"I don't see how you could've done that. It was my own stupid fault, falling for Gavin's sweet talk. I should have remembered you can't trust anybody in this town."

"Don't say that, Madge. You know they're not all as bad as Gavin and his friend. And we can't go around never giving people a chance, can we? If we did, we'd all be so cynical there wouldn't be any good left in the world."

I fell silent when he said that. His words made me think of Mrs. Henderson. If she hadn't trusted anyone, in spite of what she'd seen happen to Marissa, she never would've had the courage to get help to fight her case. She would have just given up and turned passive and bitter, like Mom.

"I guess you're right," I finally said. "Serena said the same thing. But sometimes a person's gotta listen to her head instead of her heart, you know? Sometimes a person's got to stop being stupid."

"So what's your heart saying now?" Krishna stared into his tea as he spoke, blowing on it to cool it down. My chest squeezed when I heard his words, a quick squeeze of pain.

"My heart says Gavin Winslow isn't worth even half of this dirty Kleenex. And that you're the best friend anyone in this world could ever have." And to show him I meant it, I pulled off my hood.

Krishna looked up from his teacup, smiling. But then his smile dropped away and his eyes grew huge.

"Oh," he said with an intake of breath.

I put my hands over my face. "It's hideous, isn't it? Mom says I look scalped."

I didn't hear anything for a moment, so I peeped through my fingers. And this time I was the one who was shocked. Krishna's eyes were filled with tears.

Half an hour later, the two of us were standing in the bathroom, staring into the mirror. Krishna was behind me, holding Mom's electric razor (the one she used for her own ugly buzz cut), and looking much too nervous for my liking. The idea was that he was going to even out my stubble so at least it would have a little style, but the jittery expression on his face didn't exactly fill me with confidence.

As for me, I could hardly stand to look at myself. My stumpy hair made my face seem huge, my neck long as a goose's, and my eyes wide and surprised. I looked like E.T.

"Maybe I should let my aunt do it," I said cautiously. "She is a real hairdresser, after all."

"No, no, I can do it. I shave myself every day, don't forget."

"Well, I better wash it first and get the tangles out."

"Can I shampoo?"

"Uh, okay." I filled the sink with warm water and dunked my head in it so Krishna could scrub in the shampoo. "See if you can ease out the twists. No yanking necessary." His long fingers felt good massaging my scalp and prying apart the knots in my hair. Even though I was scrunched over the sink, I almost went to sleep.

"All right, follow me," he said, the expert now, and he draped a towel around my shoulder and led me back to my room. He sat on a chair and suggested I sit on the floor with my back against his legs. "Now I can see what I am doing." For a long time, he gently worked on what was left of my hair, sometimes with my hair pick but mostly with his fingers, separating the tangles, undoing the twists, and he hardly hurt me at all. It was like my dream about having a kind old grandma to do my hair, only this was my best friend instead.

"Madge?" he said after a while. "You don't have to tell me if you don't want, but why did you do this to yourself?"

I closed my eyes. "I'm just an idiot."

Krishna kept working at my hair with his gentle fingers. But after a long pause he said, "I've felt like that, too. It's tough when you feel other people's hatred. It seeps under your skin and makes you hate yourself. But you mustn't, Madge, you mustn't let them do that to you. You aren't an idiot. You're smart and brave and good-hearted. Don't let them spoil it."

I thought that was so kind. But then Krishna didn't know half of what an asshole I could be.

"Thanks," I said quietly. "I wish you were right." And I told him how I'd accused Mom of stealing the CDs, and how I'd only found the receipt just before he came. "I remember now, she said to ask you about it. Do you know what she meant?"

"Yeah. She called me for a list of your favorite bands. She said not to tell you because it was for a present."

"Shit. She probably saved for weeks to afford all those. And I wrecked every one of them!"

"That is too bad. But you can make it up to her, right? All you have to do is say sorry. I've got a feeling she doesn't hear that word too often."

I shrugged. Krishna was always lecturing me about how I should be nicer to Mom—it was the only thing about him that annoyed me. If he'd known her like I did, he would have known that being nice to her never got a person anywhere.

"Krish?" I said to get off the subject of Mom. "You remember that little boy Timmy I met in New York?"

"Yeah." He was concentrating on a particularly tough tangle. His fingers were so gentle they sent tickles down the back of my neck. "Why?"

"I've decided to go back to see him, like I promised. I've left it way too long. I'd really like you to come with me, if you want. Trouble is the bus costs almost fifty bucks round-trip."

"I can use the money from my pizza job." Krishna delivered pizzas at night, at the same time as getting those straight A's and helping his parents with the motel. I was always amazed at how much he could cram into one life. But then we all had to work and help out our families, given how short money was around here. I babysat for Maggie Donahue's kids and helped Liz at the beauty shop. Jamie got up at dawn to work on his family's farm every day before school. Serena delivered papers and cleaned people's houses on weekends so she could buy all those spooky black clothes her parents couldn't afford. Every kid I knew did something like that, except for maybe the spoiled ones like Sophie and Gavin.

"But I thought you were saving that money for college."

"I am, but I can spare some for a trip as important as that. Okay, I'm done. Stand up now and tell me what you think."

It was hard to pull myself out of his gentle fingers, but I clambered to my feet anyway and went to look in the mirror. The dreads were gone and my hair was back to the half-inch layer of fuzz I'd had when I was little. Only this time the fuzz looked like it had been attacked by moths.

"It's horrible."

Krishna came up behind me and put his arms on my shoulders.

"Madge," he said, looking at me in the mirror, "don't worry about your hair. It makes those big eyes of yours look even bigger. I don't think you understand this, but you are very beautiful."

nine

"HUH. YOU LOOK like an African queen," Mom said when she saw my hair the next morning. Krishna had evened it out to a quarter of an inch and made three zigzag partings in parallel rows, like I'd seen in one of my aunt's hair magazines, then I'd used a little gel to take out the frizz and added some silver hoop earrings. I wanted a style bold and black, and I wanted to show people they weren't going to make me ashamed. If it made me look like an African queen, so much the better.

"Not bad, for a scalping victim," Mom added, handing me a cup of tea. Neither of us breathed a word about our scene the day before. But I wasn't ready to apologize about the CDs, whatever Krishna said. I was still too mad.

When I got to school, Serena and Jamie were real kind about what was left of my hair, but mostly I got stares, snickers, and rude remarks. "Oh, look, somebody mowed her head!" "Is that a bowling ball?" I didn't care. I was looking forward to meeting Krishna at the end of the day to plan our trip to see Timmy, and I wasn't going to let myself mind how all those idiots behaved, let alone that shithead I'd pushed over and punched. As for Gavin, I couldn't even stand to think about him. He still looked beautiful, he still looked sexy, and that confused me because the anger I felt at him was so close to hate. I was just grateful we hadn't gone any further than we did. If I'd let him have sex with me, think where that would have left me now.

It turned out Krishna and I didn't need to take the bus to New York after all, because he had the idea of asking Jamie to drive us in one of his family's old farm trucks, so that Serena could come, too. I hadn't really wanted to drag all of them to see Timmy—it seemed like too many people to spring on him at once. But I realized it'd be cheaper this way, as well as a lot more fun. Jamie still needed us to chip in for gas, though, but between the money I'd made sitting for Maggie Donahue and the fifty bucks Bob sent me (easiest dough I'd ever made), I had enough for gas, and even some to spare.

Getting up early on a weekend morning was usually my idea of slow and senseless torture, but that Saturday I was out of bed and washed by eight. I yanked on my jeans and hooded sweatshirt—I wasn't quite up to walking the streets in my baldness just yet—stuffed my wallet into my pocket, and I was done. I could hear Mom snoring in her bedroom, so I chugged down some cold milk and left quietly as I could. It wasn't that I was being considerate, though; it was that I wanted her to wake up and find me gone. I wanted her to feel what it was like.

Krishna was waiting for me at the bus stop down the hill, where we'd agreed to meet the others so as not to invite nosy parental questions. The stop was nothing but a pole in the ground with a tiny sign on top. You'd never know you could get all the way to Philly or New York from there. Only people who'd been born here would ever figure that out, and most of them were too suspicious of the outside world to ever actually try it.

While Krishna and I waited, we shared a Styrofoam cup of hot coffee. He offered me half of his glazed doughnut, too, but I shook my head. I still didn't like to eat in the mornings. I woke up every day with my stomach so tight and scared, wondering whether Mom was home or gone, or what shit might come my way in the next twenty-four hours, that I never had any appetite. I had to wait for the day to reveal itself before I could face any food.

Jamie's muddy green pickup rattled up pretty soon, snorting and stinking in that way old farm trucks do. Serena was in the front next to him, so Krishna and I climbed in the back. I knew it was going to be windy as hell in the open air like that, and that we'd have to duck down whenever we saw a cop car, but that was okay. I was just happy to be getting out of our trap of a town with my friends. *See, Gavin,* I said in my head, *I don't need you and your kind.* I couldn't imagine him or any of his buddies going to see some poor kid like this. They were way too indifferent.

Krishna and I huddled under an old blanket and watched the mist lift off the fields while the truck rolled along. "What did you tell your mom you were doing today?" I yelled over the wind. I hoped he hadn't lied. It was one thing for me to lie to my mom—what did it matter when she was such a liar herself? But it was another to lie to a mother like his.

"I told her that you wanted me to go with you to New York to visit this injured boy you know."

"You mean you told her the truth? What did she say?"

He leaned into me, resting his head on mine a moment. Sometimes Krishna smelled of the sandalwood soap his family used, other times of minty toothpaste, but it always made me feel at home, the way you feel about the smell of your own room.

"She said to say hi to you and have a good trip."

"You're so lucky! If I told my mom what we were doing, she'd throw a fit."

"Well, I can't tell my mother everything. She doesn't know I drink Brandy's brandy, for example, or smoke Mrs. Jenkins's weed."

"Yeah, but you tell her the important stuff. I could never do that."

"Perhaps you should try."

There he was, lecturing again. He didn't know that Mom wasn't the type you could confide in. For one thing, she didn't listen. For another, she had a whole slew of subjects she refused to discuss, including what she did with herself for most of the day. That's why I had this backup mom in my head, the one who was married to my fantasy father with the green car and the helicopter. That mom was dignified and wise, black and beautiful. She didn't have a criminal past, either, and she didn't pretend to be color-blind.

For the rest of the trip, Krishna and I talked about school, howled a few Stylofone songs into the wind, and whenever Jamie drove over a bump, bounced like a couple of seeds in a rattle, laughing and tumbling. The hurt from Gavin was still there and so was the anger, throbbing like a burn, but I had a mission now, and I had my friends. I didn't need Gavin's summer-morning eyes and velvet kisses. I didn't need his lies.

When we spotted the sewage park sticking out over the Hudson River, I tapped on Jamie's window to tell him to park and we all hopped out, talking about everything we'd seen. Serena and Krishna knew the city pretty well, but Jamie had never been there before. "Is it safe here?" he said, looking around nervously. "I mean, isn't this Harlem?"

"Don't believe everything you see in the movies," Serena said, pulling her long black coat around her. "We'll be fine."

After we'd locked the truck, I led my friends over to Timmy's block. I remembered it pretty well, since it was right across the street from the park. It didn't seem so bleak this time with Krishna and the others beside me, but it still looked rundown and lonely. When a street has only two trees, and those nothing but spindly sticks, it doesn't look welcoming; it doesn't look alive.

"Madge," Krishna said, "what about that man Timmy lives with? You said he wasn't too friendly last time. You think he'll let us in?"

"I don't see why not. We only want to see how Timmy's doing."

"Still, maybe it'd be better if all four of us don't show up at the same time, you know? Might be hard to explain."

"Yeah, you're right." I turned to tell Jamie and Serena, who were walking behind us, and I got a shock. They were holding hands. Serena blushed but she didn't pull her hand away. Jamie looked so pink and happy I thought he'd float up to the sky like a balloon.

A lot seemed to have happened while I'd been tangled up in Gavin.

"Uh, guys?" I said, disconcerted. I was happy for them, but still, it felt weird. I didn't mind that Jamie had switched his crush from me to her—that was a relief—but it did change the dynamics of our little foursome. We were off-kilter now. "Um, why don't you wait here while I go in with Krish?" I said. "I think we'll look less threatening if we don't all show up at once."

"Sure," Serena replied serenely. "We'll wait for you in the park, okay?"

Jamie put his arm around Serena, and they took off down the street, stuck together like a peanut-butter sandwich.

"When did that happen?" I whispered to Krishna as we walked up the block.

"Last week, I think. Sometime after Sophie's party."

"You don't mind?" I glanced at his face. I was still pretty sure he had a crush on Serena, whatever she said to the contrary.

"No, why should I mind? I think it's great. She's had a thing for Jamie for such a long time. And I'm glad she's not with that prickle-head she was dancing with at Sophie's. He is not, I believe, a good person."

"Watch who you're calling a prickle-head." But I pulled my hood off my shorn scalp so Timmy would recognize me.

We walked up the stoop to number 548 and pushed the front door open—the lock was still busted. "It's on the fourth floor, if I remember right," I said, and sure enough, facing the stairs was the door with the fish eye.

Krishna looked around before we knocked. "This building's in terrible shape. It must be owned by one of those criminal landlords." It was true. Old gum wrappers and wads of spit were all over the stairs, the mosaic floor was splattered with stains, and the squashed bodies of at least four roaches were right under our feet.

"It's disgusting," I said. "Almost as bad as my house."

Krishna chuckled.

"Ready?" I asked him. All of a sudden I was nervous. Krishna was right—I was scared of that man with the stained underarms. Very scared.

Taking a deep breath, I knocked, hard, the way I'd seen Joey do. I tried ringing the bell, too, but it made no sound. We waited, my heart banging back and forth inside of me like a gong. Nothing. I knocked again, louder.

"Timmy?" I called. We waited again. Still nothing.

Krishna put his ear to the door and listened. "I think nobody's home." He looked at me. "Now what?"

I didn't know. I'd felt sure Timmy would be there, somehow. I'd had this clear picture in my head of going down that hallway again and finding him on the stained orange couch, his ankle in a nice clean bandage, his face lit up and happy to see me. The picture had been so clear for days that I'd confused it with reality.

"I guess we should look for him in the park. Maybe he'll be there. That boy Joey said they play there every day."

"Okay, let's go." Krishna touched my hand—he knew I was disappointed—and we walked down the stairs together.

When we got to the park, we found Serena and Jamie making out on a bench. I was surprised they hadn't gathered an audience the way they were going at it. "Hey, get a room," I said.

"Good idea," Jamie said with a blissful grin. Serena blushed and giggled.

I showed Krishna and the others the playground where I'd found Timmy before, but we didn't see him anywhere. They were surprised as I'd been at how green and pretty the park was, 'specially now that it had daffodils and crocuses poking up underneath the trees, and there were more people around this time, too. But even though it was late April by then and real spring, the wind was still blowing cold as snow.

Krishna said he'd read about this park but had never seen it before. "You know why it was built here?" he told us. "It was a bribe to the people of Harlem to make them allow a sewage plant right in their neighborhood. You can be sure the rich people in Manhattan wouldn't have put up with this stink."

I was sure Krishna was right, but I kind of liked the park myself.

We did find Timmy at last. He was sitting behind a tree, shoving a stone around in the dirt and making engine noises.

I thought it was sad that he had to use a stone instead of a toy truck. I'd brought him some candy, but I wished I'd thought to bring him a little truck, too.

He didn't see me at first. He was too absorbed in making his stone rev up its engine so it could climb a dirt hill.

"You wait here," I told my friends, and walked over to crouch in front of him. "Is that a bulldozer, a backhoe, or an excavator?" I knew quite a lot about work trucks on account of my uncle.

Timmy looked up the minute he heard my voice and stared at me. I'd forgotten how cute he was, his face big-eyed and oval, his skin soft and brown. Without a word, he went back to shoving his stone through the dirt.

I didn't know what to do. I'd expected him to be glad to see me, not act like this. I picked up another stone and drove it up his dirt hill, then made it roll over and crash. A little smile flickered across his face, but he switched it off quick.

"Where you been?" he said finally.

Ah, so that was it. "I had to go home. I'm sorry I didn't come before, but I live pretty far away, you see."

He didn't answer, so I watched him awhile, squatting there on the ground. Then he looked back up at me. "What you done wit' your hair?"

"I cut it, nothing special. How's your ankle? Is it better yet?"

"Kinda." He had a low voice for a boy so young, raspy and hoarse. "Still hurt me sometime."

"Can I have a look?"

He stretched out his leg so I could reach over to lift the cuff of his pants. The ankle was a little puffy but the bruises had gone. "It looks a lot better. What did the doctor say?"

"Didn't see no doctor."

I beckoned Krishna over, who was standing apart with Serena and Jamie, watching us. "Timmy, this is my friend Krishna. He comes from my town."

Krishna squatted down beside us. "Hi," he said gently.

Timmy ducked his head and shrank away from him. I looked at Krishna and frowned. Something wasn't right. Timmy had deep brown circles under his eyes, his hair was tangled and dusty, and he had on the same clothes he was wearing the first time I'd seen him—loose black sweatpants and a dirty blue jacket two sizes too big. He looked tiny and lost inside them, like a lone matchstick in a box.

I pulled a bag of Sour Powers from my pocket and opened it. The crackling noise made Timmy look over at me. His eyes fixed on the bag, and before I could even offer it to him, he shot out a hand, grabbed it, and in almost one bound, scooted away. He stood at a distance, stuffing the candy in his mouth fast as he could and watching me warily, like he was sure I'd take it back. He made me think of what Bob had said about Mom all those weeks ago, and how she always ate like she was afraid someone would snatch her food away.

"He could be more polite," Krishna said.

"I think there's something wrong. Look at him, Krish—he's filthy. And look how skinny he is! And why's he always playing alone every time I see him? That man he lives with never took him to the doctor about his ankle, you know."

Krishna sat on the ground beside me, his long arms around his knees. "I think you might be right."

"I'm going to talk to him." I started to get up, but Krishna put out a hand to stop me.

"Let him come to us. We don't want to make him feel like we're chasing him."

I sat back down and sent a smile over to Timmy, who was still watching us nervously while he gobbled his candy. Krishna picked up a stone and drove it over the ground, making it roar and beep. Timmy took a step forward, then another. But he didn't come all the way back till he'd finished every last one of those Sour Powers.

We spent two hours with Timmy that day in the park. Serena and Jamie went off to explore, while Krishna and I zoomed a bunch of stones around, pretending they were backhoes and tractors. I was starving the whole time—I hadn't had a thing to eat all day—and it was cold and damp sitting there in that wind on the newly thawed ground, but I was fascinated by that kid. When we tried to talk to him, he was wary and sullen, but when we played trucks he was a different boy. He turned lively and excited, full of energy, totally focused on all the different truck sounds he could make and on maneuvering his stones over imaginary ditches and bridges, scooping up dirt. I decided right then that the next time I visited, I'd bring him a toy bulldozer. Because I was going to visit him again. And again.

"Krish?" I finally said. "I'm starving and freezing and my ass is stuck to the ground."

"Mine, too. Let's find a coffee shop and warm up."

"What about . . . ?" I nodded at Timmy, who was absorbed in hitching his stone to a fantasy Dumpster so he could tow it away.

"I'm comin' wit' you," Timmy said calmly. I hadn't realized he was listening.

Krishna and I stood up and Timmy surprised me by inserting his cold little hand into mine. We gathered up the smooching couple and the five of us walked out of the park and over to Broadway to look for a diner. It took a while, but we finally found this cheap-looking place with steamed-up greasy windows and gray Formica tabletops. Krishna counted out our money and figured if we limited ourselves to a toasted bagel and a hot tea each, we'd have enough left for gas and for me to buy Timmy a whole new outfit before we went home.

None of us said much while we thawed out. We were too busy taking turns going to the bathroom in the back and hugging our teas to suck every last particle of warmth out of them. We were also too busy watching Timmy. He insisted on sitting right up close to me, which wasn't too comfortable because he stank of dirty clothes and stale pee. Much worse than the first time I'd met him.

Once the bagels arrived, he ate his in huge bites, incredibly fast, just the way he'd eaten the candy. Jamie tried to make him laugh by hanging a bagel off his nose, but Timmy stared at it so hungrily that Jamie gave up and just handed it over. All of us did, breaking off half a bagel each for Timmy, and he ate every one. I looked over at Krishna. We both knew what the other was thinking: this kid wasn't being looked after at all.

"Anybody know what time it is?" Jamie said at last, his arm around Serena's shoulders. "Dad said I have to get the truck back by four."

Krishna looked at his watch. "Almost two."

"Damn!" I said. I wouldn't have time to buy Timmy those new clothes now. I bent over to peer into his face. "We better take you home, sweetie, it's getting late."

Then I realized something: we'd walked this child right out of the park and nobody had noticed.

"Timmy?" I said. "Don't you think somebody must be wondering where you are by now?"

He shrugged.

"What about your mom? Isn't she gonna worry?"

"My moms is gone."

"What do you mean?"

He wouldn't answer. He just clamped down, silent as a locked door.

"What about that man you live with? Is he looking after you?"

Timmy shook his head hard, but he still wouldn't say anything.

I gazed down at him, nestled up beside me. Mom may have disappeared on me over and over, but at least I'd had Liz and her family. I'd never been left by myself in a park like he was, hungry and stinky. I'd never been so alone that strangers could wander off with me without a soul even blinking. I thought back to the first time I'd met him, how he'd been outside with no adult and how Joey had said he and Timmy went to the park alone all the time. I also remembered Joey running away as soon as that man had come to Timmy's door. So I made a decision. I was going to take Timmy back to his place right then, figure out who was looking after him, and see if his home was as bad as Marissa's.

I slid out of the booth, pulling him with me. He only stood as tall as my thigh. "It's time to go now," I said gently.

He clung to my leg the same way his little claw hands had clung to my wrist the first time I'd seen him. "Don' wanna." He sounded genuinely scared.

"I'm sorry, sweetie, but I've got to take you back to your apartment. It's time for me and my friends to leave."

"No," he said, whimpering and holding on to me.

I looked down at his little head pressing into my leg, and my whole self hurt. He was scared to go back, it was obvious. That man he lived with wasn't making Timmy feel loved or safe—Timmy wouldn't be acting like this if he was. He wouldn't be so hungry and dirty, either. I thought of all those times Mom had disappeared and how frightened I'd felt, even at Liz's house—all those times when the only thing I'd wanted in the world was for Mom to come back. Maybe that's how Timmy felt. Maybe he needed a home and a mom as much as I had.

"Would you like to come home with me?" I said quietly.

"Madge!" Krishna hissed.

I ignored him. "Timmy, I'll take you back to your apartment if you want. But if you don't, you can come home with me. Would you like that?"

He nodded and leaned into me.

"What are you doing?" Krishna said in panic.

"Krish, he's neglected and starving and filthy and sad. We can't leave him like this. We can't be like all those people in the world who throw away kids like garbage."

Krishna clutched his head. "This is crazy! Think how his family would feel!"

Serena and Jamie stared up at us from the diner booth.

"He doesn't have a family! He says his mom is gone, right? And that man he lives with doesn't give a shit, it's obvious. It would be cruel to take him back there! I want to bring him home, where he'll be safe."

"But that's illegal!"

"Krishna's right," Serena said, piping up at last. "You can't pick up a kid and take him home like a lost puppy. That's kidnapping."

"I'm not kidnapping him, I'm rescuing him!"

"If it's like rescuing a puppy, then fuck the law and more power to you," Jamie said earnestly.

"I know it seems like that," Serena replied, sounding a tad impatient, "but this is a human child, not a lost pet. If we drive him back to Hollowdale with us, then we'll be committing a serious crime."

"If that's how you're all going to think, then I'll take him home on the bus by myself!" I looked down at Timmy. "Timmy, are you truly sure this is what you want? You really want to come home with me?"

He nodded again, still holding on to my leg for dear life.

"See?" I said to the others. And leaving them all gaping at me in the diner, I picked him up, stink and all, and carried him out.

Krishna came running up behind me. "Madge, wait!"

I did, still holding Timmy in my arms. His legs were wrapped around my waist, his head resting on my shoulders. He felt tiny and vulnerable, which only made me surer than ever that he needed me. Too many people were messing up this world with their selfishness and indifference, like the quote on my wall said. Too many people were cowardly and passive. Too many people were lying and breaking hearts. I didn't want to be one of them.

"Take him back," Krishna said, panting. "You know you can't do this. His family'll call the cops and we'll all be thrown in jail!"

I looked Krishna in the eyes. "You can come with me and Timmy, or you can drive back with Jamie and feel nice and safe. Up to you." And I turned and headed toward Broadway.

Krishna must have told the others to leave without him, because a minute later he'd caught up with me again. He tried every argument he could. He argued all along the street, he argued down the stairs into the subway, he argued on the train, and he argued following me back out again. But I shut my ears. I knew nobody would call any cops for Timmy. He wouldn't be begging to come home with me—a stranger—if anybody he knew cared about him, and he wouldn't smell like a bum, either. I felt it in my bones. I didn't know if his mom was dead or had only run off someplace, or if he was in a cruel foster home like Marissa had been, but it was clear he was a throwaway. I might be the only chance he'd ever have to get pulled out of the trash, and I couldn't think of anything that mattered more than that.

"Krish," I said after he'd yelled at me all the way to the door of the Shortline bus, "you'll have to buy your own ticket. I only have enough money for me and Timmy."

Krishna looked at me, all the words drying up on his tongue. We were standing on the steps of the bus by then, the driver glaring impatiently at the three of us, waiting for us to pay and move on inside. "I'm only trying to do some good in the world," I said. "Don't turn it bad."

ten

BY THE TIME I got home with Timmy, I felt like I'd been through a war. I'd dragged myself up at dawn, traveled all the way to New York, played with the kid for hours in the cold, and battled Krishna all the way back again on the bus. But the day wasn't over yet. I had to wash Timmy's hair, which was tangled up with dirt and God knows what else (he kept scratching, which worried me), and I had to clean his filthy clothes and smelly self, too. So soon as we got home, I carried him straight to the bathroom and shut the door.

"You sit here and I'll run you a nice warm bubble bath," I said, putting him down on the toilet seat and turning on the faucets. "Come on, sweetie, give me your clothes." I bent down to pull off his jacket.

"No!" he shouted, waking out of the groggy daze he'd been in since falling asleep on the bus. He lunged at the bathroom door, but I quickly leaned over and locked it.

"Don't be scared, Timmy. We've gotta get you clean, that's all. You'll feel much better."

"No, fuckin' bitch, *puta*, I won't!" He began struggling with the doorknob, which was only about level with his forehead.

I blinked. I'd never heard curses so bad from a boy his age. "Calm down, it'll be fun!" I yelled above the roar of the running water. "You're covered in dirt, you need to get washed!"

I was trying again to pull off his jacket when something solid and sharp whacked me in the guts. I doubled over, letting him go. Having punched me in the stomach, he began pummeling my face, too, his little fists surprisingly hard and strong.

That annoyed me. I wasn't going to let some three-foot-high bean sprout beat me up. I pinned his arms behind his back and wrestled him to the ground. Then I sat on his thighs, careful not to hurt his ankle, and held his wrists down with my hands.

"Now listen to me." I tried to sound calm. "If you wanna stay here, you better stop hitting me right this minute. When I say you get undressed and have a bath, you get undressed and have a bath. Understand?"

Timmy looked up at me, his black eyes wide with either defiance or fear. And he spat in my face.

Half an hour later, I heard somebody trudge up the stairs and into the apartment. I was lying on the bathroom floor, eyes closed, face scratched, soaked and panting. I'd had to fight Timmy quite a while before he calmed down enough to let me hug and comfort him, but at last he'd agreed to get in the bath and now he was having a grand old time splashing in the bubbles. The problem was he wouldn't get back out.

"Anyone home?" It was Liz. Since my uncle had died, she often dropped by after she closed up the beauty shop. "I can't face all those evenings alone," she'd told me once. "It gives me the spooks being in an empty house like that." I heard her toss her keys on the side table and let out a big yawn. "Madge, where are you?"

"Bathroom," I answered weakly.

"Hello, love," she called out. "God almighty, that cat of yours is fatter than ever." I heard her rattling around in our empty fridge, insulting Mousy some more, and then I heard her tromp down the hall to the bathroom and knock on the door.

"Come in."

She opened the door. "Aaah!" she yelped, staring. "What on earth is that in your bath?"

"His name is Timmy."

My aunt glared down at me. "Get up off the floor and explain yourself, young lady. What in the hell is that filthy-looking boy doing here? And what in God's name have you done to your head?"

I'd been planning for hours how to break the news to Mom and Liz so I could get their help instead of their disapproval, but I was way too exhausted at that point to muster any kind of tact. I sat up and looked at her, trying to control my temper.

"I've rescued him, and I'll thank you to talk about him with respect."

Liz dropped back against the wall, clutching a beer can. "You what?"

"I found him in New York. His mom's disappeared and he's mistreated and neglected, so I brought him home."

"You mean you picked him up right off the street?"

"Yup."

My aunt was so astonished she could only stare at me, taking in my soaked clothes, scratched cheeks, and swollen eye. "Did he do that to you?" she said, pointing at my face.

"So?" I scowled.

"And what happened, he shaved off all your hair, too?"

That I refused to answer.

"Lord, Madgy, what have you done?"

Half an hour later, Liz, Timmy, and I were squeezed around the kitchen table, and my aunt was looking about as worried as I'd ever seen her. Timmy was on my lap, smelling good at last and cute as a pea wrapped up in my old white bathrobe, munching his way through one of Mom's leftover powdered doughnuts. (I'd finally got him out of the bath by promising him a treat.) I was having a cup of tea. My aunt had pushed aside her unfinished beer and was smoking one cigarette after another. And Mousy was whining and rubbing his head against her ankle.

"Now let me get this clear," she said, kicking him away. "Was the boy lost or running away or what?"

"Neither. He was abandoned. I found him all by himself outside, no grown-ups in sight, hungry, and so dirty he stank."

"Then why didn't you take him to the police? That's what people normally do when they find abandoned kids."

"'Cause I don't trust the police. 'Specially after what happened to Marissa."

She dropped her head in her hands.

"You would've done the same thing if you'd seen the state he was in. He was dying to come home with me, weren't you, Timmy?"

"Uh-huh," Timmy mumbled through his doughnut.

Liz lifted her head and looked at me like I'd grown horns. "Listen, you daft girl, I'm calling his family straight away to tell them he's safe. Oi, little guy, what's your phone number?"

"Don' got no phone," Timmy said, taking another bite of doughnut.

"You sure? Come on, you must have a number."

He shook his head.

My aunt flopped back in her chair. "Jesus, Madgy. This is such a pain in the arse."

"I know and I'm sorry, but you don't seem to understand how he was when I found him," I said as patiently as I could. "He had a sprained ankle nobody had done anything about. It's real swollen, look." I picked up Timmy's bare little leg to show her. "His clothes were too big and worn out. He was starving. And he was all alone outside. Nobody was looking after him, Aunty. He was so scared! We can't call the people who treated him like that."

"Where do you live, Timmy?" Liz said, ignoring every word I'd spoken. "Do you know your address?"

I held my breath. Timmy kept chomping on his dough-nut, getting powdered sugar all over my legs. Finally, he swallowed. "Big building."

"But where? Do you know the street and the number?"

"Uh-huh. New York City."

"Where in New York City?"

He shrugged. "Don' know."

I exhaled with relief. Of course he didn't know. He was way too young.

Liz sucked on her cigarette, frowning. "We better call the coppers, then, whether you trust them or not, Madge. They'll know what to do."

"But I'll get arrested! Serena told me I'd be accused of kidnapping 'cause I took him out of New York, and that's a serious crime."

Liz sank back in her chair, staring at me.

"Look, Aunty, he doesn't want to go back. Doesn't that tell you something?"

"Is that true, Timmy?" she said, turning to him. "Don't you want to go home?"

Timmy huddled up tight against me, the way he had on the park bench. "Wanna stay here." He hid his face in my chest.

Liz took another drag on her cigarette and let out an enor-mous sigh. "That's impossible. And who would look after him, anyway? Have you thought about that, you mad girl?"

"I will, of course. But think about it, Aunty. With you and Mom there are three of us, aren't there? We can share. Three moms seems like more than enough to me."

Shaking her head, my aunt stood up and stubbed her cigarette out in a saucer. "It's not that simple, Madgy." She paused, frowning down at Timmy. "Look," she said at last, "since we're stuck with him for the moment, let's at least get him some decent clothes and food for supper—the poor lad can't live on doughnuts. Then we'll decide what to do next."

"Thanks, Aunty. I knew you'd understand."

"I'm not saying I understand anything! But now you've brought him here, we're going to have to do what's right by him, aren't we? Come on, Timmy, let's find you something to wear so you won't scandalize the neighborhood." And plucking him from my lap, she carried him into my room, Mousy trotting after them.

In the end, we had to bundle Timmy into one of my sweaters, which was like a dress on him, because we didn't have anything else in the house he could possibly fit into. We got into Liz's car, me and Timmy in the back, and she chatted to him the whole way. She didn't say another word about calling the cops. All she said is, "When Brandy gets home, we'll sort all this out."

After we'd picked up some food in the supermarket, we went to Discount Dollars in the mall, where we could get kids' clothes pretty cheap. Timmy ran around all excited, wanting anything with a picture of a truck or a car on it, so we found some underwear covered in racing cars, a sweatsuit decorated with a smiling bulldozer, and a pair of cheap red sneakers that fit him well enough. I persuaded Liz to buy him a toy truck and a Batman doll, too, though she complained about the expense, as well as some overalls, little blue-and-white-striped ones like train engineers wear. I put them on him right there in the store and he looked so adorable I wanted to eat him up.

But all the while, my mind kept going back to Krishna. The minute the bus had arrived in Hollowdale, he'd turned his back on me and walked off. He'd only stopped to say, "Madge, I'm still your friend, but I think what you're doing is wrong. Dangerous and wrong."

Once we got back from the store, Liz and I went to work emptying the crap out of the kitchen and wiping it down. "You can't let a child eat in a pigsty like this," she said, scrubbing the tea-stained counter, and even though that's where I'd eaten all of my life, I agreed. We took out the trash, washed the plates covered with cigarette ash and mouse turds, and even mopped the floor. The kitchen still looked crummy, orange paint peeling and the linoleum curling up at the corners, but at least it was clean and crummy. Timmy, meanwhile, spent the whole time chasing Mousy around the apartment with his new truck, laughing and squealing. He was in heaven.

When Mom finally banged into the house, we were sitting at the newly spic-and-span kitchen table, eating dinner like a real family. Timmy had gobbled up the macaroni and cheese Liz had cooked, but he was staring at the zucchini she'd put on his plate like it was going to bite him.

"Mmm, smells yummy in here," Mom called out. She pulled off the old gray jacket she always wore and threw it on a living-room chair, then clumped into the kitchen, stamping her muddy work boots all over the floor we'd just mopped.

"Fuckin' hell!" She stared at Timmy. "What's that the cat's dragged in?"

"Shut up!" I glared at her.

"Don't you two start, you'll scare him," Liz said. "Sit down, Brandy, and keep your voice quiet."

Mom took a beer out of the fridge and dropped into a chair with her legs spread and her shoulders squared. "All right, you two. Out with it." She looked over at Timmy, who was staring at her with his huge eyes. "What are you gawping at?"

He picked up a zucchini slice and threw it at her. It landed on her leg. She glanced at it, shrugged, and popped open her can of beer. "Well?"

"Madge has decided to become a child-welfare agency rolled into one person," Liz began, but I interrupted and explained all over again how I'd rescued Timmy. I left out the part about the man he lived with, however. I knew if I told them Timmy did have a home, they'd ignore every word I said and force me to take him back.

Mom listened, her eyes wide. She didn't even remember to drink the beer in her hand. "You mean you took this kid across the state border?"

That wasn't exactly the first question I'd expected her to ask. "Well, yeah."

"How many people other than us know about this?"

"Only Krishna and Jamie and Serena. I'm sure they won't tell anybody, though."

"Jesus effing Christ." The piece of zucchini, I noticed, was still stuck to her leg.

She turned to Liz. "How long have you been sitting here with that boy, not doing anything? Are you out of your mind? We've got to take him back right now, before somebody reports him missing and gets the fuzz after us. And it isn't going to be me who does it—it's too dangerous. I'm an illegal, remember, and if the cops find out about me because of this, I'm fucked. It's got to be you, Liz, in the car. No buses, no Port Authority—that place is crawling with coppers. You, Madge, the kid—all of you, driving carefully, no accidents, no stopping for a piss, right back to his house. Put him on the doorstep, don't even ring the sodding bell, and skedaddle. And, Madge, if any of your mates spread one word about this, you'll be done for kidnapping and I'll be booted out of the States right on me arse."

"We thought of all that, Brandy, we're not daft," my aunt said. "But we can't take him back, not just yet. He doesn't know where he lives or his phone number, and the poor lad says he doesn't want to go home."

"I don't care what he wants." Mom turned to Timmy, who was leaning over his plate, shoveling his zucchini into little piles. "Come on, little fella, tell us your address, eh?" she said in a wheedling voice. "You're a big lad. I bet you're smart enough to know, aren't you?"

But Timmy wasn't going to fall for that crap. He looked at her a moment, then yawned. "You got prickly hair," he said sleepily, and rubbed his eyes. He didn't seem afraid of her at all.

Mom put her beer can down on the table. "All right then, we'll have to bloody well find out where he lives by ourselves, won't we? You've got to take that boy back now or we'll all be in the nick. Kidnapping is a felony, you know—you can get twenty years for that in this state. And I don't know about you, Liz, but even though Madge is a fuckin' nuisance and thinks she's Queen of Sheba to boot, I'd rather see her on this side of the bars."

I scowled and stabbed my fork into a hole in the red plastic tablecloth. Liz took such a long drag on her fourth cigarette she almost smoked it in one breath. Mom swiped the zucchini off her leg and glared at us. Only Timmy didn't seem to notice the tension. He was too busy humming some private tune, yawning, and dropping his zucchini slices on to the floor, watching them go splat.

Before any of us said another word, Timmy slid off my lap, went over to Mom and stared up at her. Then he clambered on to her knees and stood up, wobbling so much she had to hold on to him to stop him falling. He ran his hand along the top of her bristly head. "Tickles," he said. He dropped into her lap, laid his head on her chest, and fell instantly asleep.

Mom looked down at him in astonishment, but she couldn't help wrapping her thick arms around him. "He reminds me of our Bobby when he was little," she said, a watery smile on her face. "Remember, Liz?" Why him and not me? I was thinking, but then her usual hard expression came back. "Madge, go ring up Bobby and see if he knows how to find the boy's address."

"No."

"Madge!" Mom hissed—we'd all lowered our voices now, so as not to wake Timmy. "This is no time to throw one of your scenes. You've put yourself in danger, this boy in danger, and me in danger. You can't really be this stupid, can you? Go on, get going."

"No."

Mom rolled her eyes. "What's the kid done, put a spell on you? He's a street brat, that's all, conning you out of what he can. I've seen enough of them in my day. Borstal was full of them."

"That's the point! If they'd had decent lives, you wouldn't have met them in prison, would you? If those kids hadn't been abandoned or sent back to cruel homes, like you want to do to Timmy, they wouldn't have been as screwed up as you, either."

"And what the hell is that supposed to mean?"

"Madge," Liz said warningly, but I ignored her.

"It means I know about you, Mom. I know what you did to your mother. I know what a fuckup you are. You want Timmy to be like that, too?"

Mom blinked, opened her mouth, then closed it again. She was stroking Timmy's back unconsciously, rubbing her hand up and down, around and around.

"Look, Mom, why don't just listen to me a moment?" I said more calmly. "I found him alone on the street, okay? Twice. He was cold and hungry and filthy. And when I said I'd take him back to his place, he cried and begged me not to. He wanted to come home with me! You think he would've wanted to come with me, a complete stranger, if he was happy where he was?"

Mom did listen for a change, her eyes moving from me to Timmy on her lap and back again. "Did you find any bruises on him?" she finally said. "Aside from his ankle, I mean?"

"No. I looked when he was taking a bath. I think he might have lice, though."

"Bleedin' hell!" She leaned back from him with such a look of disgust on her face I had to laugh. "Stop that cackling and get him off me, right now!"

I lifted him gently off her lap, carried him to my red room, and put him in my bed, lice or no lice. His face was so tiny against my pillow as I tucked him in. I bent down and gave him a kiss. "Don't worry," I whispered, even though he was fast asleep and couldn't hear me. "You'll be safe now."

When I walked back into the kitchen, Mom and Liz were having a serious talk.

"Bobby knows all types of coppers because of his work on the paper," Mom was saying. "He could snoop around without letting on Madge kidnapped the poor lad and find out if anybody's reported him missing. Maybe he could find out where the boy lives, too."

"But what if Madgy's right and nobody wants him?"

"Come on, Liz, be realistic. We can't keep the kid—he's not our responsibility. And the last thing I need is even more staring and gossiping in this town. He can stay tonight because it's too late now to do anything. But tomorrow we're getting him out of here."

"No, we're not!" I said fiercely. "You're wrong, Mom—he *is* our responsibility. I know it's a shock for you and I'm sorry. I'll do most of the work, I promise. But we've all got to be responsible for the suffering of others—it's the only thing that'll stop the world turning evil. That's why I took him."

eleven

THE VERY NEXT morning, Bob hightailed it down from New York to see us—Mom must have called him right after I'd gone to bed to get him there so fast. He didn't say much at first. He just sprawled in one of our armchairs, smoking and frowning and shooting glances at Timmy and at my shaved head. He looked pretty tense, as if a whole snowfall of troubles had tumbled onto his shoulders and stuck there, like dandruff. I wondered who was worrying him the most: Julie, Ruth, or me.

Mom plunked herself on the couch next to me and Timmy, who'd been watching TV practically since dawn. She was wearing jeans and a man's white undershirt that morning, a cigarette packet rolled up in one sleeve. With her arms bare we could see the blurry tattoos she had on her biceps and forearms; a few she'd made herself in prison, others she'd gotten back in England. They mostly looked like some jerk had doodled all over her with a ballpoint pen. She yawned and rubbed her eyes. I wasn't feeling too perky myself. Timmy had kept me awake all night, whimpering and flailing around next to me in bed. It was like sleeping with a windmill.

Bob finally spoke up. "Madge, you're such a screwball. I can't believe you did this."

Timmy glanced at him, startled, then climbed into my lap and hid his face in my chest. (He didn't have lice, I'd checked—it was just that his hair had been so dirty.) I'd dressed him in his new engineer overalls that morning, and he looked unbelievably cute. I gave him a hug. I loved the way he nestled into me like that. It made me feel like I could really protect him. "Shh," I said to Bob. "You're scaring him."

He lowered his voice. "Okay, but you can't keep your little visitor, you know. It's illegal and immoral." He gazed at Timmy, who was playing now with the Batman doll Liz had bought him. "So I've thought of three options. First, I could drive the two of you back to New York right now, so we can go to all the places you might have found him and hope he recognizes his home."

"No way!" I put my hands over Timmy's ears. "I don't know where I found him, and even if I did I wouldn't tell you. Anyway, he wouldn't cooperate 'cause he doesn't want to go home. And you know what would be really immoral? Forcing him to go back to that cruel life. Don't you remember Marissa?"

Timmy pulled my hands off his ears impatiently, and Bob scrunched up his face and rubbed it. "Second option: we take him to a police precinct in New York, leave him on the doorstep, and split before anyone sees us."

"Are you off your rocker?" Mom said quickly. "That's way

too risky. If the coppers catch us, or anyone gets our license plate, we'll all be in the shit."

"Perhaps Madge could've considered that before she took up kidnapping," Bob replied sourly.

"It's your kind of cowardly thinking that stops people doing good in the world," I retorted. "Anyway, you can't leave a little kid stranded at a police station like that. Or anywhere else, for that matter. It would scare the hell out of him. Jesus, have a heart, Bob."

My cousin leaned forward, his bald head pink and crinkly. "Listen, Miss Preachy, hasn't it occurred to you that some loving relative might be crying her eyes out over him?"

"Go to hell! If he had a loving relative, he'd want to go home, wouldn't he? But he doesn't."

"All right." Bob sighed. "That leaves option three. You keep him while I get my police contacts to look into missing-persons without using your name. Once the boy's been reported, I'll have his address, and we can take him back without the cops finding out. I hope."

"You don't have any faith in me at all, do you?" I said. Then I stopped, thinking of Timmy on my lap. He didn't seem to be paying attention to what we were saying—he was too busy bending Batman's leg all the way up to his head till the poor superhero was doing an agonizing split. Still, I didn't like talking about all this in front of him.

"You're right, you know, Bobby," Mom said then, crossing her arms over her hefty chest. "If anybody's filed a report with missing-persons, or someone is breaking her heart over him, we'll do what we should, of course, and the coppers need never know a thing about it. But, Bobby, I've been watching this lad since last night, and I bet my front teeth you won't find out a thing. What we've got here is an abandoned . . ."—she glanced at Timmy—". . . bird. I can tell all the signs. I met enough of them inside. I was a runaway kid myself, you know. I know what I'm talking about."

I looked at Mom in surprise. "You mean you agree with me now?"

"I never said that. But if you *are* right and nobody wants our little bird back, we'll have to find a way of getting him to the child-welfare people without them figuring out who we are. It's not going to be easy."

"No! I didn't rescue him to have you dump him into a system where nobody cares! Look at what happened to Marissa. She was put in one hellhole after another!"

"Calm down," Bob said. "It's way too early to worry about foster care. Let's deal with one thing at a time. I'm not going to tell the cops anything, and I'm not going to get you arrested, but we have to find out if anybody wants him back. You say he was abandoned, Madge, but maybe he was only lost."

"If he was lost, he'd be crying to go home, wouldn't he?"

"Look, he's only four years old. He doesn't know what he wants."

"That's exactly the kind of attitude that makes people so cruel to children!"

Bob closed his eyes. "Jesus, Madge. At least tell me his last name."

"I don't know his last name."

"Rivera," Timmy said.

I stared down at him, startled. Had he understood every word?

Bob leaned forward in his chair. "Do you know your address, too?"

"No, he doesn't!" I clamped my hand over Timmy's mouth. "Ow!" He'd bitten me.

"Well, do you?" Bob asked.

"Fuck your mama," Timmy replied, then wiggled off my lap and sat on the floor. I couldn't help smirking.

Bob looked at me impatiently. "Come on, don't make this harder for me. He's the kid you told me about, isn't he? The one with the sprained ankle?"

I paused. "Yeah," I said cautiously. "So?"

"Did you find him in the same place this time?"

"No! Look, I've rescued him. Why are you trying to undo it?"

"Grow up, will you? He's not a toy. You can't just grab a human being like this and not think about the consequences!"

"But I did think about the consequences! That's why he's here and not still back in New York being mistreated and starved!"

Bob clenched his jaw. "God, you're self-righteous. You need to cool down and see reason. Anyway, I've got his name now, so I can look into it with or without your help."

He stood up and wandered over to the window to peer out. I watched him, all twisted up inside with anger and confusion. I'd been so sure I was right to take Timmy, but now I felt shaky. I wished I could tell Bob and Mom the whole truth and get their opinion. If they knew about that man Timmy lived with, who wouldn't take him to a doctor, or dress or feed him right—who wouldn't even comfort him when he was hurt and scared—then maybe they'd agree with me. But I was too afraid they wouldn't. I was too afraid they'd only make me take Timmy back, and turn my rescue into no rescue at all.

I got off the couch and walked over to join Bob at the window. Outside, it was one of those dazzling spring days that can come at the end of April. The sky was a hard blue, and the white of the sidewalk jumped out at us like it was already trying to leap into summer. Bob struggled to open the window till I reminded him that Mom had painted most of our windows shut by mistake five years ago. That's why the whole apartment had the sour stink of an ashtray.

"Let's get out of here," I said. "Timmy needs some air."

"We all need air," Bob replied. He turned away from the window. "You coming, Brandy?"

"Yeah, why not?" Mom hoisted herself up from the couch with a grunt. "Fancy going down to the Golden Harp? They have this hard cider packs a real wallop, and they've got a little back garden where we can put Timmy."

"Mom, Timmy isn't a goat. And Bob doesn't want to go to a sleazy dive like that anyway."

"Sure I do," he said, pulling on his jacket.

"All right then, prisoners, let's go," Mom said, and grabbing the keys off the top of the TV, she marched out the door.

I hated it when she got teenagery like this. Was it too much to ask that she act like an adult once in a while? It made me miss Krishna, who sometimes seemed more grown up than anybody in my whole family. He and I had never had a fight like we'd had on the bus before, and I didn't know how to end it.

The Golden Harp was Mom's favorite hangout in town and the only place where she seemed to have any friends, aside from Maggie Donahue. It was an imitation Irish pub tucked down a side street, and to my mind it was full of nothing but drunks and criminals. Mom had been taking me there pretty often over the years, but it had always made me uneasy.

She led us through a small door into a narrow, dark room. Inside, the ceiling was so low that its fake beams almost grazed the top of our heads. I glanced about while Mom kidded around with the grizzled old Irishman behind the bar. A few other people were there, tough-looking men and women eyeing Timmy curiously. I picked him up and turned his back to them so he wouldn't see their stares.

"Heavy place," Bob whispered. "Looks like a smuggler's cave."

"Well, I like it," Mom replied. "Makes me feel at home."

We followed her through a door to a tiny back patio warmed by the sun and filled with white plastic furniture. Flower baskets trailing pink geraniums hung on the walls, and the whole place smelled of damp concrete and petals. We each took a chair, Timmy on my lap again. I put my arms around him and gave him a squeeze, but I was aching from the morning's conversation. I didn't want to fight my family to keep him. I wanted us all to be on the same side.

Mom produced two bags of peanuts and a sack of potato chips from her jacket pocket. "To old times," she said, raising a glass of cider to us and winking at Bob. "You're looking good, Bobby. You've grown a nice manly jaw on you."

I couldn't believe it—Mom never flattered anybody. But I guess nothing was too good for her precious nephew. When he was little, she'd loved him so much she'd tattooed his name into her forearm. You could still see it: BOBBY, scratched in her own handwriting with a pin and darkened with pen ink. That's how they made tattoos in prison, she'd told me.

"He'd look a lot better if he had a little hair," I muttered.

"You're one to talk!" Bob said. "Why did you cut it all off, anyway?"

"She bloody well scalped herself, stupid girl," Mom interjected.

"It's not so bad. Shows off her pretty cheekbones. Makes those green eyes look huge, too."

I looked away. That's what Krishna had told me.

Timmy leaned forward on my lap, grabbing the lemonade Mom had bought for him and slopping it all over the two of us. "Jesus, watch what you're doing!" I dabbed at his chest and my legs with a napkin. The morning's conversation hadn't exactly put me in the most patient of moods.

"Leave him be, Madge," Mom said in a bored tone. "If you pick on him over little things like that, he'll only end up fighting you all the time."

"Nah, I won't," Timmy said, planting a kiss on my cheek. "Hey, babe, gimme some chips." He snatched them, jumped off my lap, and sat on the ground to play.

I was so surprised I laughed.

"Is that child really four?" Bob said.

"He says so, but I think he's five going on fifteen," Mom replied.

"If he's five, then he must be in school. We should find out if a school anywhere has reported him missing."

"He's four, not five," I said. "He's not old enough for school. Hey, Timmy, do you go to school?"

"Fuck school."

"I think that means no." I glared at Bob.

"Here we go again," Mom said. "I'm going in to talk to me mates." And she went inside.

Bob turned to me. "Madge, I can't force you to cooperate, I realize that. But you've got to face that you don't know anything about this kid. Snatching somebody you know nothing about is irresponsible and stupid." He picked up his glass. "I'm getting another cider." And he followed Mom into the bar.

After he'd left, I looked over at Timmy gobbling his chips on the patio floor. I knew more about him than Bob guessed, but he was a mystery, it was true. I didn't know whether his mom was alive, who that man he lived with was, if he had a dad, or even where he was from. I only knew that I'd found him lonely and scared. I gazed over at his little head, his shoulders thin as wings. He seemed to need so much protection—that's what Bob didn't understand. I thought of his whimpers in the night, what he'd said about his mom being gone, the way he'd clung to me so eagerly in the coffee shop, and how he wanted to sit on my lap whenever he was scared. I thought of the way that man in his apartment hadn't seemed to care about Timmy at all. I wanted to help him leave all that behind. I didn't want to be like Gavin or any of the other kids who'd jeered at me all my life—a person whose indifference to others added to the misery of the world. I didn't want to be like Mom, either, bringing up a kid as sloppily as you bring up a cat. I wanted to make Timmy safe and happy.

Given my family, I wasn't sure it could be done.

twelve

THERE'S NOTHING SO lonely as a lie. The lies I'd had to tell at home made me feel bad enough, even though I was telling them to protect Timmy, but then I had to tell even more at school the next day. I'd realized Mom was right: it was too dangerous to let anybody know about him. Suppose a friend blabbed to some adult who decided to call the cops? So when it became clear at lunch that Krishna hadn't told Serena and Jamie about Timmy, I said I'd changed my mind and left him in New York after all. And when they asked why Krishna seemed so mad at me, I said I didn't know. They kept asking me questions and I kept telling them lies till I could hardly keep track. And every lie I told opened a bigger chasm between me and my friends till I felt like they were on one side of an ocean and I was alone on the other.

I hadn't wanted to go to school at all that first day. I'd wanted to stay at home with Timmy to make him feel safe, but Mom wouldn't let me. "You can't start skipping school, kid or no kid," she said. "That's the road I went down, and I can tell you it's not a pretty one. I'll look after the lad while you're gone, don't worry. Now scat."

But I did worry, not only about the lies but everything else, too. I didn't trust Bob not to take advantage of my absence to grab Timmy and hand him to the cops. And now that Mom was in charge of Timmy, I felt nervous about her, too. I was grateful she was helping, but I knew what could happen to her good intentions. She might go out on a whim and leave him alone for hours, like she'd done so often to me, and he was much too young for that. So all that first day, while I dragged myself through classes, ate lunch with Serena's and Jamie's hormones (they'd started having sex over the weekend, Serena whispered to me, and the two of them were so wrapped up in a lust fog they could hardly see), and missed Krishna, who sat with people he knew from his chemistry class and wouldn't even look at me, I was both dying to get home and dreading it.

Soon as school was over, I scooted home to find Mom in our dim orange kitchen, smoking like a factory stack and watching Timmy wolf down an early dinner of chicken and peas. They were sitting at the table, Timmy's face barely poking over the top. Mousy was hiding under the couch (Timmy did nothing but chase that poor critter around all day), and the kitchen was already such a mess that Liz and I might as well never have bothered to clean it at all.

"You cooked him dinner already?" I said, amazed. I wasn't being sarcastic. I hadn't seen Mom cook a real dinner since I'd started high school, let alone at four thirty in the afternoon.

"Yeah, the poor lad's so hungry all the time I had to. I swear he hasn't been fed a square meal in years."

"Was he all right today?"

"Course he was all right. He's a right little devil, though, worse than Bobby was at his age. But he's smart as a whip, aren't you, Timmy?" She winked at him. "He just needs taming."

"God, Mom, he's not an animal." I tossed my backpack in the corner and gave Timmy a kiss and a hug hello. As soon as I let go, though, he reached up to grab a handful of peas off his plate and threw them on the floor.

"Timmy!" I said. "Get down off that chair and clean those up right now."

He slid off his chair so quickly I was surprised. But then he went over to the peas and instead of cleaning them up, he stamped on them, one by one.

"Stop it!" I shouted, but he was too wrapped up in his experiment to pay me any attention. Mom watched him from her chair, chuckling, her tattooed arms crossed over her chest.

"You're making it worse, snickering like that," I muttered. "You're encouraging him."

She tipped back in her chair, her foot balanced against the table leg, and rubbed her hand over her brush-bristle hair. "Leave the poor kid alone. You wouldn't eat your greens either when you were his age." She lit a cigarette.

"Then why did you cook them for him, if you knew he wouldn't eat them?"

Without waiting for an answer, I started washing the mountain of dishes in the sink. Timmy had only been in our house two and half days, but already I was drained. He'd refused to go to bed the last two nights, then jumped on me at six in the morning. He made a mess all over the apartment. He cursed like a gangster, wet my bed in his sleep, and ignored every suggestion I made. If it weren't for those moments when the softer side of him showed—when he was sitting on my lap or cuddling with his arms around my neck—I would have been yelling at him all the time.

I scrubbed the dishes, banging and clashing, while Mom slouched at the table staring off in a dream through her cigarette smoke. The peas were still on the floor, the pissed-up sheets were in the bath waiting for me to wash them, Timmy had to be bathed, read to, and put to bed, and I had a whole pile of homework to get through. How was I going to do it all, not only today, but maybe for years?

"Why are you just sitting there with all this mess all over the place?" I snapped at Mom, slinging a dish into the plate rack. "Can't you at least dry the dishes?" I felt so overwhelmed, my voice trembled.

Timmy looked up from the squashed peas, which he was now scooping into a pasty lump on the floor, and examined my face a minute. He stood and walked over to me.

"Don' cry, Madge." He put his skinny arms around my thighs, smearing pea paste on my jeans. "I don' want you to cry."

I looked down at his curly head, and I felt ashamed. "It's okay, sweetie, I'm not crying," I said gently, bending down to give him a squeeze. "Don't worry." I glared at Mom but she didn't notice. She was staring at Timmy.

"He's uncanny, he is. I told you he was smart. I think he sees right through us all, don't you, Timmy?"

"Don't talk to him like that. It's not appropriate."

"Hah! When have I ever been appropriate?"

She stood up to stretch, her big face splitting into a yawn. "Who shopped and cooked and looked after him all day, eh? Dragging him round with me to the salon and the supermarket and the devil knows where. Something I didn't ask for, did I?"

She picked up her cigarettes and slipped them into her shirt pocket. "I don't know what you were thinking when you snatched the kid, Madge, or if you were thinking at all, but it's like Bobby said—he's not a toy. Looking after a kid is hard work, you know, and it never lets up for a second. That's what I did for you, in case you forgot. So I'd thank you not to lecture me. In fact, a little appreciation might be nice, instead of all this moaning."

I scowled down at the gray suds in the sink. "All right," I grunted. "Thanks."

I washed another dish, trying to calm down while Mom went to get her jacket off the living-room couch. "Did Bob call today?" I said when she came back.

"Yeah, I talked to him this morning. He said he's hitting nothing but dead ends. No missing-persons reports, nothing. We'll just have to be patient. It's early days yet."

"He won't find anything. I told him."

"We'll see about that." Mom picked up the car keys from the table and hooked them to her belt loop. "Right, then, I'm off to work." She came up to me and put a muscular arm around my back, her head only reaching my ear. "There's something I have to do tonight, but I'll be around tomorrow, all right?"

"What do you mean there's something you have to do?"

"Not for your ears, ducky."

"Mom, don't disappear again, please? Not now. Not with Timmy here."

"See you later," is all she answered. And she zipped out the door.

After she left, I sent Timmy into the living room to watch some kids' show and got on my knees to clean up the peas and crumbs under his chair. I felt bad about planting him in front of the boob tube like this, but how else was I going to get the cleaning and my homework done? I was scrubbing at a particularly stubborn squashed pea when the phone rang. Hoping it was Krishna, I ran into the hall to get it.

"Hey, Madge." It was Bob.

"Shit."

"Well, hi to you, too. Did your mom fill you in on our conversation this morning?"

"Yeah. She said you haven't found anything." I lowered my voice so Timmy wouldn't hear. "He's abandoned, just like I said. Nobody cares about him. That's why he hasn't been reported missing."

"Not so fast. Missing Persons isn't everything. There could be lots of people who care about him but are scared to go to the cops. Illegal immigrants, for example. I need to poke around his neighborhood and find out if anybody's been looking for him, but I can't do that unless you fess up and tell me where you found him. I know you remember, I'm not an idiot. Was it Harlem or near my house or what?"

"How many times do I have to tell you? I'm not a New Yorker, I've no idea where it was."

"Was it in Riverbank Park, by any chance?"

"What's that?"

"The park on top of the sewage plant I told you about."

"No, I never went there in the end. Sorry, Bob, gotta go. Timmy's calling." And I hung up.

I didn't like to lie to my cousin any more than I did to my friends; it made me feel horrible. But he didn't know what I knew. If that man Timmy lived with hadn't reported him missing by now, it was obvious I'd been right about him. The man didn't care, nor did anybody else. Imagine letting a kid disappear like that and not doing anything about it! No, Timmy was safer with me. I just wished Bob would see it.

After I'd finished in the kitchen, I went to check on Timmy in the living room. He was curled up on our balding red couch, still watching TV, his chin resting on his little round knees. I stood at the door awhile without him noticing, wondering for the hundredth time what had happened to him in his short life. I'd tried to pry information out of him all weekend, but he only ever said he didn't want to go home. And each time I asked about his mom or that man in his apartment, he clamped down the way he had in the diner, silent as a pebble. At least I hadn't found any obvious signs he'd been abused, like Marissa had, or those other kids Bob was writing about. I'd taken a book out of the school library to read up on it. The book said to look out for bruises or scars, for unusual flinching at sudden sounds or movements, or for "an extraordinary amount of fear or sexual knowledge." I hadn't found any of that in Timmy. He didn't even mind taking a bath anymore. But who knows what had been done to him that didn't show on the surface? He could be clingy one moment, rough and stubborn the next, and he had those flashes of understanding and capability in the middle of being foulmouthed and defiant. He hardly ever cried, but he couldn't stand it when anybody else did, and he seemed more frightened of Krishna and Bob than he'd been of me or Liz and Mom—I was sure these were clues, but I couldn't read them, didn't know what they meant. All I knew was that Timmy acted like somebody who'd been forced to fend for himself for a very long time.

"Timmy, I'll be in my room if you want me, okay?" I said quietly, but he didn't answer, too mesmerized by the television. "Timmy?" I had to say it three more times before he turned to me. I smiled. He looked so sweet with his tiny nose and round mouth, those big eyes, black as olives. That floppy mop of curly hair. I kissed his forehead. "Call if you need me."

In my room, which was now Timmy's room, too, I kicked off my shoes and sat at my dressing table to do my homework. I'd only managed about three hours sleep since bringing Timmy home, and I was so tired I wasn't sure I could do a thing. But I had to try. Before I opened any books, my eyes drifted up to the quote on my mirror, the one I'd had in mind ever since I'd clapped eyes on Timmy: "The opposite of love is not hate, it's indifference." Krishna had always loved that quote.

An almighty crash came from the living room. I jumped up and ran out.

"Didn't do nothin'!" Timmy blurted the minute I appeared. He'd knocked over the table Mom kept by the couch, the one covered with souvenir ashtrays and her trinkets from England. Shattered glass and china lay all over the floor, and ashes and cigarette butts were already grinding into the rug under his bare feet.

"Shit, what did you do with that table, play football with it? Get back on the couch and don't touch anything. You might cut yourself."

I closed my eyes, struggling to hang on to my patience. "The opposite of love is not hate, it's indifference," I chanted silently. That's what's important. That's why Timmy's here.

When I came back into the living room with a dustpan, I found Timmy crouched over the mess, crying. "I broke Brandy's toy!" he wailed. He was holding something in his hand and rocking back and forth, like he was in pain.

"What is it, sweetie? Are you hurt?" I sat down beside him and pried what he was holding out of his fingers to see if he'd cut himself. He hadn't. "Oh, don't cry about this, little love. It's all ugly junk, anyhow." It was one of Mom's china figurines, a boy peeing into a pond. The head and legs had broken off; it was nothing but a peeing torso. I put it back on the table and cradled Timmy in my arms. He was sobbing so hard his body shook, so I held him tight against me, wondering what had made him so afraid.

"Nobody's going to hurt you 'cause of this," I said, the first words that came into my head. "Don't worry, it's all right."

"You gonna send me away now?" he finally managed to say between sobs.

"No, no, little love! Nobody's going to send you away."

So that was it, I thought—he was scared we were going to run off and dump him. I knew what that felt like. Poor kid.

After Timmy had calmed down, I threw the broken junk into the garbage, vacuumed up the cigarette ash, and told Timmy to turn off the television and get ready for bed. First, he refused to budge from the TV, so I had to turn it off for him, which made him scream with rage. Then, once I'd wrestled him into the bathroom, he wouldn't open his mouth to brush his teeth but stood in front of the sink, lips clamped tight as a zipper while I poked at them uselessly with the toothbrush. He hit me when I tried to get him into our bedroom, and once I'd pulled off his clothes, he ran away and hid in the closet.

"Come on, Timmy!" I begged. "If you don't come out now, I won't read you a story." At last, losing my patience, I grabbed the door handle and wrenched it open, sending Timmy, who'd been hanging on to the other side, sprawling naked across the floor.

"Timmy, for God's sake!" I picked him up off the ground and shoved the pajama top over his head. When his little face emerged, though, I had to smile. He looked so adorable with nothing on, his belly round, his legs sticking out from under his pajama top like toothpicks, his little penis like a baby's toe. He let me lift him to his feet, suddenly calm, and yawned while

I pushed his legs into the diaper pull-ups Mom had bought for him to use at night.

"Can I have that story now?" he asked.

"You don't deserve it, but you can." I climbed into bed, pulled him up close, and read him *The Little Engine That Could*. His body was so tiny, and his hair tickled my chin. When I held him like that, all my anger melted away. Still, by the time I left him asleep in my room, I'd spent an hour and a half just getting him to sleep.

At eleven o'clock, I sat on the floor of the living room, my homework spread out on the coffee table and my eyes stinging with fatigue. I gazed down at my book, wishing I could pay attention. I was supposed to write a book report about *Brown Girl, Brownstones* by Paule Marshall, normally the kind of assignment I loved, but how could I when I was too tired to think or see? I forced my eyes over the words, wrote some notes, and the next thing I knew a door slam woke me up and I was lying with my head on the table.

"What're you doing here?" Mom said, flinging her jacket down on a chair. "It's a school day tomorrow. It's one in the friggin' morning—you should be in bed."

I stared at her with what I hoped was bitter irony.

"Are you taking Timmy with you to the beauty shop tomorrow?" I asked. Liz had agreed to fire her part-time assistant and let Mom work mornings at the salon instead. I knew that was her way of giving us money and keeping an eye on Timmy, which I thought was real kind and tactful. What Mom thought of it, I had no idea.

"Maybe. I'll see how I feel. I think I'm getting a cold." She blew her nose. I watched her suspiciously. When Mom claimed to be sick, it was usually a lie.

"Where have you been this late, anyhow?"

She raised her eyebrows. "And why should I tell you? You got Timmy to bed all right, did you?"

"Yeah, but . . ."

"Oi!" she interrupted, spotting the now bare side table. "What's happened to my things?"

"Timmy knocked them over. He cried about it, too. They were crappy anyway." It was true. The porcelain figure of a boy being spanked, an ashtray in the shape of buttocks, deformed-looking glass animals, and that peeing boy—they were all stupid and embarrassing. I was glad to see the last of them.

"But that stuff meant a lot to me, it did! I collected those glass animals for years, and Liz gave me that little boy pissing when I moved down to Brighton after getting out of the nick. It's always symbolized freedom to me."

"What, the freedom to pee wherever you want?"

"Yeah, something like that. Where did you put them?"

"In the garbage. They're broken."

"Jesus Christ." Mom stormed out to the kitchen and I could hear her swearing and rifling through the garbage can. Finally she came back in, carrying the pieces of her ornaments, her wrists smeared with cigarette ash and Timmy's squashed peas from dinner. "These can be glued together, you know. You shouldn't have thrown them away. How would you like it if I'd done that with your things?"

I didn't bother to answer. Mom was being secretive, and that scared me because that's how she always acted before she disappeared.

She put the ornaments back on the table, wiping her hands on her jeans. Then she sat down on the couch, lit a cigarette, and stared at the dark television. In its blank screen I could see a dim reflection of Mom smoking, me in the background, my shaven head like a fuzzy basketball. How could Krishna have said I was beautiful? I picked up my book, trying to focus on it, but then Mom heaved a sigh.

"What's the matter?" I said quickly. "You sound worried."

"What? Oh, yeah." She scratched her head. "Got a bit of a tangle to sort out, that's all. Nothing concerning you, love."

"Why won't you ever tell me anything?"

She stood up, yawning, then walked over to me and tweaked my ear. "That's for me to know and you to wonder, isn't it? Now off you go to bed."

thirteen

TIMMY'S FIRST WEEK with us went by without Bob finding out a thing. He called every day to keep us posted and to try to make me help him, but I could tell he was getting discouraged. He'd been working through all the Riveras in the Manhattan phonebook, even though I'd told him Timmy said he didn't have a phone, but none of them had heard of Timmy or reported anyone missing. And the cops had nothing on him, either. I guess Bob thought he was doing right, but I found it insulting. Why wouldn't he just believe me and accept that nobody but us gave a damn about Timmy?

May had arrived by then, so everybody at school was buzzing with talk of proms and summer vacations. Coats were put away, boots shoved into the back of mudrooms, and people started wearing flip-flops, bare legs, and T-shirts. My shaved head wasn't so shaved anymore—I was wearing it in stubby little twists now, which looked a little bit chic but mostly messy. But none of this meant anything to me. The idea of going to the junior prom, where Snake Eyes would be playing, was pure misery, and I had too many responsibilities anyway.

I had to come home right after school to look after Timmy, so Mom could get to her supermarket job. And I had stay home nights to look after him, too, because lately she hadn't been coming back till past one in the morning. Between that, feeding and washing him, taking him outside to play, cleaning up, and my homework, there wasn't time for anything else. No time to go for ice cream at Dale's Diner with Serena, like we always used to when the weather turned warm. (She and Jamie still didn't know about Timmy, so I had to tell even more lies to cover up why I was so busy.) No chance to hang with Krishna either, since he was still avoiding me, nor to spend those long Sundays together, trading dreams on the floor of my room. It had been only a week, but already I felt so far away from my life before Timmy, I might as well have turned middle-aged overnight.

Well, as Mom kept saying, "That's what happens when you decide to be a mum. That's what it's like."

At the end of Friday of that week, I was heaving my backpack on to my shoulders for the lonely walk home and an even lonelier weekend ahead, when I felt somebody's eyes on me from across the classroom. I turned to see who it was, expecting some kid or other from one of my classes, probably wanting to ask me about homework. But it was Krishna, standing by the door and looking at me with such a sad expression on his face that it made my heart hurt.

I didn't know what to do. The sight of him was so precious. His long, skinny self, those big dark eyes. But I was afraid he hated me now. I was afraid he thought I was immoral.

For a long time I stood in the classroom, staring at the

floor, not moving. I wasn't trying to play games, I only felt paralyzed. If I acted friendly, he might lecture me again and we'd have another fight. If I acted cold, I might drive him away. I was stuck.

The two of us stood there, not doing anything, till every last student had left the room. Finally I heard a rustle and looked up just in time to see him walk away. I still couldn't move. I wanted to, I wanted to run up and tell him how much I missed him. But my pride was too strong.

I trudged the thirty minutes home slow as I could, my spirits sinking with every step. I don't like who I'm being, I thought. I don't like myself at all.

When I got in, Mousy was cowering under the couch, Timmy was in the living room, watching afternoon cartoons, as usual, and Mom was nowhere to be seen. It made me furious that she'd left him by himself like that, even though I'd known she probably would.

"You okay, Timmy?" I gave him a kiss. He was so absorbed in the TV he didn't even notice me. His eyes were going to turn square if we kept this up. I was just about to turn the damn thing off when Mom waltzed in, whistling.

"Why did you leave Timmy alone?" I said through clenched teeth. "You can't do that! He's too little!"

"Don't have a cow, I was only gone a minute. Listen, go into the kitchen where the lad can't hear us. I've got something to tell you."

I sat on a kitchen chair and looked at her warily. "What is it? Did Bob find out something?"

"Nope." She sat opposite me and leaned forward, her square face serious. "Listen, love. I've decided you and Timmy have to move to Liz's place till we know what to do with him."

"What? Why?"

"Because people natter about you and me too much in this town. You know how they look at us, you know how we stick out. It's a pain in the arse and we've got to be careful, for Timmy's sake and mine. 'Specially mine. It'll be much safer in Riverbend, where people don't know us so well. Me and Liz decided you can pass him off as your cousin. We'll call him Timothy Botley and say he's come to visit from Philadelphia, if anybody asks. That way he'll be hidden better, right?"

"I guess so," I said, but suddenly I felt terrible. A made-up name, a pretend family, and a phony hometown? I'd never imagined doing all that to him when I took him. And what made us think we had the right? Suppose Bob was right and I had taken Timmy from someone who loved him? Suppose I'd made a huge mistake and Timmy wasn't neglected or abandoned after all, only poor? How could we justify hiding him like this then?

For the first time, I really felt like a kidnapper.

"Don't look so worried, love," Mom was saying. "It's only while we've still got him. And Liz said she'd be happy to have the two of you with her. She's taken a real liking to the little fella all those mornings he's been in the salon with us. And anyway . . ." She squinted, her narrow green eyes shifting away from me. "Well, I'm sorry to say I can't really afford to look after the lad. He eats like horse and I couldn't pay the last phone bill as it was. So go pack up now, all right?"

"Now?" This was going way too fast for me.

"Yeah, the sooner the better, Madgy. People are giving me the eye already. It's not exactly easy to hide a little black boy round here."

"But I don't understand. Why do I have to pack now?"

"'Cause you're moving in tomorrow, love."

"Tomorrow?"

"Yeah. Liz is giving Bobby's old room to Timmy, so you can have a room to yourself. Isn't that nice? I can see how knackered it's been making you, sharing with him. I'm keeping Mousy, by the way. Your aunty said she couldn't cope with old scaredy-cat on top of the two of you." Mom chuckled. "So, you can spend tonight packing, and off we go in the morning! That's great, isn't it, eh?"

But it didn't feel great at all. I knew I should be thankful to Liz for taking us in like this, and that she'd look after Timmy much more reliably than Mom while I was at school, but I didn't want to live with her. I didn't want to be stuck in Riverbend, far away from my friends. I didn't want to have to face the school bus twice a day, and I didn't want to leave my wonderful red room either, or the possibility that Krishna might come around to hang out there again. As for leaving Mousy behind, I hated the idea of that—sometimes he was the only being in the whole world who could cheer me up. I didn't even want to leave Mom.

I said nothing. Just went into my room, shut the door, fell on the bed, and stared at the ceiling.

The next thing I knew, Mom burst into my room without knocking, as usual, and stopped dead. "You haven't done a thing!" she exclaimed. "I told you to pack, you big lug!"

I glanced at the window. It was already dark. "I guess I fell asleep."

She looked down at me a minute, her tattooed hands on her hips. "Yeah, I'm not surprised. You have been looking a bit peaky lately. I'll fry up some hamburgers when you're ready."

"I'm not hungry, thanks."

Mom gazed at me with a concerned expression on her square face, an expression I only saw about once a year. "Listen, love, I know it's been hard on you, dealing with Timmy. He's a handful and you're not used to being a mum like I am. It'll be easier when you've got Liz to help. Tell you what. Given this is your last night here, I'll look after the lad for you so you can go out. I'll call in sick to work."

"Thanks," I said, genuinely touched. "Thanks, Mom." I looked at my squat, rough mother for a minute, standing at the foot of my bed all tired and harried, and suddenly I felt so bad about all the troubles she'd had in her life, and all the times I'd made it worse. "Mom?" I added quietly. "You know those CDs you gave me when I got back from New York? I'm sorry I said what I said about them. It was real generous of you. I've been meaning to tell you that for a while. I wish I hadn't wrecked them up."

She looked at me in surprise, then cracked a grin. "Oh, don't worry about that, lovey. We all say things we don't mean. Now, how about my offer? You want to go out?"

"No, it's okay, I don't have anyone to go out with. I'll get up and pack."

"Don't be daft. Why don't you ring up your Krishna bloke? He always wants to see you. He's smitten as a kitten, if you ask me."

I looked away. "Not anymore he isn't. And he was never smitten, anyhow. We're just friends. Or we were."

"Rubbish! He must have rung you at least four times the other day. Sounded all wobbly and lovelorn, he did. Pathetic."

I sat upright. "Why didn't you tell me?" All my tenderness for Mom went right out the window. "*Four* times?"

She shrugged. "I got a lot on my mind, young lady. Much more important stuff than a moony teenager."

I jumped off the bed and ran into the hallway, praying the phone hadn't been cut off yet. I picked up the receiver. Dead.

"Shit!" I yelled. "Why didn't you tell me when I could've called him back?" I thought of Krishna standing in that classroom, looking at me without saying a word. He must have been so hurt, thinking I hadn't called him back on purpose. How could one mother wreck so much so fast?

Mom didn't hear me—she was making too much noise clattering around in the kitchen—so I grabbed my wallet and jogged down the hill to the public phone near the closed-down movie theater. That phone was broken half the time, too, but it was all there was. The only other choice was the pay phone in Rooney's Bar way down the road, in the kind of neighborhood where no female in her right mind would ever venture at night, especially if that female was me.

The phone did work—I was so relieved. I pushed in the only change I had and waited, my heart jumping about in my chest. A few cars rumbled by, their headlights glaring in the dark, but the rest of the street was as dead, as usual. The phone rang and rang. Was nobody home? *Answer before it cuts off,* I prayed. At last somebody picked up.

"The Hollowdale View Motel. Hello, may I help you?" It was Mrs. Sharma, Krishna's mom, speaking with that lilting Indian accent of hers I thought was so pretty.

"Hello, it's Madge. Can I speak to Krishna, please?" I always put on my best manners for her.

"Oh, good evening, Madge. I hope you are well? I have not seen very much of you lately."

"Yes, I know. I've been, um, busy." Hurry up, I yelled inside my head, my money's running out! "I'm at a phone booth, Mrs. Sharma, so . . ."

"Oh, I am terribly sorry. Please wait a minute while I look for my boy."

That could take time, I knew from experience. A boy can be in a lot of different places in a motel. I waited, jiggling up and down with impatience.

"Please deposit twenty-five cents for the next three minutes," the operator's voice whined in that nagging, nasal tone they always have. *Hurry up, Krish!*

Finally I heard the phone clatter. "Yes?"

"Krish, it's me—"

Beep, beep, beep. "Please deposit twenty-five cents."

"Oh God, I don't have anymore money. Mom didn't tell

me you called till just now. I'm so sorry, Krish, I want—"
More beeps drowned me out and the phone cut off.

Swearing, I shook my wallet and knelt on the ground to look for dropped coins, but no luck. Then I heard a car drive up behind me and stop. I jumped up and turned around, but I was too dazzled by the headlights to make out anything except a man's head sticking out of the driver's window.

"Hey, girly," he called. "Come over here."

I backed away.

"Know what? You looked real pretty crawling on the ground like that."

I turned and ran.

"Hey, nigga' girl, get back down on those knees!" he shouted after me, laughing.

I ran all the way up my steep hill, my breath ragged, through people's yards, past their barking dogs, over their front porches. I was sure I could hear the car roaring after me. It wasn't until I'd fallen through our front door and locked it behind me that I realized the man hadn't followed me at all. Only his ugly words had, searing my skin like burns.

"Your supper's cold," Mom said when I stumbled into the kitchen. She was standing at the sink with her back to me, washing up—unusual for her. I dropped into a kitchen chair, my chest heaving. Timmy had bitten his hamburger roll into the shape of a gun and was pretending to shoot her in the back. I didn't say a word. Mom turned around to look at me.

"What's the matter?" she said when she saw my face.

"Madgy, what happened?" She came up to me and put her rough hand on my cheek. "You all right, love?"

I pushed her hand off, too choked up with anger and humiliation to answer. I didn't want to tell her what had happened anyway—it made me feel too dirty.

Mom stood there awhile, waiting for me to say something, but since I wouldn't she shrugged and lit a cigarette. "You going to eat your burger, then?" I shook my head, stood up, and went to my room.

Closing the door, I shoved a chair under the handle to block out Mom and Timmy and pulled my green duffel bag from the closet. I was going to pack, not think, and get out of there. I only wished it wasn't Liz's house I was escaping to. I wished I could get on a bus to New York and leave this white place and all its white bigots behind, forever.

I'd just stuffed the last of my clothes into the bag and was struggling to zip it up when Mom knocked on my door. She'd left me alone till then—she never did really want to know what was wrong with me—but curiosity must've gotten the better of her. At least she'd knocked this time, instead of trying to storm right in.

"Go away!" I yelled.

"Madge, it's me."

Krishna! I flew to the door and dragged away the chair to let him in, blocking the door again behind him. Then I flung my arms around his neck and burst into tears.

He held me tight, his special Krishna scent curling around me like petals. "Hey, what's the matter?" he said. "Please don't cry."

"I thought you hated me," I said between sobs. "I thought you'd never speak to me again."

"I'd never do a thing like that!" He stepped back a little and wiped the tears off my cheeks with his hand. He was looking down into my face and I don't know quite how it happened, but then he was kissing me. It felt so natural, Krishna kissing away the tears in my eyes, then my cheeks, then my lips like that. Gentle kisses at first, and then not so gentle. I was confused about everything else, but this one thing felt right. We fell on the bed and kissed for a long time, running our hands over each other. I'd thought I knew his skinny boy's body so well—I'd leaned on him, hugged him, and horsed around with him so many times. But this was different. Now he felt solid and strong. Now he didn't feel like a scrawny boy at all. He felt wonderful.

Mom, for once, had the tact to leave us alone. I knew she couldn't wait to get Timmy and me into the car so she could dump us with Liz and be free, but I guess she figured she'd let me have my good-byes with Krishna first. After all, she was about to be rid of me for a nice long time. She could afford to be a little generous.

Krishna and I talked a lot between kisses. I told him about the bastard down by the phone booth, and he got so mad he wanted to call the NAACP right away. Then I asked him when he'd first started liking me like this—a while ago, or just at that very moment.

"It's been forever. That night of Sophie's party? I was so jealous of Gavin I couldn't see straight. I walked all over town, picturing gruesome ways of murdering him."

"I thought Serena was the one you liked."

"No. It was always you."

"I wish I'd known. I was so dumb to fall for Gavin's act."

"But it showed you've got a heart, even if he doesn't. You do have a great heart, Madge."

Mostly, though, Krishna wanted to hear all about Timmy. I told him how it had been going and that we had to move to Riverbend the very next morning, which made him real upset. Then I told him how Bob had been looking into Missing Persons but hadn't found anything.

"Do you still think I did a terrible thing?" I asked cautiously.

Krishna kissed me again before answering. "It's difficult," he said finally. "And I'm sorry for avoiding you all week like that. I was just so blown away by what you'd done. But I've been thinking pretty hard since the day you took him, and I've talked it over with Serena and Jamie . . ."

"You mean you told them?"

"Yeah, I had to. All week they've been asking me why we weren't talking to each other and why you ran home every day, so yesterday I finally told them the truth. Don't worry. They won't tell anybody else."

"Do they think I'm wrong, too?"

"Not exactly. It's just that we're all so confused. Jamie thinks what you did is totally cool, but me and Serena, well, we half believe it's crazy, and we half believe it was the bravest thing we've ever seen."

"You do?"

"Yeah. People are always talking about helping the

unfortunate, right? You've heard me talk that way enough. But what do most of us ever actually do? We yak about it, maybe we give money, if we've got any. We dream. But that doesn't help anybody. You did something real. Reckless and crazy, maybe, but real."

"Thanks, Krish."

Instead of feeling pleased by his praise, though, I felt uneasy. Even if I had rescued Timmy from people who were cruel—and I wasn't so sure of that anymore—was I any better? I thought of all those times in the past week when I'd yelled at him or stuck him in front of the TV, and how Mom and I were always bickering in front of him. And what made me think he'd be any safer in Hollowdale than he'd been in New York, with racist maniacs around like that man by the phone booth?

Maybe I hadn't helped Timmy at all. Maybe I'd made his life worse.

fourteen

TIMMY TOOK A WHILE to get used to Liz's house. I don't think he'd ever had a whole bed to himself before, let alone a room to go with it. When I took him upstairs to see it, he stood in the doorway for a long time, staring at the bright blue curtains she'd sewn for him and the bedspread covered with cartoon trucks. He didn't say a word.

"This is your very own room, Timmy," I said. "How do you like it?"

He looked up at me, his dark eyes wide. "You not gonna sleep here wit' me?"

I stroked his head. "No, sweetie, but I'll be right across the hall. I'll leave our doors open at night so you can see me, okay?" He looked doubtful. "You don't like your room?"

He clutched my leg and hid his face against me. "Too big." But it wasn't long before he was jumping on the bed and squealing with glee.

In a few days, we had a routine. Timmy went to the local day care while I was in school, then either stayed late till I got home, or hung out in the beauty shop with Liz, coloring in magazines and humming along to her piped-in music. They both seemed pretty happy with this, though he still couldn't sleep in his own bed the whole night through. Whenever a bad dream woke him up or he wet himself, he'd crawl into my bed and huddle up to me for comfort till he fell back asleep. It happened every night.

After about a week, I called Bob.

"Ah, it's the kidnapper," he said.

"Jesus!"

"Sorry. Bad joke. I hear you and Timmy are all cozy with Mom now."

I thought he sounded a little jealous. "Yeah, it's going pretty well."

"Just don't let her forget this is temporary. I don't want her getting too attached."

I ignored that. "Have you found out anything new?"

"Of course not, since you won't cooperate. I've gotten nowhere calling all those Riveras. . . ."

"I told you he didn't have a phone."

"Shut up and listen, will you? I went to the Department of Health to find his birth record and hopefully an address, but they couldn't find a Timothy Rivera anywhere. They said they need his parents' names and his date of birth, at the very least. Does he know his birthday?"

"Nope. I've asked him but he has no idea. I've got a feeling he's never been given a birthday present or a party in his life."

"Well then, I'm stuck unless you help out."

I took a deep breath. I'd done a lot of thinking since my conversation with Krishna, but Bob was always so ready to jump on me it was going to be hard to admit.

"Look, I'm sorry you've gone to all this trouble," I said finally. "That's why I called. I'm going to help now."

"You are?" I could practically feel his surprise vibrating the phone cord. "How?"

"Well, I do in fact know where Timmy was living," and at last I told Bob about the man in Timmy's apartment. "I've decided to go back there to find out more about him."

My cousin let out a low whistle. "I knew you were hiding something, you jerk! I've wasted hours on the phone because of you. Christ."

"I know. I'm sorry."

Bob sighed loudly down the phone. "Okay. But I don't want you going there on your own. Given that you've kidnapped the kid, you could get into a lot of trouble. I'll go with you."

"I don't need you. Krishna's coming."

"I thought Krishna was a Hindu god."

"Very funny. I've told you about him before. He's my boyfriend now." That felt so good to say, like a caramel melting in my mouth.

"How are you going to explain what you're doing there?"

"I'll say I've come to see how Timmy's ankle is doing."

"Madge, he sprained his ankle more than a month ago. They won't believe you. Look, if we go together, I can tell them I'm doing some kind of story for the paper. That can be our cover in case things get sticky. We have to be real careful not to let on that we took him, unless we find a family who only wants him back, of course, and isn't interested in getting us into trouble. What do you say?"

"Okay," I replied reluctantly. I didn't really want Bob interfering like this.

"Good. Hey, what made you want to do this all of a sudden? How come you changed your mind?"

I fiddled with the telephone wire awhile before I could screw up the courage to answer.

"I just want to make sure, Bob. I want to make sure there isn't anybody out there who loves him."

Krishna had a hard time getting his parents' permission to take their car all the way to New York. At first they thought he was nuts to even ask, so he told them it was about the same boy we'd visited before and that we were trying to help him find a good home. They only knew half the story but they were sympathetic. They were good people. Still, he had to promise that this was the only time he'd borrow the car for such a long trip and that he'd pay for the gas. Krishna did so much for me in those days.

He'd been borrowing his parents' old station wagon a whole lot lately to drive me home from school and visit me in Riverbend. It was lucky he could because the car was the only place we ever got to be alone. Liz turned out to be much stricter than Mom—she wouldn't let him stay with me in my buttercup room at all. "That's the quickest way to unwanted babies and a ruined life I know," she said. "And don't give me any crap about safe sex. I remember only too well what it's like being a hot-blooded teenager. One unexpected kid around here is enough."

She was right about us being hot-blooded. But she couldn't control what we got up to in Krishna's station wagon.

Krishna and I were pretty much in the same state as Serena and Jamie were: wrapped up in a sex fog. Krishna had kissed a few girls before me, but he was just as much a virgin as I was. Maybe that's why we felt so safe together. People say boys don't know what they're doing the first time and a girl should find an experienced guy to lose her virginity with, but I don't agree. When you're both beginners and you know it, nobody has to feel inferior. You can be embarrassed and excited, proud and clumsy together, without either of you feeling stupid about it. We did a lot of giggling over how to work the condoms, and a lot of panting, too—we were so heated up we didn't know what had hit us. Krishna said he wasn't surprised because he'd been lusting after me for so long already, but for me it was more of a shock, though a wonderful one. I wasn't sure at first how much I liked the sex part of it, though—it hurt when he pushed into me and made me kind of scared. But I loved the cuddling and kissing, the feeling of each other's bodies, the exploring and the closeness. And after a few times, I loved the sex part of it, too.

We left that next Friday after school and cuddled up the whole drive long. The car was so old it had one of those bench seats in front, so I could lean up against him while he drove.

We couldn't keep our hands off of each other—I'm surprised we didn't end up in a car crash. Every minute I was away from Krishna I wanted to be with him, and every minute I was with him I wanted to hold him and smell him and kiss him all over. Just because he was driving didn't make any difference.

"I wish we could pull over, make love in a field, and not even go to New York," I said to him on the way. I was only half kidding. I knew what we were doing for Timmy was right, but I was scared. Liz was, too. I'd told her my plan and she'd approved once she heard Bob was in on it, but she didn't like it much. She was happier with Timmy around than I'd seen her since Uncle Ron had died, and I knew she wanted to keep Timmy as much as I did now, even if she wouldn't admit it.

When we arrived at Bob's place, he was already waiting outside the front door in his reporter's suit and bald head. "Hi," he said, looking at Krishna curiously and shaking his hand through the car window. "You mind driving? I'll hop in the back."

"Which way?" Krishna said.

"You tell me. Madge has always refused to give me the address."

"This is scary," I said, hesitating. "Suppose something bad happens and it gets out of control? What if that man calls the cops?"

"We won't give anything away, don't worry," Bob said. "I'm a reporter—I'm used to doing this kind of thing. It'll be all right."

I told Bob the address and he directed Krishna there. It

was easy to find, since the streets of Manhattan are criss-crossed like a wire fence. You don't need any imagination to find your way around New York; you only need to know up and down, left and right. And if you happen to miss Riverbank Park up on the sewage-plant roof, you can always smell your way there.

When we got to Timmy's block, Krishna double-parked like most everybody else, and we climbed out of the car. "Uh, Krishna?" Bob said. "I don't think you should come in with us. Reporters don't usually turn up with more than one teenager in tow. Sorry."

"I understand. I'll wait here."

I gave Krish a long, sexy kiss before we went into the building. I needed it for courage. When I turned around, Bob was red as a traffic light. He'd never seen me kiss anyone before.

On the way up to the apartment, I was so nervous I felt sick to my stomach. "This is it," I whispered when we got to the door with the brass fish on it. I couldn't say anything else.

Bob took a deep breath and knocked. Nothing. He knocked again, this time with his fist. Another long pause, then we heard the thump of footsteps. My stomach twisted into a knot.

"Who is?" a deep voice barked from behind the door.

"I'm a reporter from *The Daily Register*." Bob took off the press pass he had hanging on a chain around his neck and held it up to the fish. "Can I speak with you a minute?"

A long silence, then an eye appeared in the fish's belly, just like before. The door opened an inch, a chain hooked across it, and a man peered at us through the crack. It was the same man I'd met the first time.

"You?" he said, recognizing me after a moment. "What you want?"

"Hi," I answered in the friendliest voice I could. "I came to see how Timmy's doing. I brought my cousin."

"Timmy ain't here." The man began to close the door.

"Wait, where is he?"

"Why you wanna know?" He glared at me suspiciously.

This time Bob answered. "Let us in and we'll explain."

The man hesitated, running his eyes over both of us again. "Open jacket," he grunted, lifting a cigarette to his lips.

Bob spread his jacket wide like wings. The man must have thought he had a gun, or maybe a hidden police badge. But at last he undid the chain and opened the door. "Come," he barked, and led us down the dark hallway and into the living room.

Three other people were in the room this time, two young men and a woman. The men were lying sprawled on the orange couch, looking like they'd just been knocked down, and the woman was sitting sideways in an armchair, her skinny legs sticking out over the edge like broomsticks. She was small, bony, and dark brown, with her hair tied back in a stiff ponytail. I wondered who all these people were, if they were related to Timmy, and whether the man at the door had let us in because he actually cared about the poor kid.

He pointed at another old armchair, its springs coiling out of the seat. "Sit," he commanded me.

I lowered myself on to it, hoping I wouldn't get poked, and took a quick look around. The room looked as drab as the first time I'd seen it: the same shabby furniture, no tables or lamps, no rug, nicotine-stained walls, and only a bare bulb in the ceiling.

The man stood in the middle of the room, staring at us with his cigarette dangling out of his mouth. His gray mustache was almost the same color as his face, and his stomach sagged over his baggy brown pants.

"Who you again?" he said to Bob.

"My name is Robert Dunbar. I'm her cousin, like she said." He tried to pull himself up taller. "Do you read *The Daily Register?*"

Nobody spoke. Nobody moved an inch. What a ridiculous question, I thought.

"Look," Bob said then, "I'm not a cop, I'm a newspaper reporter. I've come with nothing but my notebook. See?" He took off his suit jacket, shook it like a stripper, and dropped it over a chair. The people in the room all watched him, their bodies still as the furniture, but still none of them said a thing.

Finally, the man spoke. "Why you come here, asking 'bout Timmy?"

"Because we wondered where he is."

The man narrowed his eyes. "Why?"

Bob hesitated. "We've been told the kid is missing," he said quietly, "and I'm doing a story on missing kids."

The woman spoke up then, in that same breakneck Spanish

I hadn't been able to understand before. She sounded upset. The man replied to her briefly, then ran his eyes over Bob again.

"You talked to the cops?"

"No, of course not."

"Then who tell you the boy, he is missing, huh?"

Bob opened his mouth, then shut it again.

"It was me," I said quickly, my voice coming out a squeak. "I went to the park to see how Timmy's ankle is doing, and some kids there told me he'd disappeared. So we came here to see if it's true."

The man took a long drag on his cigarette, then dropped it on the floor and stepped on it. I couldn't breathe.

"You got him, don't you?" the woman said suddenly in English.

Bob looked at her, startled. "Who are you?"

"She my lady friend," the man answered for her. "Why you wanna know?"

"Why do I want to know?" Bob sounded exasperated now. "I want to find out if anyone cares about this poor boy, of course! Who *are* you all, anyhow?"

"We his family," the man said. "Me, I am the boy's *tío*, you understand? And sure, we care about him. His mama, her heart is broke since he been gone." He looked at Bob in silence for a moment, puffing again on his cigarette. "The lady, she is right. You took our boy, no?"

"Of course we didn't!" Bob said, flushing.

The man turned to me. "You, girl. You know where the boy is?"

"No!" I squeaked.

"Mr. Rivera, listen," Bob said, trying to sound calm. "Is it Rivera?"

"Garcia."

"Look, Mr. Garcia, we only came here to help. My paper is doing a series on missing children, running descriptions and backgrounds so people can look out for them. It's a public service."

What bullshit, I thought. These people will never believe that.

The woman jumped to her feet. "You got our boy!" she yelled. "I see it in your face. You got him! What you doin' wit' him, huh? He okay, is our baby okay?"

"*¡Cierra la boca!*" Garcia barked at her. She dropped back into her chair, scowling, and he turned to Bob. "Listen, you and me, we gonna have a little talk, huh? You take our nephew, you worry us so bad. For this you owe us big." And he rubbed his fingers together, like people do when they talk about money.

Bob grabbed his jacket off the chair. "What do you mean, we *owe* you?" As soon as he said that, the two young men on the couch sprang up and glared at him.

Garcia spread out his hands, acting surprised. "I only say we work out a deal so we all can be happy, yes? Come, sit down, Robert Dunbar, and we talk like men, huh?"

"There's nothing to talk about, Mr. Garcia, you've got it all wrong," Bob said, backing toward the hall and signaling me to follow him. The woman jumped up again and yelled something more in Spanish about Timmy, but Garcia ignored her and followed us down the hall, the two other men close behind him. When we got to the door, he pushed past me and flipped Bob around as easily as flipping a pancake. He snatched the press pass out of his hand.

"I keep this so we don't lose touch, yes?"

Bob opened the door and we ran.

When we reached the car, I hurtled into the seat next to Krishna, and Bob dove into the back pretty fast himself. "Drive!" he barked. "Quick!" Krishna took off with a screech and soon we were zooming down Riverside Drive. Neither Bob nor I said anything for a while. We were too shocked to speak.

"I thought you said you'd know how to handle this," I finally said when I'd recovered enough to talk.

"Yeah, well." Bob cleared his throat. "It got a little out of hand. I didn't expect them to see through us so fast. Sorry, Madge."

"Now they've guessed we've got him and that stinks." I turned around to face my cousin, who was sitting hunched up in the backseat, looking pretty rattled. "There's no way that Garcia is Timmy's uncle! He doesn't give a damn about Timmy, just like I thought. He didn't ask us to give him back. He didn't even ask if Timmy's okay—he didn't ask anything about him at all! And when that woman asked, he just shut her up. All he wants is money!"

"I know." Bob's forehead wrinkled into a row of straight lines. "I didn't like the look of that scene one bit."

Krishna and I didn't start for home till almost eight that night. Bob took us to the same restaurant he'd taken me to on my Easter visit, where we gobbled down some pizza and talked over what had happened. Then we said good-bye and headed back to the highway.

"I don't understand why your cousin thought he could bluff those people," Krishna said once we were alone. "It must've been obvious you knew too much."

"I know. They completely took control." I paused a moment, playing with Krishna's long fingers. "What if that man comes after us now?"

"At least he doesn't know where you and Timmy live."

"He knows where Bob works, though. Shit."

Krishna squeezed my fingers. "You think Garcia was telling the truth about Timmy's mom?"

"I doubt it. I think everything he said was a lie. Anyway, Timmy keeps saying his mom is gone, whatever that means. But I wonder who that woman was? At least she seemed to care about him."

"Yeah. But thank God you took him away from those people."

"You mean you think I was right now?"

"You bet I do."

I swallowed. "Thanks, Krish. That means a lot to me."

We drove in silence after that, holding hands and thinking over what had happened. But when we got to the outskirts of Hollowdale, I said, "Let's not go home yet. Nobody knows when to expect us anyhow."

"Excellent idea. Your mom's house?"

"Yup." We both knew she'd be out. She always was.

Mom's apartment was its usual mess when we got in—worse, now I wasn't there to clean up—and Mousy was as frantic as ever. We fed and petted him a little, then went into my old red room, which Mom hadn't touched. My posters and weeping flag were still on the walls, but otherwise it looked lonesome without all my clothes and books. I shoved the chair under the door in case Mom took it into her head to come home early and barge in, and wondered for the thousandth time where she went at nights. She didn't have a boyfriend, or not one that I'd ever met—or a girlfriend either, which is the way I sometimes thought she was inclined; nor had she ever introduced me to any of her friends aside from Maggie Donahue. I knew she went down to the Golden Harp a lot, but I had no idea who she saw those times she disappeared. Most of her life was a mystery, which was exactly how she liked it.

The night was warm, so we opened the windows, pulled the curtains closed, and turned off the light. Krishna began kissing me right away, and peeling off my clothes. He'd gotten pretty expert at that lately. I still felt kind of shy about being undressed in front of him, but he was so natural about it that I never minded for long. He loved kissing and stroking me all over, telling me I was beautiful. It wasn't long before we were on the bed together. Somehow it was more intense than ever that night—maybe because we needed relief after Garcia, or maybe only because it was a balmy night in May, with the kind of silky soft air that's created just for making love.

I felt like I was in a dream that night, the best dream I'd ever had. It was the perfect way to stop thinking about Timmy and the mess we were in.

fifteen

"AS IF IT ISN'T difficult enough running the salon and looking after Timmy, now I have to worry about Brandy as well!"

My aunt was standing in front of the fireplace in her living
room, waving her arms like a panicked chicken and shouting
because Mom had gone AWOL again, this time without even
leaving a note.

"Bob, are you listening to me?"

"Yeah, yeah." He squinted up at her from the couch, where
he was lying on his back, drinking a beer. It was the Friday after we'd gone to see Garcia and he'd taken the day off to come
talk over what to do next.

"I'm worried sick," Liz went on. "I've told her a million
times not to do this to us! Now she's left me and Madge to
cope with Timmy all alone, and Madge barely old enough to
fry up an egg!"

Bob looked over to where I was sitting on the floor trying
to get some homework done before Timmy came home from
day care. He winked. "I think Madge can do a lot more than
that."

"That's what I mean! She's liable to turn up pregnant next, now she's got that boyfriend, or bite off all our heads." My aunt turned to me. "You're like a pot of boiling oil you are, snapping about this or that all the time."

That hurt, but I had to admit it was true. So many things had been piling up lately: end-of-year finals and the SATs were coming, and I'd had hardly any time to study. Krishna's parents hadn't let him have the car all week. Liz was so bossy it was driving me nuts. And now Mom had run off again, just like I'd been afraid she would. On top of it all, I was terrified Garcia would turn up with a gang and a gun. None of this exactly put me in a mellow frame of mind.

I turned to Bob. "Have you heard anything more from Garcia?" I knew the man had called him at work, demanding money. It made me scared for Bob, for Timmy—for all of us.

My cousin sighed, the beer can he'd balanced on his chest rising and falling with the movement. "Yeah. He called me three more times this week. He says he wants five thousand bucks or he'll turn us into the cops."

"Jesus!" my aunt exclaimed. "Why's the bastard doing this?" She picked up an ornament from her mantelpiece, a porcelain shepherdess without a nose, and fiddled with it anxiously.

"Because he's a crook, of course," Bob replied. "I think he's running a cocaine operation out of that apartment—I saw a pair of scales hidden behind the TV. My guess is that the woman he calls his 'lady friend' cuts and packages, and those two men do the selling for him."

"You think Timmy's mom was involved in that, too?" I said.

"I don't know. But whatever the case, it looks like she died and Garcia got stuck with Timmy against his will."

"What makes you so sure she died? Maybe she just ran away."

"I'm not sure, but it seems likely to me. Who knows, Garcia could even have murdered her."

"Murdered her?"

"That, or it was an OD." Bob rubbed his eyes. "I wish we'd never gone anywhere near that place."

"Well, it's not your fault," Liz said. "You and Madge were only trying to do right by the boy. How were you to know you'd fall into a nest of criminals like that? All I can say is thank God Madge got Timmy out of there."

"But if Garcia's a dealer, then wouldn't he be too scared to call the cops on us?" I said.

"You'd think so, but we can't count on that, can we? I've figured out a way of getting him off our backs without giving in to his blackmail, though." Bob took the beer can off his chest and sat up, staring down between his knees at the neon flowered rug. "I'll ask my cop friends if they've got anything on him, then I'll threaten to turn him in myself unless he leaves us alone."

"But that's blackmail, too."

"You got a better idea?"

I looked down at my schoolbooks. I didn't.

"That sounds awfully dangerous," Liz said.

"Don't worry, Mom, I can handle it." Bob held up his beer can. "Got any more?"

Liz put the shepherdess back on the mantelpiece, along with a row of other cutesy-pie figurines and a picture of Uncle Ron choking in a stiff 1970s collar. Her slim figure was packed tightly into black jeans and a yellow T-shirt that day—she looked like a wasp.

"Not for you, I don't. Anyroad, it's time to fetch Timmy. Put on your shoes. The walk will do you good."

A few minutes later, we were headed up the hill toward Timmy's day-care center, breathing in the warm May air and the piney smell of the woods. The center was perched on the crest of a hill overlooking the Delaware, and on the way, as Liz was chatting to Bob, I dropped behind just to look. The sky was a shiny blue, and the woods were all happy and fresh now it was almost summer, but I couldn't really enjoy it. I was too worried. Was Timmy's mom really dead, and could Garcia truly have murdered her? And if the man was that dangerous, what would he do to us? But most of all, why did my goddamn mother have to choose now, of all times, to disappear again?

We turned a corner on top of the hill and saw Timmy waiting for us inside the day-care gates. I'd dressed him in a new navy-blue sweatsuit that morning, and he looked tiny and neat, even though he'd already torn his pants at the knee.

"Gramma!" he shouted when he saw us, jumping up and down. "Look what I made!"

"'Grandma?' Is that what he calls you?" Bob said.

"Better than 'illegally adopted great-aunt,' isn't it?" Liz muttered.

We squeezed through the crowd of parents at the gate, and Liz picked Timmy up to give him a hug. I saw the other mothers staring at her, a white woman holding a black child. They'd stared at me and Mom like that, too. Mom's way had been to glare back at them till they looked away. My aunt's way was to act like she hadn't noticed them at all.

"See what Timmy made for me?" she said proudly. She handed Bob a little box made of Popsicle sticks, scribbled over with crayons, a blue plastic bead glued to its lid.

"It's for your earrings," Timmy said. "You like it?"

"Yes, it's beautiful, little one. I love it." She put him down and rubbed his head. "I'm going to keep it right on top of my dressing table where everybody can see it. Isn't it wonderful, Bob?"

"Yeah. It looks like it was bought in a store."

Timmy beamed and I couldn't help feeling a little jealous. He hadn't even said hi to me, let alone given me a present. Ever since we'd moved in with Liz, he'd glommed on to her like a possum to its mother's back. He treated me more like a big sister now than a mom.

"Do you remember your uncle Bob?" Liz said to him then. Uncle? I thought. Oh, well, why not? We had to invent this family somehow as we went along.

Timmy gazed at Bob for a second but quickly lost interest. "You got candy?" he said to Liz.

"Did you eat your lunch?"

"Yeah."

My aunt looked into the lunch box I'd packed for him that morning. "You didn't eat your carrots. No sweets till you eat your carrots."

"Ah, shit!" He stamped his foot.

"I'm warning you, Timmy. No cursing or else no treats. Come on, eat up. If you're hungry enough for sweets, you're hungry enough for carrots."

"I hate carrots!" He was pouting now, his delicate face crumpled and grumpy.

"She used to make me eat carrots, too," Bob said. "But they help you see in the dark, you know. They give you super-powers."

Timmy looked at him scornfully. "You lying."

"No, it's true. I've tried it. Look." Bob took a carrot out of the lunch box and wiggled it. "Eat me, please," he said in a squeaky voice. "I wanna make you see in the dark!" A little smile crept over Timmy's face. He grabbed the carrot and took a bite, keeping his eyes on Bob challengingly. "Ouch! Eeek, that tickles!" Bob squealed. Timmy laughed.

Liz took Timmy's hand, and we walked to a nearby playground, where Timmy finished the carrots with more encouragement from Bob, then grabbed the chocolate bar Liz had brought him. He held it in both hands while he ate, his eyes fixed in front of him, like a squirrel eating a nut.

"Gramma?" he said through his chewing. "Am I bad?"

"Of course not, lovey. I'm not saying you're bad, I just don't want you to curse."

Timmy pointed at me. "Is Madge bad?"

"Who told you that we're bad?" I said quickly. I knew this wasn't about his cursing, even if my aunt didn't.

"Johnny said brown people is bad." Timmy kicked the ground with his foot.

I squatted down to look him in the face. "Timmy, we're not bad. It's white people who say things like that who are bad."

"Don't tell him that!" Liz snapped. "That's not going to help!"

"What will then?" I turned back to Timmy. "Some people like to be mean, that's all. They're gonna pick on you 'cause you have brown skin—they pick on me for that, too. But we don't have to listen to them. Next time somebody tells you it's bad to be brown, you tell them they're bad to say that. And then come tell me about it, okay?"

Timmy finished his chocolate and threw the wrapper on the ground. "I'm bad!" he yelled, and shot off to the climbing bars. I don't think he'd listened to me at all.

The three of us walked over to a bench on the side of the playground and sat down to watch him. "They're giving him the same damn shit they gave me," I said. "They're going to make him feel terrible about himself."

"That boy is such a handful," Liz commented, ignoring me completely. "I have to keep an eye on him on all the time. He's so rough with other children. If he wants a turn on the swing or something, he just pulls the other kids right off it. Oh, Christ." She jumped up and ran over to scold Timmy for hitting a child on the ear.

"Why won't your mother ever talk about the racism in this place?" I said to Bob.

He sighed and rubbed his face. "Makes her feel too helpless, probably. But she's doing her best by Timmy, just like she did for you and me. Give her a break, Madge."

I gave up. My family was always like that. If they couldn't cope with something, they just pretended it wasn't there. It burned me up, but I was stuck with it. For now.

That evening, after Liz had bundled Timmy into bed while I finished my homework, Bob asked her if he could take me out to dinner for a treat.

"All right, but no boozing," she said severely.

"Where the hell are we going to have dinner?" I said. "There's nothing but sleazy bars around here for miles."

"There's the hotel. Or we could go into Hollowdale."

"Okay, let's do that. Can I bring Krishna?"

"Well, I was kind of hoping we could have some time alone."

I was about to object but Liz caught my eye.

After we'd driven to Hollowdale and parked, we walked down Market Street, poking fun at the drab old-lady clothes in the one shop that hadn't gone bust. The street looked so naked without people or open stores, the buildings squat and sad. Some of the old brick storefronts must have been pretty once, but since most of them were shut down now, their windows dark or nailed over, the charm had long since got up and left. I'd seen old pictures of Market Street back when it had been bustling in the fifties and sixties, with hardware and clothing stores, diners and barbershops, and those clunky old cars parked in front of them. That was back before the factories had closed and when the racetrack was still a success. It was sad to see how the heart had gone out of the place.

"Choose wherever you want to eat," Bob said grandly, making a joke of the fact there were only two restaurants in town, Dale's Diner and Chung Ho's Chinese Palace, which was about as Chinese as a hot dog. I picked Dale's Diner. The food wasn't any good, but I'd been going there all my life and I felt like being somewhere cozy and familiar right then. I only wished Krishna could've come with us.

We chose a booth near the back and sat opposite each other. I don't think Dale's (short for "Hollowdale," of course) had changed since it was built in 1949. The orange seats were cracked and leaking foam rubber. The walls were fake wood, peeling along the edges, and covered with posters of forgotten movie stars and old root-beer ads. Dusty plastic flowers stood on each table, and cheesecake and lemon meringue pies sat under a yellowing pyramid stand on the counter. The diner was only big enough to hold about seven families and I knew most of the people there, at least by sight, including Sophie O'Brian and her parents. A few of them nodded to me or said hi. Sophie didn't, though. Surprise, surprise.

Debbie, the waitress who'd been there forever, came over to us, her orange hair sprayed into a stiff bubble, and her eyelashes so thick with mascara I expected them to stick together each time she blinked. She was squeezed into a pink shirt and white pants, and her face was round, fat, and friendly. Debbie had always been like a grandma to us kids. She gave out advice and ice cream if we were sad, kicked out the boys when they got rowdy, and generally provided a haven for those of us who didn't want to go home to drunken dads or fucked-up moms with criminal records and a taste for disappearing.

"Hiya, Madge, how you doin'?" she said. "You here for ice cream or dinner?"

"Both, I hope. You remember my cousin Bob? He lives in New York now."

Debbie winked and said, "Hi, handsome, you've gone and grown up on me," but I could tell she didn't remember him, probably because of his baldness. We ordered spaghetti and meatballs for me, a burger and fries for Bob. After she left, I asked Bob why he'd wanted to be alone with me.

He reached over the table and took my hand. "I know you must be upset about your mom. I thought you might want to talk about it away from Liz and Timmy."

"Thanks, but I can handle it," I muttered.

"Come out of yourself a minute, Madge. Stop playing sulky teenager."

"I don't want to talk about it! Okay?"

"Jesus. All right."

We fell silent then, both of us staring at the tabletop. I knew Bob was only trying to be kind and I felt bad for snapping at him, but, like I said before, I couldn't stand it when he questioned me like this. He was always either trying to get into my head or scolding me. I was sick of it.

"Did you read my follow-up on Marissa?" he finally said to change the subject. I shook my head. Bob had been sending me his articles, but I hadn't got around to reading them all. They were too upsetting.

"Mrs. Henderson won the case, you know. She gets to keep Marissa, and that sets a precedent that might help a lot of other kids, too."

I sat up, my bad mood suddenly gone. "Really? That's great! You think your story helped?"

"I don't know. I hope so."

"But does that mean you're done with the foster-care series now?"

"No, I've still got two more cases to cover. Didn't you read that horrible piece I wrote about Lucy and Pablo?"

That one I had read, and it was horrible, he was right. Lucy and Pablo were twin orphans who'd been born HIV-positive, so nobody would adopt them, and by the time they were two they'd been in five different foster homes, beaten and abused wherever they went, and had been given no medical care at all. Pablo died at three and Lucy at four. It had killed me to read that. I could not understand how people could be so cruel as to beat up a dying child.

"That's why I'll never let those people get their hands on Timmy," I said fiercely. "It'd be like throwing him in the ocean to drown."

"Not necessarily." Bob leaned over the table and lowered his voice. "Listen, I understand why you feel that way, but foster parents aren't all bad—think of Mrs. Henderson. I'm just writing about the worst cases. Madge, you've got to realize that if you never find Timmy's family, he's going to be a burden on you for the rest of your life. And if you fail him, it'll break your heart—that is, if Garcia doesn't tip off the cops first and get you arrested. I hate to be so blunt, but before you reject foster care completely, you've got to face the facts."

Debbie brought over the food then, so I diverted my anger into chomping a rubbery meatball. "I am facing the facts," I said between my teeth. "I'm gonna find out if Timmy's mom really is dead or not."

"How? You don't even know her name."

"That's why you never found anything—you're too negative. I'll figure it out—you'll see. Birth records, death certificates . . . There are ways."

Bob leaned back, shaking his bald head and smiling. "Good for you. You're a born reporter, you know that? Ruth was real impressed by how you won over Mrs. Henderson that time."

"Oh, yeah?" I knew he was only complimenting me because he felt bad for what he'd said about Timmy. "Speaking of Ruth, what's going on with you two these days?"

Bob poked at his fries with a fork. "Don't ask me."

"What's that mean?"

"Well, we were kind of getting back together after she dumped me the first time, you know? Then suddenly she started avoiding me again, big-time."

"Why?"

"No idea."

I put down my fork and looked at him. "Is it anything to do with Julie, by any chance?"

"It might be."

I looked at him a minute. "Maybe Ruth thinks you're still hung up on her."

Bob scrunched up his face, his brow pinching into those straight little lines of his. "Maybe."

"Well, are you?"

He shifted in his seat, looking miserable. "No. Not anymore. At least I don't think so. But I guess I do tend to talk about her a lot, it's true."

"You idiot! No wonder Ruth's avoiding you! She's probably scared you'll hurt her. I saw how she felt when I was in New York—she's crazy about you. You should give her another chance. I think you're made for each other."

Bob gazed at me a moment, then burst into a laugh. "Boy, have you turned into a romantic!"

Debbie came over to ask if we wanted dessert, so I ordered my favorite pecan ice cream and Bob asked for a coffee. She'd just finished serving us when two men I'd never seen before came into the diner. They wore scruffy denim jackets and buzz cuts, their faces lean and rough. They took a table by the window and ordered coffee and pie, glancing around the room with a sneer. I watched them, feeling uneasy.

Bob sipped his coffee and stared blankly into space, while I took a spoonful of ice cream. I didn't feel like talking to him anymore. He never took me seriously. Who knows, maybe he'd made Ruth feel like that, too.

"Hey, Ray," one of the two men said loudly to his friend, so loud the whole diner could hear. "What d'you think of this coffee, huh? Tastes like pig swill to me."

The man called Ray guffawed and everybody in the diner froze. I glanced at Debbie, who was standing behind the counter, cutting a pie. She looked over at the men, her mouth pinched up tight. "That ain't what bothers me," Ray replied even louder. "You know what bothers me?"

"What's that?" the first guy said. The people in the diner stared down at their plates.

"What bothers me is eating with a nig-nog."

It took me a few seconds to realize what he'd said. Then he spoke again. "I sure don't get why they let filth like that eat in here with all us decent citizens. It ain't Christian, that's what I say."

"Ray." Debbie stayed behind the counter, but her voice came out firm. "You got no business talking like that in here. You're gonna have to leave."

Ignoring her, Ray leaned toward his friend. "I know who it is. It's that colored bitch in the high school. My brother told me about her."

"Madge," Bob whispered, "let's get out of here."

I didn't pay him any attention. A rage had started up inside of me and I couldn't stop it. It was the same rage I'd felt when Gavin's friend had dissed me so bad, the same rage I'd felt when those white mothers stared at Timmy—the same rage I'd felt deep inside of me my whole life.

"Fuck you!" I shouted, struggling to stand up in the booth.

I was too angry to even see the two men, let alone anybody else in that diner.

Ray raised his voice again. "We gonna put up with that kinda talk, or what?"

Debbie edged over to the wall phone hanging behind the counter. "Ray, you and your buddy gotta leave right now, or else I'll call the police and tell 'em you're causing a disturbance." She picked up the receiver. "I mean it."

Ray sat back, and a long silence filled up the room. I was on my feet now, staring at him and shaking with fury. Bob pulled at my sleeve but I ignored him. Debbie began to dial.

Ray pretended to laugh. "Okay, Debbie, we'll go. For you. But if I see that nig-nog in here again, somebody's gonna have to teach her a lesson."

Snickering, he stood up, scraped back his chair, and strolled toward the door of the diner. But just before he got there, he made a sudden turn, loped right up to me, and lunged.

I jumped back, hitting the wall behind me.

He laughed, turned again, and swaggered out, his friend trailing after him. The door slammed behind them. Silence.

Nobody made a sound. Nobody moved.

I let Bob pull me back down to my seat.

Debbie came over to me in the silence. "You want me to call the police?" she said in a low voice.

I shook my head. I was trembling too hard to talk.

"Those goddamn fuckers!" Bob hissed. "Look, I'll make sure they're gone and get the car. Wait here and don't go outside, okay?" He waited for me to nod, then walked to the door of the diner, peered out, and left. Nobody else moved a muscle.

"I'm real sorry about that, hon," Debbie said then. "That Ray, he's always been trouble. Cracked in the head, I think. Listen, your meal's on the house. Want a cup of coffee or a milk shake or anything?"

I shook my head again and tried to thank her, but no words would come out. All I could do was sit in that booth and wait, the whole sky pressing down on my skull.

A few minutes later, Bob's car pulled up outside the diner window. I stood and walked out, my heart still slamming with anger. Every soul in that diner was silent as a stone, and every soul stared down at his or her plate like it was the most fascinating thing on earth. At least Gavin wasn't there to see this, I thought, or that asshole friend of his who'd insulted me. Sophie was, though, sitting in her booth with her parents, looking frozen with embarrassment. Why was she always there at the wrong moment? Shit.

Outside, the street was quiet, silver under the moonlight. Some torn-up paper lay on the sidewalk, a puddle gleamed in the dark, but there was no sign of Ray or his friend. I looked at this street, so familiar and ordinary. It looked calm as a Sunday, calm as I'd always thought of it. You'd never know it was filled with hate.

It wasn't until we'd been driving for ten minutes that either of us could speak. "Madge," Bob said, "are you okay?"

"Oh, I feel just great, thanks. How are you?" My voice was shaking.

"I'm sorry, that was ugly. Who were those maniacs? You got any idea?"

"Nope."

"You come across a lot of that kind of thing here?"

"What do you think?" I shouted. "That's what I was talking about in the playground! That's what I've been telling you my whole fucking life!"

"Then why didn't you let Debbie call the cops? Those guys threatened you!"

"'Cause it's no use. Half the cops in this town are as racist as those rednecks and the other half are dating their sisters. I don't want to talk about it anymore."

We drove the rest of the way to Riverbend without speaking, but when Bob pulled up in front of Liz's house, he put his arms around me and pulled me to his chest. "I'm sorry that had to happen, little cuz, I really am. You okay now?"

I pushed him away. "No, I'm not okay. I'm mad as hell."

We got out of the car and walked down the alleyway to my aunt's door. The curtains were drawn, lights out. Nothing moved except our shadows as we crossed under the streetlamp. "I'm real sorry, Madge," Bob said again as he unlocked the door. "I'm sorry about everything." And he pulled me back into his arms.

This time I let him hug me. "It's all right," I said, calmer now. "It's not your fault."

When we stepped through the door, we found Liz standing in the hallway, her arms folded across her chest, looking grim. I thought for a moment she already knew what had happened, though I couldn't for the life of me see how. But it turned out not to be that. It turned out to be something else entirely.

"Madge," she said, "your mum's been arrested."

sixteen

WALKING INTO SCHOOL that Monday, I felt branded. It'd
been bad enough on the bus, feeling all those stares boring
into my back, but making my way down the school hallways
was like walking on to a stage naked. I knew the whole town
had heard what had happened in Dale's Diner by then. I only
hoped they didn't know about Mom as well. Gossip was like
that in Hollowdale, spreading fast as a virus. Same as in any
small town, I suppose.

By lunchtime, I was worn out from avoiding all the stares.
I didn't want to know if they were looks of pity or sympathy, curiosity, or glee. I only wanted to be the way I'd felt on
that subway in New York—nobody remarkable, just one of
the crowd. I was in a strange state of mind, too, shocked and
kind of manic, looking for anything that could stop me thinking about Mom's arrest or last night. So it was a relief to see
Serena and Jamie at our usual table in the cafeteria, huddled
together like two halves of a clothespin.

"Madge!" Serena whispered to me soon as I sat down. She
reached out from under her long black sleeve and squeezed

my wrist. "I heard about what happened with those bastards in the diner. You okay?"

I nodded and sat down, too worked up to speak.

"I know who those guys are," Jamie said. "It's Ray Kruger and his sidekick. They're crazy fuckers, the Krugers, the whole lot of them."

Krishna joined us while Jamie was talking, scraping his plastic cafeteria chair up next to mine and putting his arm around my shoulder. He kissed me. Serena looked startled, even though she'd seen us do this for a couple of weeks now. It was taking all of us time to adjust to being two couples instead of four buddies.

"Are you talking about what happened to Madge?" Krishna said. I'd called him the night before to tell him all about it. I didn't want him to hear it through the gossip line. I'd told him about Mom's latest adventure, too, and how mad at her I was. I didn't know why she'd been arrested, but I did know that I was ashamed, not to mention scared that she'd get thrown out of the country now. Krishna and I agreed not to let anybody know all of that, though.

"Yeah, we are," I replied. Krishna looked so wonderful right then, with his wide brown eyes and cinnamon skin. Honey cinnamon, I'd call it, the warmest color in the world. How could the Krugers of the world hate a person like him? Or me or Timmy, for that matter? And then I had a thought: what would have happened if I'd been a teenage boy, like Timmy would be at my age? How much more violent would Ray and all the rest of those racist fuckers be then?

"Serena," I said, "you're pretty good at computer research, right?"

"Kind of. Why?"

"I need you to help me with Timmy. I want to find out who his mom is and whether or not she's alive."

"Wow. Why?"

"'Cause if she is, I've gotta give him back. I don't want him growing up around here. It's too dangerous."

"What?" Krishna said. "But I thought you wanted to keep him! What's the matter? You think Hollowdale is more dangerous than New York?"

"Oh, I don't know, I'm confused."

Krishna pulled me closer and stroked my back. "If his mother is alive and capable of looking after him, yes, you're right, you should give him back. But don't let those Ray Kruger types scare you away from doing what you think is right, Madge. Don't lose sight of your heart."

I swallowed and looked down at my lap.

"Let's go over to my house after school and see what we can do," Serena said. "Jamie can help. He's pretty good at computers for a farm boy."

"I can't, not today," I said quickly. "I've got to catch the bus right after school." Liz had told me to come home soon as possible so we could get ready to visit Mom's jail early the next morning. If I missed the school bus, I'd be stuck in Hollowdale for hours, waiting till she had time to come get me.

"I'll drive you back to Riverbend, don't worry," Jamie said. "Anything to avoid homework."

"You will?" I looked around at my little cluster of friends, touched. "Thanks, guys."

Krishna stayed by my side as much as he could the rest of that day, and so did the others. None of them said so, but I think they wanted to prove they were proud to be my friends. I don't think anybody noticed—the kids in our school were used to seeing us together anyhow—but it meant a lot to me. The only real bad moments were when I saw Sophie O'Brian in gym, who looked away from me quickly, and when I realized that Dave Kruger, the guy who'd danced with Serena at Sophie's party, was the little brother of that maniac Ray.

When the day finally ended, I was hurrying across the parking lot to Jamie's pickup when I felt a touch on my shoulder. Startled, I looked around.

"Oh, hi. I'm sorry, I didn't mean to make you jump." It was Gavin Winslow.

I spun on my heels and walked away, fast.

"Madge, wait up, I got somethin' to say to you."

I kept going. He scurried after me.

"Listen, I know what you think," he said quickly. "But it ain't like that, honest. I just wanna say I heard what happened last night and I think it stinks. That Ray Kruger is an asshole and I don't hold with what he believes at all. A lot of people are like that here, but I'm not, I swear. And I'm real sorry about what my friend said to you. I was just too embarrassed to . . ."

I stopped and looked Gavin right in his shifty blue eyes. He faltered and fell silent. "I don't need your charity," I said.

"If you believe what you're saying, then act on it. Go out and stop them. They're your friends." I walked over to Jamie's truck and jumped in.

I didn't know whether Gavin was telling the truth or not, and on the way to Serena's house I realized I never would know. But Gavin was going to have to struggle with his conscience without my help. It wasn't up to me to save him.

Serena's house was on the edge of town and it looked like a haunted mansion, with pillars holding up the porch and vines holding up the pillars. Her mom had hung hippie decorations all over it: rainbow peace signs in the windows, wind chimes singing by the door, flower baskets hanging over the front porch; and she'd painted it lavender, with dark purple trim on the doors and window frames. Hippie slogans were plastered all over on her front door, too:

GRASS, NOT GUNS.

MAKE BABIES, NOT WAR.

PEOPLE DIED FOR YOUR RIGHT TO VOTE: USE IT.

Inside, the house was even more of a hippie haven. Woven panels of messy wool hung on the walls, and Buddha statues dotted the bookshelves, along with more books than I'd ever seen outside of a library. An Indian bedspread lay over the couch, printed with little red elephants holding each other's tails. It was heaven.

"The computer's upstairs in my room," Serena said, so we all followed her up. I wondered if I could get her parents to adopt me so I could live with those books and red elephants, and leave my crazy mom and all my troubles to Liz.

For the next two hours, Serena and Jamie huddled in front of the computer, and soon it became clear that they didn't need me or Krishna, so we wandered downstairs to smooch on the elephant couch awhile. Then we went to look for Mrs. Jenkins's marijuana plants in the vegetable garden. Like most people in Hollowdale, Serena's parents had to work two jobs each to make ends meet, and they never got home till past dinnertime, so we weren't worried about being caught snooping.

"Krish, I've been thinking," I said. "If Serena and Jamie can't find out anything, I'm going back to see that horrible Garcia again."

"But why? He's a crook. He's blackmailing your family!"

"I know. But I can't get that woman who lives with him out of my mind. She seemed so upset. I think she knows more about Timmy than she could say in front of Garcia. I want to find her again and get her to talk."

Krishna shook his head, but he was smiling. "You're pretty brave, Madge, if a little crazy. I'll come with you, of course."

"You will?" I hugged him, breathing in his soapy boy scent.

By the time I was finally able to tear Jamie and Serena away from the computer, neither of them had found out anything except that Rivera was a popular name. There were a whole lot of people with that name, they told me. Some of them were living. And some of them were dead.

The minute I woke up the next morning and remembered this was the day we were going to visit Mom in jail, my whole chest cramped up with worry and shame. I couldn't believe she'd gotten herself arrested. How could she have been so dumb? How could she have done this to Timmy, and to me? And how bad of a criminal was she, anyhow?

The jail was three hours away and the only time we were allowed to visit Mom was at exactly ten A.M. on Tuesdays. To make it even more of a pain in the ass, we had to get there by nine to sign in, so because it always took an hour and five pounds of patience to get Timmy up and dressed, I had to drag myself out of bed by five.

"Come on, Timmy, up you get," I said, stumbling into his room with yawn. A flash of red pajamas as he dived under the bed. I closed my eyes. Here we go again.

Broken toys and clothes lay scattered all over the room. A plate of grapes he'd had for bedtime snack lay spilled across the blue rug. And all I could see of Timmy was one pajama-clad foot.

"I wonder where Timmy is?"

A giggle from under the bed.

"Is he in the closet?" I opened the door to look inside. "Nope. Unless he's small enough to hide in a shoe."

A squeal.

"Oh, look, somebody's left a foot under the bed."

Timmy erupted into laughter and his other foot appeared. I grabbed both his ankles and pulled him out, while he wriggled and laughed. "My goodness, a real live boy!" I lifted him to his feet and gave him a hug. "Come on, mischief mouse, time to get dressed."

"For Christ's sake, hurry up!" Liz said, coming into the room. "We have to leave in half an hour." The two of us knelt on the floor, peeled off Timmy's pajamas, and shoved him into his clothes while he sat limply on the bed, absorbed in a picture book. He was perfectly capable of dressing himself, but lately he'd been getting pretty lazy about it.

"Why don't you cooperate a bit, Timmy?" Liz said. "Oi, I'm talking to you!"

He didn't respond, so she lifted his chin in her hand. "Did you hear me?"

He blinked. "Where we goin'?"

"We're taking a drive to see your other grandma."

"She got any presents for me?"

My aunt looked grim. "I doubt it." She glanced over at me. "Madge, you can't go dressed like that."

"Why not?" I was wearing my silver hoop earrings, jeans, and a white T-shirt with a black peace sign on the front.

"The jail sent me a set of rules about how visitors have to dress. Here." She pulled a piece of paper out of her pocket and read. "No tank tops, no sheer clothing, no white T-shirts, no shorts or short skirts, and no jewelry other than a wedding ring."

"What do they think, somebody's gonna stage a jailbreak with an ear stud? And why can't I wear a white T-shirt?"

"I don't know. But your mum's in enough trouble. Let's not make it worse."

Liz had told me that while I'd been out with Bob getting hassled by racist maniacs, Mom had called her at home to tell her the bad news. "They're holding me in this jail for women and it's fuckin' miles away," Mom had said. "They're trying to decide what to do with me. They'll probably turn me over to Immigration and boot me out of the country."

"Did she sound upset?" I'd asked.

"Not at all. You know your mum. She sounded like she was telling me she'd gone to the cinema. All she did was ask for some extra undies, ciggies, and sweets."

"But what did she *do* to get arrested, Aunty?"

"I've no idea, darlin'. She wouldn't say. But they'll probably be hard on her, since she's an illegal, no matter what she's done. 'Specially now with the new security laws against terrorists."

"Mom a terrorist?" I'd laughed. I couldn't help it.

"It's exactly what I've been warning the daft bugger about all these years. The only way she could have avoided this was to have stopped her shenanigans altogether and stayed out of sight of the law."

"Once a criminal, always a criminal, I guess," I'd muttered.

After I changed into a plain red shirt and no earrings, we bundled Timmy into Liz's car, the streets dead and dim in the first light, and set off for Mom's jail. The drive was so long and quiet it gave me way too much time to think. Timmy fell asleep right away, lying on my lap in the back, and Liz didn't want to talk at all. She just lit one cigarette after another and fiddled with the radio dial, trying to find anything that wasn't country or preaching. I rolled down the window and gazed out at the highway, stroking Timmy's head and wondering again why Mom couldn't have stayed out of trouble, and what the hell she'd done.

When we finally arrived, Liz pulled into a wide parking lot, and the two of us climbed out of the car, leaving Timmy asleep inside. We stood there awhile without saying a word, staring at the flat building in front of us. It was nothing but a white concrete block, not so different from my school, in fact, except that it was surrounded by a twenty-foot hurricane fence, topped with roll after roll of razor wire. The walls were studded with tiny barred windows, and spotlights were perched all around the roof, ready to catch the first sign of escape. The whole building reeked of despair.

"Oh, Madgy," my aunt said at last. "This is just like all those times before, when I visited your mum in that Borstal back in England. I hated it. All those power-hungry guards lording it over everyone, all those poor girls looking bloated and miserable. I thought I'd never have to go through that again. But look at me—look at Brandy. Here we are, all these years later, repeating history as if we've got no more will than a horse on a merry-go-round."

I didn't know what to say. I only knew I felt cold and dank inside, like the bottom of a basement.

Liz woke Timmy and we walked over to a gate in the fence, where we were stopped by a fat guard with a face like undercooked hamburger. He ushered us into a trailer, made us sign in, and told us to wait with the other visitors on a row of hard plastic chairs. I glared at him. Already he seemed evil to me, as if all the forces responsible for locking up Mom had congealed into his ugly mug.

At last an escort guard arrived, a squat white woman with a cross around her neck and blood-red hair. She led us across the dusty ground to the prison entrance. A few inmates were out working a vegetable patch, and they stared at us, chomping gum. I looked away. I couldn't stand the thought of Mom hanging out with those losers. They looked dumpy and ugly in their orange jumpsuits, the dye half grown out of their hair and their faces heavy with boredom. It wasn't what they'd done that bothered me, it was that they'd been caught. Most of the women in prison these days weren't serious criminals anyway, I knew that from reading Bob's newspaper. They were just drug dabblers locked up for way too long because of the stupid drug laws, prostitutes, or women taking the rap for their men. But still, I thought, only the dumb ones get caught.

"I'll never let the fuckin' pigs get their hands on me again," Mom had said to me once. "I'm too smart for them now."

Before any visitors were allowed into the jail, we had to pass security. I stood glowering while a hefty female guard rifled through the underpants and bras I'd packed for Mom in a plastic bag. Already I hated the guards with the venom of an ex-con. Maybe it was in my blood from Mom, or maybe it came from the stories she'd told me about the "screws," as she called them. "They're like little dictators," she'd told me once. "They get twisted by all that power. It goes to their little brains. Even the nice ones get corrupted in the end."

"You got permission to bring these in?" the guard said to me, jabbing at Mom's underwear.

"Yes, Officer, I cleared it beforehand," Liz said before I could answer, showing the guard a piece of paper. I stared at Liz. *Officer?* Where did my aunt learn to grovel like that?

"Well, you can't bring them into the visiting area. She'll get them later." The guard shoved the bag into a locker behind her. I was sure Mom would never see those things again.

"What's this?" the guard barked at me then, pulling out a packet of M&Ms.

"What the hell does it look like?"

"Open it. And watch your mouth, young lady." The guard's long face was hard and blank as the bottom of an iron.

"Shit." I tore open the paper pouch.

"Pour them on the table."

"But they'll be ruined!"

"Go on!" The woman folded her big arms.

Gritting my teeth, I poured the M&Ms into a brightly colored heap and shook the torn pouch in the guard's face.

"Ooh!" Timmy cried, reaching out to grab a handful.

"Stop it! Those are for Mom!" I swatted his hand away. He burst into screams and half the M&Ms scattered to the floor.

"Hey!" I shouted. "Those are Mom's favorite!" I was close to tears myself by then.

"Calm down, love," Liz whispered to me, laying a hand on my arm while the guard rifled through her purse. "Let Timmy have a few. They'll only make your mum sick if she eats them all."

Finally, the guard finished checking our stuff and let us

through a door into the visitors' room, but not till she'd confiscated all the candy we'd brought for Mom. Or so she thought. In Timmy's coat pocket, where I figured nobody would look, I'd hidden two of Mom's favorites: a Kit Kat and a Mars bar.

I was surprised at how ordinary the visitors' room looked. All the prison visitors' rooms I'd seen in movies had been sealed off by a wall, with wire mesh windows and a phone you had to talk through, but this was open like a school cafeteria, except that the tables were bolted to the floor. The guard told the three of us to sit down at a round table in the corner and stay put. "Botley will be brought out in a minute," she said tonelessly.

I looked around at the other visitors, most of them worn-down grandmas trying to hush the small children running at their feet. It was so sad that these people had to be in a place like this, with their daughters and moms in jail. At least my own mother hadn't put me through this when I was little. Then it hit me like a wet towel. Who was I to talk? I was one of them now: the child of a no-good stupid convict.

At last the first inmates were marched in. Many of them weren't any older than me, and I watched them out of the corner of my eye, curious about what they were in for and what they were like. I couldn't help wondering if I'd end up like them one day. Like mother, like daughter, they say.

Finally, Mom strode in with a mannish swagger, wearing the same orange overalls as the rest of the jailbirds and the cockiest of her grins. The fact she was so at ease in this hell-hole only made me feel worse.

"Hello there, peanut!" she said, scooping up Timmy for a kiss. "Did you bring those sweets I asked for, eh?"

He held out a chocolate-smeared hand, offering her his crushed and sweaty M&Ms.

"Lovely." She sat down, legs spread, and popped them into her mouth. The orange jumpsuit reflected in her pale face, making her look washed out and unhealthy. At last she turned to me. "Good of you to come, sweetheart." She gave me a pat on the head. "Did you bring any fags?"

"Yeah, here." I furtively handed her the few loose cigarettes I'd hidden in my bra, smirking at having outwitted the guard.

Liz glared at me. "What are you trying to do, get locked up along with your mother?"

"Shut up, Liz." Mom winked at me. "Thanks, love. I can't live in this place without my ciggies." She pulled out a small tobacco tin from under her overalls and balanced it on her knee, where it was hidden from the guards. Then she put all the cigarettes inside it but one, broke off its filter and opened it along the seam, as neatly as if she was unzipping it. She emptied the tobacco into the tin, folded up the cigarette paper, and put that inside, too. Timmy and I watched in fascination.

"I'll use it to roll a teeny ciggy with later on, you see," she said, catching his eye. "Waste not want not, right, Timmy?"

"Brandy, put that thing away before we get kicked out of here," Liz said sharply. "What's going to happen to you now, eh? Are you going to be deported, are they putting you on trial, or what?"

Mom closed the tin and slipped it back under her overalls. "They're talking about a trial, but I don't know. They're still trying to decide who I belong to, the coppers or ICE—that's what they call Immigration now. Great name, isn't it? Says it all." She chuckled.

"Jesus. Have you got a lawyer?"

"Yeah, they gave me some cheapo public defender. I told her to do whatever it takes to get me tossed out of the country. I don't want to end up in some fuckin' pit of a prison, do I?"

"You mean you're going to let them deport you without a fight?"

"I've got no choice, Liz. What would I tell them—that I'm here without a visa making my living on the fiddle?" Mom threw herself back in her chair, tipping it half off the floor.

"What fiddle?" I said, glaring at her. "What were you doing to get arrested anyway? I've got a right to know."

"No, you don't." Mom turned back to Liz. "As I was saying, I'm sure they'll throw me out as soon as they can. It's much cheaper than locking me up, and that's what it all comes down to for them, isn't it, saving money?"

"Oh, Lord." My aunt plucked at her fingers, looking distressed.

"I know, Liz, I'm sorry. But never mind, I'm homesick anyway." Mom leaned forward again and lowered her voice. "Listen, my lawyer said she'll try to get me Voluntary Departure from ICE. That means if we come up with the money for a plane ticket within four months and I agree to split, they'll march me right out of jail on to the plane and I can avoid doing prison time. Think you can do it? One-way, cheap?"

Liz rubbed her temples. "Jesus, Brandy."

"I know, I know. I'll pay you back one day, I promise."

"But if they boot you out as a criminal illegal, they'll never let you back in again. Do you realize that?"

"Is that true?" I said.

Mom yawned and ran her hand through her brush of hair. "Oh, I'll get back before you know it, love, don't worry. I have my ways. And maybe you can visit me for a nice little holiday in England, eh?"

She grinned and sat back, her legs spread and her arms crossed. Her whole macho act made me sick. I'd known she was tough, but not this tough. Mom was a veteran convict, anyone could see that.

"What about Timmy?" I hissed. "Are we going to get into trouble now 'cause of you?"

She shook her head. "Don't worry, I'm not going to tell them a thing about the little squirt here, even if they pull out me fingernails!" She winked and rubbed her head again, then turned to my aunt. "Listen, Liz, as soon as you've got the time, will you pack up all my stuff and take it back to your house with you? Now they've got me locked up in here, there's no way I can pay the fuckin' rent, so I reckon I'll just let the place go."

"But that's my home!" I said. "You can't do that!"

Mom looked at me impatiently. "Don't be daft, Madgy. How am I supposed to pay the rent locked up in here like a rabbit in a cage, eh? They've been threatening to evict us for months anyway—good riddance. One more headache out of my life."

After that, Mom chatted about stupid stuff to Liz, completely ignoring me and Timmy, who'd found the candy I'd hidden in his pocket and was busy eating it all up. The two of them were acting like we'd stopped by for coffee on a shopping trip, not driven for three goddamn hours to come to this horrible jail and hear all this bad news. It was sick, my whole family was sick. I glowered at Mom but she avoided my eyes and kept yabbering to Liz, winking at Timmy once in a while. Finally I couldn't stand it anymore.

"I almost got killed Saturday night!" I blurted.

Mom turned to me. "You what?"

"I got hassled by some KKK types, right in Dale's Diner. I swear they wanted to kill me."

"Don't exaggerate. That's my job." Mom chortled.

"No, I'm serious! Debbie threatened to call the cops on them." And I told her what had happened.

Liz got real upset when she heard this because I'd kept it from her till then, but Mom only got mad.

"You should know better than to go downtown on a weekend night," she said coldly. "You know it's not safe, stupid girl, I've told you."

"Thanks for the sympathy." I glared at her.

"What do you expect if you take risks like that, eh?"

"It wasn't a risk! I went with Bob, and Dale's Diner isn't anywhere near those redneck bars. It's not my fault those assholes were there!"

"Stop it, you two!" Liz hissed, but we ignored her.

"You can use your head, though, can't you?" Mom snapped, her voice rising.

"Keep it down, ladies, keep it down." A guard walked over to us, calm in all her power. "Any more of this and the visit's over."

Mom waited for her to walk away again, then dropped her voice. "Listen, my girl," she said through her teeth. "I don't know who you think you are, but your head's been getting too big for your boots lately. Ever since you picked up Timmy, you seem to think you're Martin Luther King or someone, walking round all high and mighty. You're still only seventeen, there's a lot of people in that town who don't like who we are—you or me—and I want you in with Liz every night by ten, or else!"

I put my hands on my hips and thrust my head at her. "And what the fuck are you gonna do about it? You can't do anything stuck in here like a pig in a pen, can you? You're helpless."

"Madge, shush!" Liz laid her hand on my arm in warning, but it was too late. Mom leaped out of her chair, her face reddening with fury.

"You little bitch!"

At that the guard scooted over and grabbed her by the arm.

"That's it. You'll have to say good-bye."

"Let go of me, fuckin' screw!" Mom shouted in a coarse voice I'd never heard before. She tried to twist out of the guard's arm and a whistle blew. Before I could blink, three guards had closed in around her. They clamped her arms behind her back and marched her out of the visiting room while she yelled in protest.

"Mom!" I shouted, jumping to my feet. "Mom, I'm sorry!" But she was hustled out of sight before she could say another word.

I fell back on to my chair and put my head in my hands. Timmy shoved the rest of the Mars bar into his mouth, staring at me as he chewed.

"Well, that was pleasant," Liz said. She stood up and took Timmy's hand. "Let's get out of here."

I dropped my face on to my arms, the tears spilling over my wrists.

That night in Riverbend, after a nightmare drive back during which Timmy threw up the chocolate he'd gobbled all over the car, I screamed it served him right, and Liz screamed at me for screaming at him, I waited till he and my aunt were asleep and crept downstairs to call Krishna. I'd never needed to hear his voice so bad. Settling into a living-room chair, the room dark and shadowy around me, I dialed his number.

"Hollowdale View Motel." It was his mom.

"Hi, Mrs. Sharma, it's Madge. I'm sorry to call so late, but is Krishna available?"

"Oh. I am sorry, Madge, but this is not a very good moment for him to talk."

"It's not?" I couldn't keep the dismay out of my voice. I needed him so much. Mrs. Sharma must have heard it, because she changed her tune.

"Well, wait a minute please, dear. I will see if he is free."

I had to wait a long time before Krishna came to the phone, which puzzled me. Usually his family was so aware of the cost of phone calls they never kept me waiting this long. At last, however, I heard him pick up the phone.

"Madge, I can't talk. This isn't a good time."

"Why, what's wrong?"

He paused before answering, and when he did, his voice dropped so low I could hardly hear it. "I'm afraid we've had some bad news." He stopped and I could hear him swallowing. "My father told us tonight that the motel isn't doing very well. In fact, it's failing. We might have to move. We might have to go back to Queens, where my uncle runs a gas station. He's offered my father a job."

"You're going to have to move?"

Krishna took a long breath. "Oh Madge, I've never seen my father so ashamed."

seventeen

"ARE YOU LISTENING to me?" It was Liz in her wasp outfit again, buzzing around her kitchen. I was sitting at the table the morning after our trip to Mom's jail, poking my oatmeal with a spoon. I didn't feel like eating. And I didn't feel like listening.

My aunt pulled up a chair and sat opposite me. Timmy was alone in the bathroom, supposedly brushing his teeth before she took him off to day care, but I wasn't interested in that, either. "You haven't heard a word I've said, have you?"

I shrugged.

"Here then. Read this." She thrust an official-looking envelope under my nose. It was from the Educational Testing Service—my ticket to the first set of SATs I had to take to get into college. "They're the weekend after next, aren't they, love?" she said gently. "What are you going to do?"

I pushed away the letter and squeezed my eyes shut. I hadn't studied properly for weeks, not since I'd brought Timmy home, as my aunt well knew. I'd blown my math and Spanish finals, too. Even my favorite teacher, Mrs. Gough, was disappointed in me. There was no way I was ready for the SATs. But Liz had spent seventy bucks for me to take the tests, and that was way too much to throw away.

"I'll take them," I said. "I don't see the point, though. I can't go to college anyway. Not with him here." I nodded toward the bathroom.

Liz looked at me, her penciled eyebrows raised. "Don't talk like that, Madgy. Of course you're going to college. I'll look after Timmy."

"No." I shook my head. "That's not what I promised."

My aunt stood up, smoothing down her yellow shirt. "That's a load of rubbish, but we'll talk about it later. You better get off to school. Timmy, you ready?" she called.

Timmy appeared in the doorway, looking polished and perky in clean shorts and a red shirt. Liz had cut his mop of hair down to an inch, which made his shiny black eyes look bigger than ever. He loved day care—it was the only thing he ever cooperated about. He even had his Batman lunch box ready in his hand.

"Bye-bye, Madge," he said, starting for the door. Then he stopped and came back to me. Planting himself in front of my chair, he stared up into my face.

"What?" I grunted. I wasn't in the mood for his little-kid nonsense.

He kept on staring at me, his face serious. Then he reached up and touched my cheek. "Why you sad?" he said. "You look sad, like my moms."

That made me sit up. He'd never mentioned his mother

voluntarily before. "Your mom was sad?" I said quickly.

He nodded, his eyes filling. "Big sad."

I reached out to hug him, but he turned and ran out of the room.

Soon as I got to school that morning, I looked for Krishna. I wanted to tell him what Timmy had said, and I wanted to comfort him, too. For the first couple of hours, I didn't see him, but at last I found him walking out of social studies between periods. His eyes were ringed with brown and his thin face was ashy.

I gave him a kiss. "You okay?"

He pulled me to his chest. "No, I'm not. I couldn't sleep all night. This is so shitty, what's happening to my family."

"You want to talk about it?"

He took my hand in his long fingers and we walked down the hallway, ignoring the people bumping around us as they rushed to class.

"It's pretty simple. My father has to move away this week, and then we'll follow. He'll have to work in my uncle's gas station—it's the only job he can find." Krishna paused, his face drawn. "He's worked so hard for this motel. My mother, too. And now they've lost everything. It's this dead town, I think; they could never get enough customers or make enough money to pay back their loans. Now the bank's taken away the motel and we've got nothing left except some linens and a few junky old chairs." He shook his head. "They worked so hard, Madge. They did everything you're supposed to do in America to make money, you know? I don't understand how this happened."

I squeezed his fingers. I wished I could say something helpful, something to cheer him up, but I was also scared. If Krishna went to Queens, what would happen to us?

"When exactly will you have to go?" I said shakily.

"In three weeks, soon as school's over."

"Three weeks! But that's so soon!"

"I know. And it's real bad for my brother, too. How's he going to pay for the rest of college now? Don't tell anybody about this, not even Serena and Jamie, please? It's too shaming for my family."

I opened my mouth to reassure him but the bell went off for next period, drowning me out.

"See you at lunch," Krishna mouthed, and hurried away.

We didn't get to talk at lunch, though, because Serena and Jamie were already at our table, glued together, as usual, and eager to discuss their investigation into Timmy. "We figured out how to find out if his mom's dead or in jail or in a hospital somewhere," Serena told me the minute I sat down, "but we can't do anything unless we know her full name. We just can't get anywhere without that, Madge, I'm sorry."

I glanced at Krishna, who hardly seemed to be listening. "Okay, then I'm going back to Garcia's place. I want to talk to that woman he lives with. I've already thought about it, and it's the only way."

"You shouldn't do that alone—it's too dangerous," Jamie said quickly. I'd told him and Serena all about Garcia, so they knew everything by then. "We'll go with you for protection. I'll drive us in the truck again. I kinda like this chauffeuring job. It beats shoveling cow shit."

We agreed to go the next Sunday, the day after the SATs were done. Serena and Jamie were excited, but Krishna didn't say a word.

I didn't get to talk to him again till the end of the day, when he walked me over to the bus. He told me more about his moving plans and how crushed his parents were, but neither of us mentioned how all this would affect our future. I knew this wasn't the time to talk about that, or about my seeing Mom in jail. I did tell him what Timmy had said that morning, however.

"Do you think you can come with us on Sunday?" I said as we crossed the parking lot. "I know you'll be busy, but I'd love it if you could."

"Of course I can't! Haven't you been listening to me? I'll be packing up the motel for our move. I can't leave for a whole day. My mother needs me."

I swallowed and looked down at the asphalt under my feet. Krishna had never spoken to me like that before.

I won't even talk about how the exams went that following week. Let's just say if the SATs had been asking about moms in jail and boyfriends falling out of love, I would've done just fine. As it was, I stank.

Jamie and Serena picked me up at the bus stop again Sunday morning at nine. We'd decided to stake out Garcia's house from down the block and wait till we could catch the woman coming or leaving, in the hopes we could avoid seeing Garcia at all. It was risky, we knew, but it was better than actually going into that scary apartment again. Meanwhile, as I rattled around in the back of the truck, all alone this time, a big ache about Mom and Krishna swelled up inside of me. It was a sprained ankle kind of ache, painful and sharp. I wondered if there was such a thing as a sprained heart.

When we reached Garcia's block, we parked the truck down the street and took turns sitting in the back, watching the front of his building and nibbling on the tasteless organic corn chips Serena's mom had made her bring along. We waited almost all day, getting hotter and hotter under the late-May sun (Serena even took off her goth coat, revealing a black spaghetti-strap shirt with little skulls all over it), but nobody I recognized came in or out. Serena and Jamie chatted about the SATs and this and that, but I didn't listen. I was too busy worrying. If Mom did end up getting kicked out of the country, would I ever see her again? And when Krishna moved, would he be gone forever, too? He hadn't called me all week, and when I'd seen him at school he'd acted distant and irritated, like I was nothing but an interruption. I knew he had a lot of worries, but still, it felt like his mind had already moved to Queens and he'd lost all interest in boring hicks like me.

"Madge, is that her?" Serena hissed, jerking me out of my thoughts. I'd told them to watch out for a short, skinny black woman, and we'd had two false alarms already. But this one really did look like her. She was the same wiry build, her hair was scraped back into the same stiff ponytail, and her face was as bony and knotted as I remembered it. She was dressed in tight blue jeans and a purple tube top. She stopped at the top of her stoop, looked around quickly, and took off up the street.

"Stay here," I said to the others, and ran after her.

"Excuse me!" I called. She walked on quickly. "Excuse me, ma'am?" I ran till I caught up with her. "Hi," I said. "Remember me? I came to your apartment . . ."

She glanced at me, then slowed down, looking surprised. "Yeah, I know you. What you doin' here?"

"I want to ask you something about Timmy."

She peered at me, her eyes huge in her bony face. "What about him? You got him, right?"

That startled me so much I couldn't do anything but stare back at her. But then something, somehow, told me to tell the truth this time. "Yes, I've got him."

She ran her eyes over me quickly. "Why you take him like that? He ain't yours." I backed away when she said that, but before I had time to think of an answer she added, "He okay?"

"Yes, yes he's fine. He's real happy, in fact." I swallowed. "Can we talk a minute? I've got some questions. Please?"

"I got questions for you, too, honey."

"Okay," I said nervously. "Let's find a diner. We'll buy you a coffee, if you'd like."

"We? Who else you got here?" She edged away from me.

"Just my friends." I pointed to Serena and Jamie down the block. "We're only kids. No reporters this time."

She looked at them a second. "How come all your friends

are white? Okay, follow me." And she scooted around a corner.

She led us down four blocks and over three more before she stopped at a narrow little coffee shop squeezed between a dry cleaner and a bodega. She ducked inside. By the time we'd joined her, she was already sitting at a table in the back. She looked as jittery as I felt myself, one leg bouncing up and down and her fingers twisting together.

"Sit down, kids," she said. "We gotta make this quick. Tony sees me talkin' to you, there's gonna be hell to pay." Her voice was ragged from smoking, with such a mixed up New York and Latino accent I couldn't tell where she was from.

"Would you like some coffee?" I asked, wondering who Tony was.

"Sure. Black. Get me a muffin, too, honey pie."

"I'll get it," Jamie said quickly, looking eager for escape, and scooted over to the counter. We were all pretty jittery.

"What you wanna know?" she asked then.

Jamie came back with the coffee and a blueberry muffin, which she dunked and bit into, sucking at the wet part.

"Well, um, I was wondering . . ." I stopped, remembering Timmy's little face the morning when he'd said his mom was sad. What if I found out something that would hurt him even more?

"Come on, baby, I ain't got all day. What's your name, anyhow, and your friends'?"

"I'm Madge; this is Jamie and Serena."

"I'm Marisol. You don't need to know the rest."

I smiled at her awkwardly.

"So?" she said. "What you wanna ask?"

"Well, I guess first . . ." I swallowed. "Are you Timmy's mom?"

She took another bite of muffin and a slurp of coffee. "Hell no," she mumbled through her chewing. "His mama's dead. He didn't tell you that?"

"Not directly."

Marisol finished off her coffee in three gulps, even though it was still steaming hot. "Well, she is. OD'd 'bout a month 'fore he twisted his ankle that time. Broke me up real bad, losing my sister like that."

"She was your sister? Your real sister?" My eyes grew wide.

"Yep, my baby sis, Alicia, God rest her soul. We came over from the D.R. together, scared as two cats in a sack. Stuck by each other ever since."

"Her name was Alicia? Alicia Rivera?"

"Rivera, Quesada, Rodriguez . . .We use a buncha names. Tony make us."

"Tony? You mean that man Garcia?"

Marisol nodded, chewing again.

"Is he from the Dominican Republic, too?"

She broke off another piece of muffin. "No, honey pie, he from someplace else."

"So he's not really Timmy's uncle, like he said?"

Marisol ran her eyes nervously around the room. "Hell no. He made up all that shit to scare you."

"He's not Timmy's father, either?"

"No, no. Tony, he's my man, not my sister's." She peered at me. "How old are you, anyhow, honey pie? You don't seem to know a whole lot 'bout the world."

"I come from a small town," I said defensively. "We all do."

"Well, small towns got their troubles, too. Hey, carrot-top, get me more coffee, huh?"

Blushing, Jamie jumped up to get it, while I watched Marisol chew her way slowly through the rest of her muffin, thinking over what she'd told me. Was she really Timmy's aunt? Or was she just as much of a liar as Garcia?

Finally, Serena spoke up for the first time. "Can I ask a question, too?" She peered at Marisol through her panels of black hair.

"Go ahead, spooky girl. Don't mean I'm gonna answer."

"Did Timmy's mom really die of an overdose, or was it AIDS?"

Oh my God, I thought, of course. Junkie, AIDS—why didn't I think of that before?

Marisol shrugged. "No, it was just too much Big H all at once, honey pie. She got hooked real bad—that's what kept me off of it, watching what happened to Alicia." And to my surprise, her eyes filled with tears. She'd seemed so tough up till then, but suddenly her thin little face was crumpled and sad. And that's when I saw she looked just like Timmy.

"I'm sorry, but I have another question, too," Serena said, reminding me of how pushy Bob had been with Mrs. Henderson. "Are you in touch with your family back in the D.R.?"

Marisol stared down at the table awhile before answering. "Baby," she finally said, "me and Alicia, we ran away from our people a long time ago. Don't know if they dead or alive. Two country *chicas*, that was us, tryin' to make a better life for ourself." She stopped talking a moment and gazed at us, her eyes black and sunken. Then she leaned toward me. "Timmy ever ask for his *tía*?"

I had to tell her no.

"'Cause I miss that little *niño*, I do. Poor Alicia. She tried real hard to give him a good life. Me, I love that baby just like she did. I been missing him so bad since he been gone."

"Then how come you never reported him?"

She stared into her coffee cup. "Problem was Tony," she said, half to us, half to herself. "I went out and looked everyplace for that kid, asked all kindsa people if they seen him, but nobody knew nothin', and Tony, he wouldn't let me go to no cops. Said it would only get him busted. So when you showed up and we could see you had him, I was real glad to know he was safe. I could tell you was good peoples."

She stopped talking a minute and peered over the table at me. "You, what's-your-name, you listenin' to me here?"

"Yes, I'm listening."

"I tell you what life was like for me and Alicia, okay? We grow up in a family with ten kids and one chicken, get it? We run to Santo Domingo, where we work the streets awhile, but it's rough. Then she finds this man to protect us, right? First he's real nice. Takes us to New York, gives us money, gives her a home, gives her the kid. But soon he turns mean. I get out right away, 'cause I'm not the one he wants, but when she tries to leave, he beats her up. She tries to keep her baby safe, he beats her up again. She tries to find a better man . . . You got the picture? So she gets hooked on junk, he kicks her out, and the next thing I know she moves in with me an' Tony to die."

I thought of Bob's words in my aunt's living room. "Did Tony kill her?"

Marisol looked surprised. "What? Of course not! Tony, he took her in 'cause she was my sister. No, it was the horse did that, honey. And maybe that man she had. She wouldn't of needed no junk without him." Marisol seemed to be talking to herself again. But then she focused back on me. "So listen, how come you took Timmy, huh? You ain't told me yet."

I swallowed. "Because he was scared and dirty and he didn't want to go home. He was hungry, too. He wasn't being looked after very well." I stared hard at Marisol to see what she'd say to that.

She nodded. "Yeah, things were kinda rough back then. We went through a bad time after my sister, she died. Tony and me, we had a fight, I left for a while . . . but all that's over now. When you gonna bring him back?"

"What?"

"That's what you came here to talk about, ain't it? You had him long enough. It's time for that baby to come home now."

"I can't do that!"

"Oh, yes you can."

"But what would Tony do?" I said in a panic, grabbing at

the first objection I could think of. "Won't he call the cops? He keeps threatening to."

Marisol snickered. "If Tony calls the cops, honey pie, they gonna arrest him 'fore he's even hung up the phone." She paused. "Tell you what. You showed up kinda sudden here, and this ain't the best time for me right now. So, since you took the kid already an' you say he's so happy, you keep him a little longer, okay? I gotta straighten out a few things 'fore he comes home. Gimme your phone number and I'll call you when I'm ready."

"But what if Timmy doesn't want to go back?" I said quickly. "He didn't when I found him. He begged to come home with me."

"That's 'cause he was real upset 'bout his mama being dead, honey pie. He was all shook up back then—we all was, I told you. It ain't gonna be a problem now. We his family, an' he knows it. He loves us. An' I miss him so bad! Now, you got a pen so I can write down that number?"

Serena found a pen and I told Marisol Liz's telephone number, which she wrote on the back of her hand. I wanted to give her a fake number, but my conscience wouldn't let me. If Marisol really was Timmy's aunt, she might be the only relative he had left in the world. And if she was telling the truth, he might even love her. How could I cheat him of that?

"Okay." She tossed the pen back at me and shot out of the coffee shop so fast the three of us were left sitting at the table, blinking, like we'd seen a ghost.

On the way home, I squeezed on to the passenger seat with Serena instead of sitting in the back, so we could talk about what had happened, but the fact was we were too shocked to talk much at all. Jamie was so out of his depth he couldn't even think of a joke, and all Serena managed to say was she thought I'd better get Timmy tested for AIDS, since his mom had been a junkie. I couldn't think about anything but what would happen now. Would Marisol insist on taking Timmy back? Would he want to go? And if he didn't, how could I prevent it?

When Jamie dropped me off at Liz's house that night, I found her waiting for me at the kitchen table, drinking her nightly beer, surrounded by the remains of dinner. Timmy was in bed, listening to some music on a little boom box Liz had bought him. Nothing helped him sleep better than half an hour of folk music or reggae. He'd lie there, humming along till his eyes drifted shut, happy as a clam.

"Where in God's name have you been?" Liz shrieked. "I've been worried sick about you all day, I have."

I dropped into a chair. "I need a beer. Can I?"

"Absolutely not." She glared at me. "Come on, out with it."

I told her everything. "I'm scared, Aunty. I don't know what to do."

Liz sucked in her breath and looked at me, her pointy face drawn. "That was a bloody dangerous thing you did, Madgy. You know what a maniac that Garcia is. Jesus. But are you sure you should believe the woman? Maybe she's not his aunt at all. Maybe she's just trying to get money out of you, like Garcia is with Bob."

"I don't think so. She didn't ask for money, she only asked for Timmy. And, Aunty, she looks just like him."

Liz's whole body sagged. "Oh, Lord."

"There's something else, too. We need to get Timmy tested for AIDS. His mom was a junkie." I dropped my face into my hands. This was suddenly too much.

"I already did."

I looked up. "You did? When?"

"Right after you and Timmy moved here. He was a kid off the streets, Madge. I'm not daft."

"Is he okay?"

"Yeah. Healthy as a hippo, as a matter of fact. Your mum got him a fake birth certificate and a social security card, too, so I could take him to the doctor for a checkup and enroll him in school. She's quite good at forged documents, it turns out." Liz pulled a face. "She tells me illegal immigrants do that all the time."

"Oh." I was a little dazed. "Why didn't you tell me all this?"

"Didn't want to worry you." Liz sat up again, leaned forward, and squeezed my hand. "Look, love, I know you had to find out if he had a family sooner or later—if any of what that woman told you is true. But we can't give him back to those criminals, even if they are his relatives. He's better off here. And I can't help it, but I've grown to love the little bugger."

"I know you have. Me, too. But we've got to do what's best for him, not us."

She gazed at me, puzzled. "I don't understand you, Madgy.

I thought you'd decided long ago to keep him, no matter what."

I shook my head. "It's different now that I know he might have a family. I'll go see if he's awake. I'm going to ask him if Marisol really is his aunt."

"Careful!" Liz called after me softly. "Don't frighten the poor lad."

I went upstairs and pushed open Timmy's door quietly in case he was asleep. I did this every night to see if he wanted a kiss or a hug. He got scared at bedtime if he thought nobody was close by. I think he was still worried we'd walk out of the house and leave him forever.

He wasn't asleep. I could see his eyes glinting in the glow of his nightlight. He seemed to be watching the headlights from the occasional car outside flicker across the room, and he was humming along to his music, as usual. Jimmy Cliff this time, "The Harder They Come," some old song Liz had loved back when she was young.

I sat on the edge of his bed. "Hey there, how's it going?"

"Where you been?" he said in his raspy little voice, turning on his side to face me. "You been gone all day."

"Sorry, sweetie, I went to visit somebody." I stroked his head a moment. "Timmy? You know how Grandma is my aunty?"

"No she's not, she's Gramma."

"Well, in any case, do you know if you've got an aunty of your own?"

His shoulders shifted under the sheets. "Don' know."

I took his bony little hand. His skin felt so soft and new. "You don't have an Aunty Marisol? Your *tía*?"

Timmy looked up at me from the pillow, his oval face solemn in the shadows. "*Mi tía.*"

"You do have a *tía*?

"Yup." He turned over on his back, his hand still in mine. "Can I have some chocolate?

"Is her name Marisol?"

"Uh-huh. *Tía* Marisol."

I closed my eyes. I hadn't expected it to hurt this much.

"Did she live with you and your mom in that apartment in New York?" I made myself say.

"Yeah. I want some chocolate. Can I, huh, huh?"

"Do you miss her?"

"Hot chocolate! Hot, hot choc-o-lot!"

"Timmy, please answer me. Do you miss *Tía* Marisol?"

He didn't say anything right away. He sat up in bed, letting go of my hand and pulling his knees to his chin, and stared over them into the shadowy room. Then in a low voice he said, "Miss my moms."

I wrapped my arms around him and gave him a long hug. "I know, little love. I know you do."

"Hot chocolate," he said again, and turning away from me, he curled into a tiny ball and lay down.

I went back downstairs to make it for him, but I could hardly see where I was going. I wiped away the tears, quick.

"Well?" Liz said from her kitchen chair, blowing out the smoke from a cigarette. "What did he say?"

I leaned my back against the sink. "She is his aunt." My voice shook. "He calls her his *tía*. Oh, Aunty, he's got an aunt just like I've got you!"

Liz frowned at the floor, drawing on her cigarette again. "Did he say if he misses her?"

"I can't tell. He only said he misses his mom."

She looked back up at me, her face grim. "Well then, I don't think that changes anything. What with Garcia and what you've said about this Marisol woman, Timmy's clearly safer with us. Those people are crooks. He needs to stay here."

"Mom's a crook, too. But she's still my mother."

Liz looked as if she wanted to answer, but then she stood up to clear the dishes off the table. I turned to the stove to heat up some milk. I felt numb.

For a long time the two of us moved around the kitchen without saying a word. But finally my aunt spoke up again in a completely different tone.

"Listen, Madgy, speaking of your mum, I talked to her on the phone today. She sent her love."

I poured the hot milk into a mug and stirred in the cocoa powder. "Is she going to get that Voluntary Departure thing she was talking about?" I said in a low voice.

"She doesn't know yet. These things take a long time."

"Can't we get her out on bail?" I couldn't stand knowing Mom was rotting in that place while we all waltzed around outside, free.

"I'm afraid not. The judge denied it. They don't trust her not to do a bunk." Liz picked up the mug of cocoa. "I'll take this up to him. You better phone Bob now and tell him what you found out about Marisol. Then get yourself to bed. You look knackered."

I nodded. "Krishna didn't call for me?" I said, trying to sound casual.

"No, love. Not a peep."

eighteen

TWO WEEKS WENT by, taking us into June and the end of
the school year, but I didn't hear a word from Marisol. Maybe
she'd been talking on a whim, I thought; maybe she wasn't really planning to take Timmy back at all. Timmy didn't say any
more about her, either, so I let myself hope there was no need
to worry. Still, every time the phone rang I jumped, scared to
death it was her.

Garcia stopped calling Bob, too, or showing up at his
newspaper—perhaps Marisol had told him to lay off. As for
Krishna, he hadn't called or spoken to me since he'd snapped
at me by the bus stop. And when I'd called him, he'd said he
was too busy to talk.

At the end of those two weeks, Friday afternoon, I dragged
myself home on the school bus, feeling lonely and blue, to find
a surprise. Ruth was there, sitting in the beauty shop with Bob
and talking to my aunt. Ruth was looking real pretty in an
elegant, dark blue summer dress, Bob was tanned and seemed
pleased with himself, and Timmy was sprawled on Ruth's
lap, his head clamped into earphones and his hands clutching

a brand-new portable CD player. He was staring into space, mesmerized.

I threw myself into one of the spongy, pink salon chairs, which was like sitting on a tongue, and swiveled it around till I had my back to them. "Hi, Ruth, nice to see you again," I said over my shoulder.

"Hey, Madge. How are you?"

Her voice was so gentle I couldn't answer. I looked down at my sandals, my toes dusty and dry inside of them. I missed Krishna terribly, my grades stank, I spent every day dreading a phone call from Marisol, and it was the day of the junior prom. In the past I'd always gone to school dances with my little crew so we could protect each other, but now that Serena and Jamie were a couple and Krishna had apparently dumped me, there was no way that was going to happen.

"I was just telling Mom that Ruth's got a photography show opening in a gallery soon," Bob said. "You should come visit us in the city and see it."

He sounded so proud of Ruth I almost liked him again. "Wow, that's great." I swiveled the tongue to face them, the room spinning pink around me. I wondered how they'd moved so fast from being a broken-up couple to visiting us together in Riverbend. Could Bob have listened to my advice after all?

That night, Liz dressed up in her cherry-red skirt and sweater, her hair pulled back in a bun, and cooked us another of her anorexic dinners: turkey burgers, broccoli, and carrot salad. She even made me set the table in her frilly dining room—her way of making things special for Ruth. Then we put Timmy on the living-room couch to watch a Sesame Street video about some orchestra, and settled down to eat. The prom was starting in half an hour and I felt like shit.

"That boy is so musical it's amazing," Liz said while she served up our food. We could hear Big Bird squeaking in the background about clarinets and violas. "His day care has a music teacher who comes in once a week, and she says he's got a fantastic ear. I want to get him one of those miniature violins and start him on lessons."

"Piano," I said. "Make him take piano. It's better." I don't know why I said that. What did I know about music lessons? I just wanted Liz to remember who was the boss when it came to Timmy.

"But pianos are so expensive," she replied.

"I think Madge is right," Bob said. "Those kiddie violins sound terrible. Like a cat dying. I'm sure you can find an old piano for him somewhere."

I looked at him in surprise. Bob hadn't taken my side about anything for months. Ruth must be doing him good.

Liz shrugged and began to eat while I glanced at the new couple. They certainly looked happy. Bob was all cocky, and Ruth, who'd swept back her bush of hair into some kind of complicated knot for the evening, was glowing and talkative and much nicer to Liz than Julie had ever been. I hoped she'd stick around. She was the most normal thing to have happened to our family for years.

"So, Madge," Bob said after he'd opened a bottle of beer for everybody but me, "any thoughts on what you're going to do about Timmy's aunt?"

I jerked my head toward the living room, where Timmy was munching on his burger and humming along with Elmo. "Keep your voice down," I hissed.

"I told you your little rescue might get complicated," Bob said more quietly.

"Bob, stop." Liz leaned over the table toward him. "Listen to me a moment before you start picking on Madge. You know what the choices are, don't you? We obviously can't give him back to Garcia or his aunt, whatever that Marisol woman says. Those people are not the kind to be bringing up children. And even if we found his family in the Dominican Republic, which sounds impossible, we'd be handing him over to people who don't even know he exists and are too poor to take him anyway."

"But there are child-welfare workers who are trained to help kids like him, Mom. We shouldn't try to handle this all on our own."

"Don't be daft!" Liz said. "They'd only put him in a foster home with strangers, wouldn't they? And who's to say if those strangers would even be kind to him? You of all people know that, Bob. He's happy here with us, we want him, and here he's staying."

"But not all foster homes are terrible. Ruth and I have met some wonderful people during our reporting, people who might be able to help. Haven't we, Ruth?'

Ruth looked nervous, but she nodded.

"Great idea," I interjected. "Traumatize Timmy by giving him to complete strangers and get me arrested at the same time."

"We'd all be arrested, I expect," Liz added. "Even you, Bob. We're all implicated."

"Unless we blame it on Mom," I muttered. "She's in the clink already, so it wouldn't make any difference."

That put a stop to the conversation. I pushed the goopy carrot salad around on my plate, feeling all mixed up inside. Everything my aunt had said about Timmy's family was true, but at the same time it seemed wrong. Just because people were poor like Marisol didn't mean they couldn't raise their kids well. Liz made it sound like we were better than his family, even with my stupid mom in jail. And I didn't see what gave us the right to think that.

Liz made small talk with Ruth awhile, which I didn't listen to, but finally Bob raised his bald head from his eating and looked at me. "Madge," he said quietly, "I saw your mom last week."

"I don't wanna hear about it."

He ignored that. "I talked to her lawyer, too."

I glanced at Ruth, wondering what the hell she must think of my nutcase family. If we weren't enough to drive her away, she must really be in love.

"So?" I muttered.

"I think you should know she's decided to plead guilty."

I couldn't speak for a moment.

"Guilty to what?" I finally choked out. "Did she strangle somebody again?"

Such a long silence stretched over the room you could hear the dust falling.

"No, love, it's nothing that bad," my aunt finally said, leaning back in her chair and crossing her arms. "Tell her, Bob. She has a right to know."

Bob picked up his candy-pink napkin and folded it into a perfect little square. "Well, I'm afraid she got caught writing illegal bets at the racetrack. She was hustling customers to place their bets with her and a bookie partner instead of going to the official window. You can make quite a lot of money that way, apparently, if you don't get found out."

"Mom's a goddamn asshole!" I hissed. "Why the hell did she have to do something like that? It's not like we need money that bad—we're not starving to death!" My voice was getting hysterical, but I couldn't help it. "So is that what she was doing all those times she disappeared, hustling at racetracks like some slimy con man?"

Bob glanced at Ruth, clearly embarrassed. "It looks like it, yes," he said quietly. "Racetracks all over the country. She and her bookie buddies had this scam going for years, it seems. Her lawyer said she'll probably get the minimum sentence, then ICE will take over with the Voluntary Departure option."

"What the fuck does that mean?"

"It means she'll have to serve time in York County Prison—how much time hasn't been decided yet. It's a state prison south of here that holds immigration detainees. It's a pretty nasty place, I'm sorry to say. But after that she'll be deported for good. She wants to go back to England, start again. But, well, Madge, I'm afraid she'll never be allowed to come back here."

"Never? Not even to visit?"

"No. I'm sorry." Bob looked at me uneasily. "It's better than prison, though, right? She asked me to tell you that she wants you to visit again soon. Before they move her."

I pushed away my uneaten dinner. My friends were getting into their fancy clothes, Gavin's band was tuning up, Krishna was who knows where, and I had a headache like a vice clamping down on my temples.

"She's lying," I said, and I went upstairs to my buttercup room, pulled the covers over my head, and for reasons I didn't want to think about, cried myself to sleep.

I don't know how much later it was when Liz called me through the door, but I could see from my window that it was already dark outside. "Madgy? You awake?"

"No."

"I need to speak to you a minute, love. I'm coming in, all right?"

I was tucked under the bedcovers with all my clothes on, hot as it was. "Hi," I mumbled when she opened the door.

"Listen, darlin'. You've got a visitor downstairs."

"It's not the cops, is it?" I sat up, scared. Had the police found out about Timmy? Had Mom broken her promise and blabbed? Had Marisol turned me in?

"No, no," my aunt said. "Go on down, love. You'll see."

I threw off the covers and thudded down the stairs in my bare feet. My head was still pounding.

Krishna was standing in the hallway, his brown eyes and thin face so gentle I wanted to cry.

I was so happy to see him I couldn't say a word. I even forgot that my hair was all wonky from the pillow and that I was wearing an embarrassing old T-shirt that said, PENNSYLVANIA GIRLS DO IT BETTER. All I did was stand there like an idiot, smiling.

"Hi," he said at last, his voice low and quiet. "I came to ask if you wanted to go to the prom."

"The prom? Isn't it too late? What time is it?"

"I don't mean that prom. Come see." He took my hand and led me out of the house.

Jamie's truck was there, its headlights on in the dark, and he and Serena were leaning against it, glued together, as usual. I stared. Serena wasn't wearing black. In fact, the lights revealed that she was dressed in cut-off jeans and a tank top in the astonishing color of cornflower blue.

Krishna turned to me. "We're going to make our own prom. I want you to come. Please."

"You don't have to do that. You don't have to skip the real thing 'cause of me. I'm sure you all want to go."

"Don't be silly." And he pulled me into a hug.

I shut my eyes and leaned against him, his T-shirt rubbing my cheek. "You're not mad at me?"

"Of course not. Why would I be mad at you?"

"I thought you didn't want to see me anymore."

"No, it wasn't that at all. I'm sorry I haven't been able to talk. I've been so busy helping my mother. This hasn't been an easy time."

"I've missed you so much, Krish."

"I've missed you, too," he murmured. "It hurts how much I've missed you."

After I'd run inside to grab my sandals and say good-bye, I climbed into the back of the truck with Krishna. He'd put a blanket underneath us, and now that the air was balmy with June, it wasn't uncomfortable at all. We cuddled up together, just like the time we'd gone to see Timmy, and my headache floated away. It was a perfect moment.

"Where are we going?" I asked.

"Down to the river. We have a picnic, we have music, we even have beer."

On the way, Krishna told me how hard he'd been working all week, helping his mom pack and clean up the motel. He hadn't even been able to go to school every day, and on the days he did go, he'd had to run home at lunchtime. "I wanted to call you, but each time I tried, my mother asked me to do something else. She's very worried, Madge." They'd not only had to clean out the whole motel, they'd had to wash and press all the linen so they could sell it to the next owners, hold a yard sale to get rid of their tools and old furniture, and find the cheapest way to ship what was left of the family belongings to Queens. They'd had to do it all by themselves, too, because Krishna's dad was too caught up fighting the bank and rearranging their lives to help, and his older brother was in the middle of finals at college. Krishna sounded so sad telling me all this that I was ashamed for thinking the reason he hadn't wanted to talk had anything to do with me.

Jamie drove us to the same part of the Delaware I'd gone

to with Gavin, but that didn't bother me anymore. We found a dry spot on the bank and set up our picnic. The water was burbling beside us and the stars were making their shapes in the sky, which was so clear we could see every crater on the half moon. We put some of Krishna's bhangra music on his CD player, and its rhythms and harmonies fused perfectly with the sounds of the river. Then we ate up the pizza Jamie had brought, drank some beer he'd stolen from his dad, and told silly jokes till we were all lying down, rolling with laughter. Serena and Jamie rolled so far they ended up disappearing under a bush.

"Madge," Krishna whispered, "come with me."

We stood up, holding hands, and jumped along the pillow-shaped rocks until we were out of sight of the others and alone with the river. We found a soft patch of grass on the bank and soon we were making love. I'd never done that out-side before, under the stars and moon, the air soft and silky all around me. It felt free and beautiful, even if there were mosquitoes biting my butt.

Afterwards, when we were lying there with the night breeze caressing our bodies, my head on Krishna's chest, I finally worked up the courage to say what was on my mind. "Krish, can I ask a tough question?"

"Sure. You can always ask me anything, you know that."

"You're leaving next week, aren't you?"

"Yeah, on Wednesday, alas. Why, what is it?"

"Wednesday?" My stomach clenched. Wednesday was much sooner than I'd expected. I'd thought at least we'd get to celebrate the end of junior year together.

"Well?" he prompted.

"It's just . . ." I paused. "It's just that I need to know what's going to happen when you leave. With us, I mean." I held my breath.

Krishna was quiet for a while. I felt his chest rise and fall under my head. I could hear his heart, too, pulsing steadily deep inside of him.

"What do you want to happen?" he said.

That wasn't the answer I had hoped for. That was way too cautious.

I took a deep breath. "I don't want to lose you." I winced. I'd said it now.

"Of course you won't lose me. I love you, Madge. I've loved you for a long time and I'm not going to stop now."

"You do?" I was so happy to hear this my voice squeaked.

"I do. I'll call you so much you'll get sick of me. But, you know," he said then, "we're still very young. It's not like my parents, like a husband and wife. We've got a lot of time ahead of us and we can't know what'll happen."

"Yeah, of course," I said quickly, but inside I was thinking, what did that mean? "But what am I going do when you're gone?" I said aloud. "I don't want to go back to that school without you. I know I'll have Serena and Jamie, but it's not enough, not now they're a couple. It's going to be awful."

Krishna shifted his bony chest underneath me. "You don't have to look at it that way. You could pretend you're going to a new school like me, and find some new friends. They're not all as bad as Gavin and Sophie."

"Yes they are. I grew up here, don't forget. I know how they think."

"Madge, that's not true and you know it. You've got to give them a chance. If you open your mind to them, I bet you'll find plenty of other people here who want to be your friend."

"Maybe," I said. But I don't want new friends, I thought. I only want you.

Krishna did leave that Wednesday, right at the end of the school day. I went to say good-bye to him at the motel. It was so depressing seeing it all empty and bare, and his family's apartment turned from an Indian home full of color and light to a bland concrete box. Mrs. Sharma looked terrible as well, tired and upset, and too distracted to even be her usual kind self. I could see why Krishna hadn't had any time for me. His mom seemed on the verge of breaking down altogether.

After their old brown station wagon was packed to bursting point, every window blocked with piled-up boxes and bags, Mrs. Sharma gave me a quick hug and climbed into the passenger seat. Krishna took me by the hand and led me out of sight behind a wall. "I can't kiss you in front of my mother. She still believes I have to stay pure till I have a wife." He sighed. "I'm going to have a big fight with my parents about that one day."

I nodded. I had no words anymore. I didn't understand whether he was going to be my boyfriend now or what he wanted. But I was too scared to ask.

Krishna kissed me and held me for a long time. "I'll never

forget you, Madge," he said. "The first love always stays in your heart, that's what they say, right? I know you'll stay in mine."

Are you saying we're over? I longed to ask. Are you saying no more romance? But all I said aloud was, "I'm going to miss you, Krish. You're the best person I've ever known."

nineteen

SUMMER CAN BE pretty bleak when you're seventeen and useless. Serena was off in the Poconos, working as a camp counselor for deaf kids. Jamie was busy on the farm. Timmy was enrolled in day camp, learning how to swim in our local pee-pot of a pool and whack people over the head with a base-ball bat. Krishna was in Queens. And Mom was behind bars.

Nobody needed me.

I tried to get an internship on our dinky local newspaper, since Bob and Ruth had said I was such a good reporter, but it turned out the entire staff consisted of the owner and his wife, so they had no room for me. The only other work in town was lawn mowing or babysitting, and those jobs were already taken. So I was stuck with helping Liz in the beauty shop, washing old-lady hair and cleaning up. She taught me how to do a basic cut and set, but my heart wasn't in it. I hated being locked up all day with the sticky, poisonous smell of shampoo and hair dye when it was shiny and hot outside. I hated even more the clients' conversation, which was about nothing but TV stars, diets, and how great it was that our president was always bombing some poor dark-skinned kids overseas. Sometimes it made me so mad I wanted to run into the street and scream.

The worst, though, were the days when Liz went to visit Mom. She went every Tuesday, in spite of the three-hour drive and the sight of her own sister as a jailbird, but she wouldn't let me go with her.

"Why not?" I asked. "Mom told Bob she wanted me to come."

"I know, love, but the two of us had a little talk and we agreed jail's not a healthy place for you and Timmy to be visiting. Anyroad, she doesn't like you seeing her there. It makes her feel ashamed."

"She should've thought of that before she started conning people at race tracks."

"I'm know, darlin', but I think it's better this way, at least for the time being."

"Why the fuck doesn't she give up on being a mom altogether?" I yelled. But Liz wouldn't budge. So I kept the beauty shop open for her every Tuesday, offering trims and sets. I took Timmy to and from camp, and played with him afternoons and evenings. And I stared at the walls, imagining Mom's life in jail, missing Krishna like mad, hoping I'd never hear from Marisol, and waiting for things to change.

And things did change. The insurance money for Uncle Ron's death came through at last, which made things a lot easier for Liz. We packed up all our stuff from Hollowdale, and said good-bye to my old apartment forever. And Mom called collect to tell me her fate had been decided.

"They've given me nine fuckin' months in York County Prison. It's going to feel like lifetime, Madgy. And after that, they'll boot me out of the country forever."

I squeezed my eyes shut. I'd taken her call in my aunt's living room and was curled up tight in one of the armchairs, clutching the phone like it might wriggle away from me.

"Where is York Prison?" I asked, my voice wobbling. Whenever Mom called from jail it made me feel sweaty and panicked, like I was about to be arrested myself.

"Far fuckin' away, that's where. Even further than this godforsaken place. It's going to take Liz twice as long to visit me now, bloody wankers. How's Timmy, by the way?"

I paused. It had always taken me a moment to adjust to Mom's switch of moods.

"He's fine. He's in this little summer camp learning to swim and play baseball. Liz wants to find him a piano teacher, too."

"Well, la-di-da. We are getting fancy. We'll have a little ponce on our hands if you're not careful."

"What's that supposed to mean? You shouldn't talk like that. God, Mom."

"Oops, here comes Martin Luther King again. I'm only joking, silly girl. Loosen up."

I fiddled with the fringe on the armchair, scowling. But I controlled myself. Mom was in jail—she wasn't allowed many phone calls. I'd better be nice.

"Mom, can I visit you in England once you get there?"

"Yeah, absolutely. I want you to. I've always wanted to show you my real home. I've got it all planned out, Madgy. I'm moving back to Brighton, where I used to live with Liz. She still has some mates she thinks might find me a job, maybe working in a hair salon, like she did. I love Brighton, all that sea and fresh air. You'll love it, too, ducky. It's got this fairground right on the beach—roller coaster, Ferris wheel, the whole shebang. I'm sure Liz and Bobby will help pay for you to come."

I shut my eyes. Something about Mom's tone, her falsely cheerful voice, her acting like she was talking about a vacation instead of criminal deportation, made me hurt all over.

"Why did you do this, Mom? Why couldn't you keep straight for my sake, and for Timmy's? I don't want you living over there. I want you home with us."

There was a long silence after I said that. Finally, I heard her let out a breath.

"Madgy, that's sweet of you an' all, but it's time you grew up. You've got Liz if you need a mum. I have to get off the phone now. Give Timmy a kiss for me." She paused. "I am what I am, you know. Love it or leave it, as they say."

And she hung up so fast I was left with a ton of words to say and nobody to say them to.

A few weeks after that, I was in the gory pink beauty shop alone, sweeping up the white hairs of all her old-fart clients, my aunt having gone to get some lunch, when Bob called me on the salon phone.

"Madge, do you have a minute? I need to ask you something."

"I've got more than a minute, I've got my whole damn life." I wasn't in the best of moods those days.

"Well, you don't have to answer this right away, but I've thinking ever since that night in Dale's Diner and, well, I wondered if you'd like to come stay with me. Live here, I mean. There are some good public high schools in New York where you could go for twelfth grade. Much better than Hollowdale High. And I've got that spare room you stayed in."

I was too surprised to speak. I had to stare at a row of liver-colored hair dryers for quite a while just to grasp what he'd said.

"Wow," I finally answered. "Wow, Bob, that's incredibly nice."

"Well, it was Ruth's idea, really. She thinks you'll be happier here, maybe safer, too, and I agree."

I didn't know what to say. Bob couldn't really want to me to live with him, I thought. Every time we got together these days, we ended up yelling at each other. He must be doing this to please Ruth.

"I'm real grateful," I said at last, "but you can't really want this. I irritate the fuck out of you, and what would I do with Timmy?"

"I know we tend to squabble, but we can work on that. I do want you to come, honest. It's too hard for you living in Riverbend and going to school in Hollowdale. It's too much commuting and it's too isolated and, you know, like we discussed, it's too damn white. Look, think it over. Talk about it with my mother. I already told her my idea."

I hung up and wandered through the back door of the salon into the kitchen, sat down, and stared at the frilly white curtains in shock. Mousy whined at my feet—we'd had to take him in the last time Mom had disappeared, even though my aunt couldn't stand him, and he was fatter than ever now because Timmy kept feeding him scraps off his plate. His orange fur seemed to vibrate against the yellow walls. What about him? I thought. I'd had Mousy since I was twelve; I couldn't abandon him. I was touched that my cousin had offered me this, but how the hell could I move to one room in New York with an obese cat and a kid?

My aunt came in from lunch then, rubbing lotion into her long, bony hands. She was always telling me how hairdressing dried out her skin. "So, did you talk to Bob, then?" I nodded and she pulled up a chair opposite me. "What do you think?"

I took a moment to answer. "It's real nice of him, but I don't see how I can do it," I said slowly. "How can I live in one room with Timmy, let alone with fatso here?" I poked Mousy with my foot. "And what about when Ruth stays over? We'd be on top of each other, we'd drive Bob crazy, and where would Timmy go while I'm at school?"

"You won't be bringing him, Madgy. You'll have to go on your own."

"My own?"

"Yeah. Timmy will be better off here with me, you must be able to see that. He's got his day care now and his little camp. He's happy here. And I can put up with that furball a bit longer, too, even if he does give me the willies. You can be free to finish school in New York and go off to college this way. It's what you've always wanted."

"But I promised Timmy I'd stay with him. I can't just walk away!" Then I remembered Marisol, and I shuddered.

Liz patted my hand. "I know you feel that way, darlin'. But you're young yet, Madgy—you've got your own life to live. I've discussed this with Bob, and he agrees. You can always come see Timmy whenever you want."

That hurt. All along I'd suspected Liz had been trying to make Timmy love her more than he did me, but now it was obvious. "So then you're the mom and I'm just some kind of visiting cousin, is that what you're saying?" I said angrily.

Liz sat back in her chair and gazed at me a moment. "I suppose it is, if you want to look at it that way. Yes, I suppose it is."

As soon as my aunt left to pick up Timmy from camp that afternoon, I went into the living room and telephoned Krishna. He'd been calling me as often as he'd promised, but it wasn't the same as having him there with me. I missed his gentle eyes, his gangly limbs, his special smell, and his warm arms holding me. I missed his kisses and caresses, too, but most of all I missed his friendship. A voice on the end of the phone, all tinny and far away, wasn't good enough. Plus, he was caught up now in a world I knew nothing about. He was working as a busboy in some Indian restaurant that belonged to a cousin.

He'd hooked up with his old friends—he was having a great time. He was too tactful to admit it, but I knew he was glad to be back in New York and free of Hollowdale. He'd probably even found a new girlfriend already and was too kind to tell me. Some days our conversations felt warm and close, like they used to. But more and more often they felt awkward and distant, as if everything we'd once known about each other was unraveling like a spool of cotton.

"I don't see how I can do it," I said after I'd told him about Bob's offer. "I'd be putting my own needs ahead of Timmy's if I left him here. And I'd hurt him, too. I don't want to be like my mom, leaving kids behind like forgotten suitcases."

"But Madge, I'm sure your aunt can look after him fine. This is your chance to get out of Riverbend and Hollowdale, like we've always talked about. And if you're in Manhattan, we could see each other more often. I miss you."

I couldn't speak for a moment. "I'd love that," I finally replied in a watery voice. "But if I left, I'd be breaking my promise to look after him. And then he'd be the only black person in this family and this whole damn town, just like I was."

But at the same time, part of me was saying, argue me out of this; give me a reason to go.

I could hear Krishna breathing. God, I wanted to hold him.

"Yes, I see what you mean," he said at last. "It's hard to know which is better, to help yourself or help him."

"Parents are supposed to sacrifice for their kids, right? I mean, my mom isn't so good at that, but look at your dad."

"Yeah, you're right."

"So, what should I do?"

"I don't know. I think you have to decide for yourself."

I closed my eyes to look for an answer. But there was a war going on inside of me. Half of me wanted to look after Timmy like I'd promised. And the other half wanted to fly to New York to be free.

I tried to work all this out calmly while I put Timmy to bed that night. He was much more cooperative now than he'd been when I'd first brought him home. He stood at the sink brushing his teeth without any fuss, cute as a button in little red summer pajamas. And without being told to, he picked out a book for me to read to him in bed. I didn't have to put up with him hiding in closets or wetting the bed anymore, either. I didn't even have to yell or plead. What was the difference? I wondered. Was it that he was happy?

I cuddled up beside him and opened the book, *Abiyoyo* by Pete Seeger. I'd gone to the Hollowdale mall with Krishna one day to pick out books about black people for Timmy, because every picture book my aunt had brought home was about one white person after another. Timmy loved *Abiyoyo* because a lot of it was song and we could sing the chorus together. I loved it because it was such a treat to read a book with Timmy where the people on the pages looked like us. And we both loved it because it was about a dad and his son who were outcasts in town, till they scared away a monster with magic and a song.

"Read it again!" Timmy said as soon as we got to the end. "Please, Madge, pleeeease!"

"Kiss first!"

He got up on his knees, planted a firm, dry kiss on my cheek—his specialty—and cuddled back down with me. I put my arm around him and pulled him up close so he could see the pictures. And I read it again and again, the two of us singing together.

How could I ever leave him?

Two nights later, I was fretting hot and sleepless in bed, when I heard the phone ring downstairs. Hoping it was Krishna, I ran down to get it. But it wasn't Krishna. It was the call I'd been dreading all summer, collect from Marisol.

I accepted the charges, my heart thudding so hard it made me feel sick.

"Who this?" she barked.

"Um, it's Madge."

"How ya doin'?" She sounded nervous.

"Fine, thanks. How about you?" I could barely get the words out.

"Good, good. And Timmy, he okay?"

"Yeah, he's fine."

"Great. Listen, I been thinking. You got any money?"

"No, I don't have money," I said warily. "Why?"

"What 'bout your family? They got money, right? Money enough to keep Timmy, anyhow."

Was Liz right? I wondered. Was that all the woman was after?

"What do you want, Marisol?"

"See, I am wondering. I am wondering how I pay for Timmy when I take him. You know, buy him clothes, food, things that like? See, Tony, he got busted, so he ain't in the picture no more. But I got this other guy now, he like me a lot, he got other kids. I'm thinking he will help some. But I'm thinking, too, maybe you, your family can help while I get on my feet, y'know?"

"What are you saying?" I was beginning to panic.

"Me? Oh. I am saying I'm ready to take him back, see? You bring him, okay? Bring him to Tony's house. Place is mine now."

I swallowed. "Are you sure about this? It's been almost three months since we talked, Marisol. Timmy's settled in here."

"Maybe. But I thought 'bout it lots. The boy, he belong with me, that's what's right. And now I got a good situation, I'm ready. That's what my sister, she woulda wanted."

"But what if Timmy doesn't want to be with you? What if he wants to stay here?"

"Hey, enough. Don't give me no hard time now. I'm family, I'm what he knows. You bring him tomorrow, okay?"

Tomorrow was Tuesday, when Liz would be gone all day visiting Mom. I closed my eyes. Tomorrow was so soon.

"I . . . I need to think about it," I said.

"You already had time to think. I'm his *tía* and I want him back. You know you got no right to keep him."

My eyes were still closed. How would I explain this to Timmy? What would I say to Liz?

"Okay," I said finally, my voice shaking. "Okay. I guess."

"Good. Six o'clock, got it? Dinnertime. Bring the kid's things. Oh, I cannot wait to see that sweet little boy!"

And she hung up.

The next morning, I sat in the kitchen, watching my aunt get ready for the long drive to Mom's jail. I kept opening my mouth to tell her what I was going to do, but then I'd close it again. I knew what would happen if I told her. She'd stop me. She'd say Marisol was no good for Timmy. She'd say we were better and I had no right to take him away from her because she loved him. She wouldn't understand that no matter how much it hurt, this wasn't about us anymore, this wasn't even about our love for Timmy. It was about Timmy's right to be with his real family, not the one we'd invented for him.

Once Liz left, I put the CLOSED sign on the beauty shop door, locked it, opened the cash register, and took out three hundred dollars. Then I went upstairs, packed all of Timmy's things in the biggest suitcase I could find, and picked him up from camp, saying he had a dentist's appointment. Finally, I called a taxi to take us to the bus depot in Hollowdale and caught the Shortline to New York City, just like before. When I got back at the end of it, then I'd tell Liz what I'd done. And I would try my best to make her understand.

I did all this without telling anybody. I didn't want a soul to know what I was doing. I could hardly stand to know it myself.

"Where we goin'?" Timmy said to me once I had him on

the bus in a window seat. He looked up at me, his big eyes so trusting I wanted to cry.

"We're going to visit Uncle Bob."

Timmy pouted. "Where's Gramma? I want her to come."

"She's too busy to come today, sweetie. You'll see her later."

He scowled but I distracted him with a bag of gummy snakes. Kids were so easy to distract, so easy to lie to. Too easy.

Timmy slept some on the way, but mostly he listened to my Stylofone CD on the portable player from Ruth. He was amazing like that when it came to music. He could sit and listen without moving for hours, whether it was rock or Mozart—I was sure it meant he was a musical genius. As for me, I'd brought a book, but I couldn't concentrate on it. A little voice kept going through my head, interrupting me, a voice kind of like Timmy's, and it kept saying, Is this right? Is this what Mrs. Henderson would have done? Am I being righteous? Or am I being cruel?

How could I be sure? All I knew was that things were different now that Marisol wanted him. When I'd thought he didn't have family or anybody to love, keeping him had felt right, and I still believed it would have been. But I'd never meant to take him away from his very own aunt. She seemed to really want him—she'd clearly loved his mom—and now that Garcia was gone, maybe she could give him a decent life, though I knew it would be a hard one. If I moved to New York to live with Bob, I could visit her and check. I could drop by all the time and make sure she was treating him right. But at least with her, Timmy wouldn't have to be like me, always the "different" one, always having to deal with the Gavins and Krugers of small-town Pennsylvania. With her, he could be with his own family, in a city where he belonged. Maybe she would even take him back to the D.R. one day. He wouldn't have to be the only olive in the peanut bowl, the black button in the white button box. He would grow up knowing who he was.

That's what my aunt wouldn't understand.

It took us longer than I expected to get to Timmy's old apartment building, what with my having a huge suitcase in one hand, Timmy in the other, and it being hot as a pizza oven outside. The subway ride seemed to last forever, and the walk over to his place did, too. To make matters worse, soon as Timmy recognized his old neighborhood, he turned jittery and strange. First he wanted to run off to the park to look for Joey, then he wanted to go home to Grandma, and after that he went silent and thoughtful. I had to pull him along with one hand while I dragged the suitcase with the other, two dead weights that didn't want to cooperate at all.

I saw Marisol right away, waiting by the stoop, even though I was half an hour late. She was peering up and down the street, looking for us. Soon as she spotted us, she came running up.

"Hey, Timmy! Hey, baby!"

He stood, staring at the ground and clutching my hand. I put the suitcase down on the sidewalk, panting.

"Ain't you gonna give your *tía* a hug?" Marisol said then.

Timmy hung back and I felt terrible. He doesn't like Marisol, I thought. If he doesn't want to be here, I'm going to grab him and run.

But then a moment later he let go of my hand, stepped forward, and wrapped his little arms around her hips.

Marisol held him a long time. "Hey, *mi cielito*," she crooned, "I missed you so bad. House been real empty without your little voice. You miss me, too, honey pie?"

Timmy nodded, still clinging to her legs. He didn't even look at me.

Okay, I thought, my chest hurting and hurting, this is it. Time for me to leave. Just tiptoe away and let Timmy be where he belongs—with his own aunt, not mine. I should never have taken him in the first place, me with my grandiose dreams of being some kind of hero. I made all kinds of assumptions I had no right to make just because they suited my dreams. The opposite of love is indifference? Yes. But the opposite of love is selfishness, too.

I waited for a chance to say good-bye, but both of them were ignoring me, like I didn't matter anymore. So I turned, feeling torn in half, and walked a few steps down the street. The sidewalk was shimmering gray, the garbage sitting hot and rotten in the gutter. The August sun was beating down, merciless and dirty. I'd tried to do right by Timmy, and now everything I'd done seemed wrong.

I could still hear his voice behind me, which made it even harder to walk away. "Where my moms?" he was saying. "What you did wit' my moms?"

I tried to keep going, but I couldn't. I had to stop and turn. He'd let go of Marisol now and was looking up into her face. Her hands were on her hips and she was shaking her head down at him.

"Now quit that, Timmy. You know your mama is dead, honey pie. You always known she's dead. You saw her laid out right in front of you."

"You lyin'!" Timmy shouted, and I could hear the tears in his voice. "Gimme my moms!"

I couldn't help what I did then. I ran back, picked him up, and held him tight against me. "It's okay, Timmy," I said, rubbing his back and hugging him. "Don't cry, sweetie."

"Put him down," Marisol snapped. "He ain't yours to hold."

"I've got a right to hold him if I want," I said, my voice trembling. "I love him."

Marisol put her hands on her skinny hips. "So what? He's mines now. Give him back."

I stood tall as I could, still holding Timmy. He'd wrapped his legs around my waist by then, his arms around my neck. "Marisol," I said more steadily, "Timmy's been happy with me and my family. He calls my aunt 'Grandma' and my cousin 'Uncle.' He's got a school he likes and people who love him. We've treated him right. I want you to know that."

She looked me in the eye a long moment, then she seemed to soften. "I'm glad to hear it, honey. I know'd you was good people. But you gotta believe me, I love him, too."

She turned her face to the sky. "Hey, Alicia," she called

out, "what you want me to do, huh? What you want for your boy?" She shut her eyes a moment and stood still, like she was really waiting for a message. Then she grabbed the handle of the suitcase.

"Bring him in. He belong with me."

She headed toward the stoop of her building, struggling with the suitcase, which was almost as big as she was. I followed her slowly, my whole body aching. And suddenly everything was clear. I didn't want to go to New York and live with Bob, not even to escape Hollowdale High and be nearer to Krishna. I wanted to bring Timmy back to Liz, where the two of us could look after him. I wanted to do what I'd promised him I'd do and give him a home. Together, we could handle Riverbend and Hollowdale—we could handle anything. And when he was older and more settled, maybe then I could go off to college, let Liz be his mom like she wanted to, and come home to see him whenever I could. But first I needed to make sure that Timmy felt safe—I needed to make sure that he knew he would never be abandoned again.

And now it was too late.

Marisol stopped at the bottom of her stoop and turned around, panting. "What you got in this suitcase, anyhow? Weighs a fuckin' ton."

I swallowed. It was hard to even speak. "Timmy's things," I just managed to say. "His clothes and toys. His books and CDs. Kid stuff."

"Shit, you bought him all that?"

"Marisol, you will let me and my aunt visit him, right?

He's going to miss us so bad and we're going to miss him, too. We'll want to keep seeing him."

She didn't answer. Only heaved the case up the first step. *"Mi dios,"* she gasped. "Feels like a dead body in here."

She dragged the bag up the rest of the steps, groaning and panting and resting between each one, and at last got it halfway through the front door, where she let go of it and bent over to catch her breath. Finally, she stood up, took another long look at us standing at the bottom of the stoop, and stared again into the sky.

"Alicia?" she said once more. "Alicia, you hearin' me? You sure 'bout this?" She waited, her face pointed up the whole time, like she was really listening.

I watched, clutching Timmy. I was trembling all over.

Marisol turned back to us.

"Hey, Timmy," she said. "What you want, huh? You wanna stay here with your *tía*? Or you wanna go back with Madge?"

Timmy didn't answer. He only buried his face in my neck.

She squinted down at us for a long moment, while I stared back at her from the sidewalk, hugging him to me.

"Timmy?" she said again. "You gonna answer me?"

He shook his head.

"I think it's got to be you who decides," I said, forcing out the words. "He's too little."

She gazed at him a long time. Then, finally, she gave a quick nod.

"Tell you what." She patted the suitcase. "I keep this. You keep the boy. I can't give him no good life, not here, not like his mama, she wanted him to have—not like you folks can give him. It's gonna break my heart, but it's what's best. Now get outta here, 'fore I change my mind again."

And with one great heave, she yanked the suitcase all the way into Garcia's building and slammed the front door behind her.

I stood at the bottom of the stoop, stunned. Half of me was weak with relief; the other half filled with a whole new fear.

I shifted Timmy on to my hip. "You want to go back to Grandma now?" I whispered. He nodded, clinging to me. And I carried him down the hot, dusty street, in the direction of home.

author's note

This book is a work of fiction, but behind it are some facts:

Three million children in the U.S. were reported victims of abuse and neglect in 2004.

More than half a million abused and neglected children live in foster care.

These figures are from a report by Children's Rights, Inc., at www.childrensrights.org or Children's Rights, 330 7th Ave., 4th Floor, New York, NY 10001, (212) 683-4015.

Madge's state, Pennsylvania, was home to twenty-seven racist hate groups in 2005, including neo-Nazis, racist skinheads, and the Ku Klux Klan. In the same year, the highest numbers of hate groups were in California (fifty-two), Florida (fifty), and Texas (forty-three).

These are statistics gathered by the Southern Poverty Law Center's Intelligence Project, a nonprofit civil rights organization that monitors hate groups all over the country and promotes programs to teach tolerance. Go to www.splcenter.org or 400 Washington Ave., Montgomery, AL 36104, (334) 956-8200. Also visit www.tolerance.org for ways to help.

acknowledgments

FIRST I MUST THANK my daughter, Emma Benedict O'Connor, who brought a wisdom and sensitivity beyond her years to helping me with this book. Her passion for justice is an inspiration, and her spirit a delight. I also want to thank my son, Simon Benedict O'Connor, who contributed sage advice on language, and his considerable musical expertise. They both helped make this book. My thanks also go to my generous friends and readers, Nicholas Boston, Slane Hatch, Ynestra King, Felicia Lee, and Rebecca Stowe, for their time and invaluable comments; to The Virginia Center for Creative Arts for summers of time and peace to write; and above all to Stephen O'Connor for his enduring faith and gifted editing.

Beth Raymer gave me essential information regarding Brandy's activities. Professor Victor C. Romero of the Dickinson School of Law at Penn State University and attorney Raphael A. Sanchez both gave me immeasurable help regarding Brandy's fate. Joy Peskin encouraged me to write the book in the first place. I thank you all.

The stories of Marissa, Lucy, and Pablo are based on cases reported by Children's Rights, Inc. I was also inspired by the courageous voices of the teenagers in foster care who write for *Represent*, a magazine published by Youth Communication in New York. See www.youthcomm.org.

Finally, I must acknowledge the following authors of noble hearts and words, whose shadows inhabit this book: W. E. B. Du Bois, James Baldwin, Richard Wright, Ralph Ellison, Zora Neale Hurston, Paule Marshall, and Harper Lee. These writers teach us what it means not to be indifferent.